62495

D1529381

DATE DUE	
OCT 24 2003	
NOV 27 2003	
JAN 27 2004	

Faithful Women

Barbara Shoup (signature)
Barbara Shoup

Guild Press of Indiana, Inc.
Carmel, Indiana

Guild Press of Indiana, Inc.
435 Gradle Drive
Carmel, Indiana 46032

Printed in the United States of America

Library of Congress Number
99-069812

ISBN 1-57860-048-0

For
Pat and Joan,
faithful friends

All the things of the past rearrange themselves, line up in rows, as if someone were standing there giving out orders; and whatever is present is utterly and urgently present, as if prostrate on its knees and praying for you.

Rainer Maria Rilke

Chapter One

This is my earliest memory. Night. The moon is round and white, framed in my bedroom window. Its light makes a shadow of the big tree on the wall above me. My swing hangs from the highest branch, motionless now. But it's mine, safe in my room with me. All my things are with me. My doll, my book, my blanket. My shoes are on the dresser. They shine, white as the moon. I can smell the fresh polish on them. I drift off to sleep with one thumb in my mouth and the other rubbing the satin ribbon of my blanket—

"My Aunt Lily remembers it," I told Cliff. "That is, when I described this to her a long time ago, she remembered that she polished my baby shoes every evening while she watched me in the bath. She'd set them on the dresser, the polish still damp. Yes, I slept with my doll, my book, my blanket. Yes, there was a big tree in the front yard. She said she had hung my swing there herself because there was no man to do it. My father and my Uncle Paul were both away, in the war."

"Ah," said Cliff. He leaned back against the old stone wall where we'd stopped to picnic, appearing to study the green English countryside spreading out beyond us.

I waited. Cliff thinks everything a person says or does means something. He's like an earnest child taking apart a toaster or a radio, scrutinizing each piece, memorizing it so he'll be able to put it back together. He's maddeningly patient. He'll look at the smallest part interminably, his pleasure at its integrity equal to his pleasure at its function. While he examined this piece of my life I'd offered him I fell into an agitated state. I felt out of balance, as if the telling had diminished me physically.

"You actually remember the smell?" he asked.

"Yes. The smell. You know the smell of white shoe polish—"

1

But I could tell he was less interested in the smell itself than he was in the smell as an integral part of the scene I'd described. His expression was still turned inward. To him, it wasn't *my* memory yet. He was examining what I'd told him the way a painting can be examined and appreciated, detail by detail, with absolutely no knowledge of the painter at all.

Then, suddenly, he directed his gaze at me. "Center of the universe. You were the center of the universe, weren't you?"

I felt myself flush, felt something like shame wash over me.

He went on, caught in the web of his own thoughts forming. "So tranquil, still. Your doll, your book, your blanket. Your shoes polished for you. Moonlight carrying your swing. You were everything. It was a perfect world, whole. Think about your work, your job."

I am a conservator of paintings. My specialty is Dutch genre painting of the late seventeenth century. Interiors, particularly. Domestic scenes. It's my job to keep them clean, to do what I can to neutralize the ravages of time. If they're damaged, I restore them.

"Your memory is like a little Vermeer," Cliff said. "Those few objects, deceptively simple. And light. I can see the moonlight slanting through the window—the white leather of the baby shoe, the satin on the blanket shining. That little room is a whole world defined by light, held by light forever in your memory. Don't you see, Ev? No wonder you love it. No wonder you're always trying to go back—

"It's made-to-measure for you, isn't it? Your work. It's as if you go straight into a painting. You guard the ideal, you keep it from changing. If it does change, you restore it to perfection. You're so fierce about it. And if anyone should shatter the moment and bring you back to the living world—" He smiled, having shattered such moments any number of times himself in the past weeks. "You, your aunt, your mum living in that little house. There must be dozens more of these perfect little 'paintings' in your head."

"Actually, no," I said. "It was more than forty years ago, after all. I was a baby when I lived with Aunt Lily. I was just three when my father came home from England, when my mother died and everything changed. There's just that one memory. A few photographs. And what my aunt's told me."

"Yes, your aunt—" He leaned toward me.

I saw Aunt Lily in my mind's eye, framed in the doorway of that memory; felt again that sense of her constant presence in my life. I didn't know how to say what she was to me. I loved her too much and was taken from her—

I missed her for a moment in exactly the way I'd missed her years ago, sleepless in my father's house. I could almost hear the branches scratching the screen in the wind, voices that never quieted. My half-sister, Vicky, breathing in the crib beside me.

"Tell me about your Aunt Lily," Cliff said.

But I could not. Instead, I feigned indignation. "Honestly," I said, "you English are supposed to be such *private* people."

I waited for him to tease back as he usually did, to affect his fake Texas drawl and say, I'm half Yank, you know, I come by my impertinence fair and square, and make me tell him more.

Instead he sighed, "Ah, Evie—" He let loose of my memory, I watched my life drain from his face. He gathered up the plates and cups, the leftover cakes and fruit from our picnic tea. Lost in his own thoughts now, he folded the tablecloth and put it in the Harrods carrier bag.

I watched his hands, rough and sturdy, well-used, freckled by the sun. Patient hands. I thought of all they had touched in this world, all they'd searched for and found deep in the earth: smooth stone, pitted metal, shredded fabrics, sharp gems—the remnants of lives more than a thousand years past. His hands had held and treasured the antiquities they unearthed, turned them over, over, over. Lifted them toward the sun.

I thought of how those hands might feel on my body. Confident hands learning everything about me; after all these years, allowing light. I turned to him, but I couldn't make myself speak.

We were high on the earthworks that support the wall surrounding the buried Roman town, Calleva. We'd left London that morning, driven narrow winding roads tunneled with hedges to get to this place. Silchester, it is called now. We'd parked the car in the churchyard, walked under a great gnarled yew tree, through the little cemetery with its crumbling gravestones, to the kissing gate, which we passed through onto a path. Shoulder-high with weeds, laced with stinging nettles, buzzing with insects, the rutted path cut through the center of a vast field, up the mound of the earthworks to the wall itself, the only part of the

Roman town still visible. We walked a ways along the top, which is as wide as a city sidewalk.

Earlier, Cliff had explained its careful design: flat gray leveling stones, sharp darker-gray flint between, more leveling stones, more flint. The dozens of layers create a striped effect. Outside, the stone face of the wall is thirty feet high; inside, the part of the wall that sheltered our picnic is just head-high. He made me imagine the Romans building these earthworks where we sat, hauling the dirt in wooden carts to build this mountain of sod that sloped up on the inside of the wall and made it impenetrable.

I had closed my eyes and listened as he described the way the town looked then, the people moving through the streets. He treasures the smallest details of ancient people's lives. When he speaks, you live their lives, you care for them as if they are members of your own family. He believes there is a plan, that everything matters. He makes you believe that the present world has been flawlessly crafted from the past.

In the month that I had known him, he had begun to make me consider that this might be true of each solitary life as well. You must know your past to know yourself. You must suffer the exhaustion, the filth, the tedium of digging. You must be patient. Brave. You must learn to cherish what you find, even if it's not what you hoped for, even if it renders meaningless all you found before. But I resisted it. I didn't want it to be true. When I left home at eighteen, I believed my real life was beginning. Now I was in the prime of that life I'd made. Come autumn, I'd be forty-five. Why look back to a time that had brought me so much unhappiness?

Cliff zipped up the pack and hoisted it on his shoulder. As if he'd read my thoughts, he stood and looked beyond our solid, touchable wall to where it curved out of sight, a long chalky line meandering through the luxuriant English summer. Where the Roman town had flourished, now wheat and barley grew. Cows and goats grazed above the buried streets.

"It's as if it never was," he said.

"Yes," I said. Again, I waited.

"Buried, gone—" He smiled at me. "We English are so sensible, you know. We've worked the site. Museums hold what we've found here, safe, and now the rich farmland is put back into proper use. But in the autumn the town reasserts itself. Evie, if you could see it from the air!

"The wheat and barley can't root so deeply where the gravel streets were, or above the remains of the flint walls. As the season changes and the plants receive less moisture, those above the streets and walls grow poorly. They're shorter than the others, unhealthy. Ripening, they reach maturity and turn yellow sooner than the other plants. From the air, you can see the grid of Roman streets in them—yellow lines on a green field. In a very dry season, you can even see the narrower lines of walls and houses."

I understood what he was saying to me, why he had brought me here. And I was afraid.

Chapter Two

*C*liff thought it was stubbornness that kept me from examining my childhood, but there were some things I really couldn't remember. I could see my beautiful young mother in my mind's eye, but the image of her was static, glamorous, like a posed photograph. I had no memory of my father coming home after the war, though I'd heard Aunt Lily tell the story of that day again and again. All my short life, I had known only women, she said: herself and my mother; her best friend, Lois; my mother's girlfriends; the ladies who came to Aunt Lily's for fittings. I was used to women's voices, to the way women moved. According to Aunt Lily, when my father came home, I took one look at him and burst into tears. "I don't like him," I said. "He's too big."

Like I said, I didn't remember it. Nor did I remember those first months he spent with us, before my mother died. We all lived together in Aunt Lily's house, the one she'd bought with the money she earned, dressmaking, during the war. I knew that because Aunt Lily told me so. But I knew about the unhappiness only much later, when I was old enough to see it in the photographs from that time. On picnic blankets, at dinner tables, beside a Christmas tree, my mother and father sat, smiling brittle smiles. Uncle Paul looked anxious, Aunt Lily, solemn. I was the only one who looked happy. I was always sitting on Aunt Lily's lap.

I learned early not to ask questions. It hurt Aunt Lily too much to talk about what had happened to my mother. It made my father's face go blank. So I learned to eavesdrop and, piece by piece, I made my own picture. My father had stopped loving my mother while he was away. He loved Peg instead. Which had something to do with a fight he had with my mother on the night she died. A car accident was all anyone ever said about her death; but it seemed to me that my father must have been glad she died, because as soon after the funeral was over he left me with Aunt Lily so that he could go back to England and marry Peg.

Years ago, teaching art history, I was often struck by the vividness with which my students could describe a painting they hated. Ask them to comment on a work they loved, and they were tongue-tied. Or vague: "Gosh, it's just so…beautiful." But they understood exactly what displeased them. "There are too many cupids in that Rubens, all flying in a frenzy. And, ugh! Those awful fat, pink ladies writhing around."

In just this way, because I hated my life with Peg and Dad, the most vivid memories of my childhood began with the time they came back from England and claimed me. I remembered the awful little house we lived in. I could still see it: the beige living room with its mismatched furniture, the windowless bathroom, the kitchen with its egg-yolk yellow dinette set, my own bedroom papered with pink roses that were so large they seemed to be alive. I remembered going to sleep every night, crying for Aunt Lily. Waking up every morning, crying. Vicky was a tiny baby then; she slept in my room in my old crib. She cried even more than I did. She cried when she was hungry or when she needed her diaper changed or when she wanted somebody to play with her. Peg cried sometimes, too. I remembered sneaking from my bed when I was supposed to be napping, seeing her crying at the messy kitchen table. She cried quietly, though. Not like I did, or Vicky. Her red hair got all wet and frizzy around the edges, her eyes got puffy. Her freckles stood out on her white skin, like measles.

Every night, my father came home and picked me up and swung me around like an airplane. "Bombs over Tokyo," he'd holler, and make shooting noises. My ankle and wrist hurt where he held them and my stomach flip-flopped and it scared me the way the stove and refrigerator and Vicky in her high chair and Peg and the window, pink with sunset, flew by. But I never cried or said, Stop. I let him swing me until he got tired of the game and brought me in for a landing on the cold linoleum. Then he'd turn up the radio and dance Peg around the kitchen, kissing her. They kept the radio on loud all through dinner, both of them talking and laughing above the noise. In fact, they kept the radio on loud all through the evening. Except when they hired a babysitter for Vicky and me and went out.

"Which they have no business doing when they have to pinch pennies just to eat!" I heard Aunt Lily say more than once to her friend, Lois. "Those kids look like ragamuffins, it's a disgrace. And Peg, pregnant *again*."

Peg hated it when I asked for the things Aunt Lily used to buy me. Cereal with prizes, Bosco, pink Sno-balls. At the check-out at the grocery, I'd beg for a dime to ride the electric pony. Peg would march me outside and set me in the red wagon with Vicky and the bag of groceries she'd bought. We'd gone a block and a half one day, and I was still whining. "Aunt Lily lets me ride the pony. How come you never let me ride the pony? I never get to." Peg stopped all of a sudden and dropped the wagon handle. I shut up in the middle of a word.

"Oh, the baby!" she said. "We've left the blooming baby!" And she turned and ran back up the street. "Stay right where you are," she called back. "You stay there, Evie. Watch Vicky."

People stole babies, I knew. And children like me were kidnapped by men who drove up and offered them candy. Aunt Lily always told me never, ever talk to strangers. Even if they're nice.

All the ladies in the store were nice. "Oooh, look at that sweet baby," they said when they saw Bets. "Leave the buggy up here," one had said to Peg that very morning. "We'll keep an eye on her while you shop." Bets was only three weeks old. She couldn't even see right yet, Peg had said. So how would she know the difference if one of those ladies stole her and took her home?

Peg forgetting the baby was my fault. I'd asked for too much, and made Peg forget her. I didn't like Bets much, but I didn't want her to be stolen. I burst into tears. Which made Vicky start, even though she was only one and had no idea what had happened.

"For heaven's sake, Evie! Stop that right now," Peg said when she got back with the baby. "I mean it. And not another word. Mind you, young lady, I'm at my limit."

When we got home, she made me go to my room. It was the same room I'd had measles in not that long before, and I lay there very still, remembering when I was sick. I'd had to lie still then, and I hadn't been allowed to look at my books, practice my letters, or draw because all that was very, very dangerous for my eyes. I could be a little blind girl right now, I thought, and I wondered if that would have made Peg act nicer to me.

I didn't cheer up until after lunch, when it was time to go downtown to get new shoes. First we went to the store where Dad worked. Peg opened the door with the gold writing on it, and there he was, bent over a piece of black velvet cloth that had been spread on the glass counter, holding a ring. The funny black thing that he used to see better was on his eye; he had to scrunch up his face to hold it there.

"Get a load of these," he said to Peg.

Tip-toe, I was eye-level with the counter-top. The rings he showed her looked like mountains on the flat glass. Big, sharp diamonds, glinting with light. The gold settings shone. Dad's blunt fingers picked one of the rings up and held it toward Peg. It had a round diamond in the middle, with little diamonds all around, like flowers.

"Oh, no," she said, and took a step back.

"Come on, hon," he said. "It's all right. Try it on."

She shifted Bets to her hip then, and held out her free hand, palm down, so he could put the ring on her. It slid on easily, her finger was so thin. Too thin—the weight of the stones made the ring fall toward the inside of her hand, and all you could see was a thin band of gold, like her wedding ring. She let the ring slide back onto the velvet.

Dad picked up another, smaller, ring for her to try, but Peg shook her head. She cradled Bets in both arms again, bent and nuzzled her, murmuring, "Oh, what a good baby you are. You'll have diamonds like that some day, you will. Vicky and Evie, too," she said.

I wanted them now. I wanted everything in the store. I wanted the big wood radios with the speakers that looked like open mouths and the typewriters like the ones in Dad's office that he let me type letters on sometimes and the cameras so I could take whatever pictures I wanted to take. I wanted the guitars and the saxophones and the trumpets. I wanted the fur coats locked up in the secret place in the back. And the heavy silver trays and candlesticks. And the emerald brooches and the pearl bracelets and the wonderful gold lockets that had places for tiny photographs inside.

I wanted them even after Peg explained to me that all the things in Mr. Rafferty's store already belonged to someone else. People brought them there because they had gotten poor and needed money, she said. Dad or Mr. Rafferty gave them some money to use and a ticket with a number on it for each thing they brought. Then when the people weren't poor any more they could come and pay the money back and take their things home again—if someone hadn't already bought them. It wasn't nice to want the things in the store, Peg said. It was like wanting the people who owned them to stay poor.

That day, she hurried us all out toward the shoe store before Dad could show us any more treasures. "Let's not dawdle, Tom," she said. "Get your jacket now. I've got to get home in time to give Bets her bottle."

I loved the Buster Brown store with the machine you stuck your feet under and you could see the bones, bright green as leaves, right through your shoes. I loved the shelves of shiny patent-leather Mary Janes, the navy blue gym shoes, the black-and-white saddles, and the penny loafers like the ones I saw the big girls wear. Every time, I got all excited and forgot that I wasn't going to get to choose what shoes I wanted. I had to get the red leather two-strap shoes with holes poked on the top, the kind Peg said that children in England wore. Every time, it was a shock to me. Every time, I behaved badly and embarrassed Peg and my dad and the nice clerk.

If I lived with Aunt Lily, she'd let me choose. She'd let me get one pair of each kind if that's what I wanted. And she'd let me wear my Sunday shoes to play in if I felt like it. She was nicer than Peg. She wouldn't make me get those stupid shoes I hated.

"What did you say, young lady?" Dad's voice. It sounded mean.

I didn't answer. It was my business how I felt about the shoes and about Peg and Aunt Lily. Nobody else's. It was my business what I said, too. I was just talking low, to myself, so it wasn't fair at all that he spanked me.

When he came home from work that night, he came into my room. He sat beside me on my bed and put his hand on me. It covered my whole shoulder, from my arm bone to my neck.

"Evie—" He reached to brush my hair back from my face. "Oh, Evie," he said. Just my name. But it was as if he'd said something really sad, and I started to cry. I couldn't stop. He picked me up just like I was a baby, the same way Peg picked up Bets. But I was so big that my arms and legs hung over his arms. My head was bent funny so that my neck hurt. Still, I held on tight.

When, finally, I stopped sobbing, he said, "Honey, just settle down a little, will you? You're a good girl. Just don't fuss about everything. Don't ask for so much. Peg's tired with the new baby and all. That's why she gets so upset with you."

I promised to be better. I ate every bit of my supper that night. I played with Vicky—I even let her hold the teddy bear Aunt Lily had given me and did not yell at her when she started acting silly with it. I went to bed without whining even though it was still light and I could hear the neighbor kids playing in the street. I thought everything was okay. But then I heard Peg crying. I heard Dad say, "Christ, I am so tired of this." The door slammed, and he went out.

It was very, very late when the noise woke me up. I knew because there was just the moon in my window, round and full. There were no lights anywhere except street lights. But there was music coming from the living room. I heard laughter. There was a sound I didn't recognize, too. Kind of like someone kicking gravel against a wall.

I got out of bed and crept to the door. When I opened it, I saw them dancing. Peg was in her nightgown and duster, her hair wound in pink curlers. Dad was still in his clothes. He still had his hat on. They were the ones laughing. It was dimes that had made the funny sound.

I had never seen so many dimes in my whole life, a silver mountain of them. They covered the whole coffee table. Every once in a while Peg and Dad stopped dancing and ran their hands through them. Dimes fell to the linoleum, ringing. I watched Dad scoop a hatful and put the hat on his head. Dimes spilled down his face and his body like rain. He didn't even pick them up. He just got another hatful and did it again. Then he put his hat on Peg's head. Some of the dimes got caught in her curlers.

That's when they spotted me.

"Come here, Ev. Try on my hat," Dad said. He slid some dimes from the table into it and tipped it onto my head. The dimes were cold, they hurt a little sliding down my face. I bent to pick them up. I didn't want to lose them. But Dad took both my hands and stuck them into the pile on the table. There were so many dimes, my hands were buried in them.

He winked at Peg. "Hey, Ev," he said, "you can have all of 'em you can hold."

At first, I was excited. I cupped my hands and lifted them, but the dimes were heavier than I thought they'd be, and my fingers wouldn't stay together. The dimes fell through them like sand in the sandbox. They made that sound I'd heard in bed. I tried again. This time I made my fingers stay together, but dimes spilled out over the top. My hands were so small. When Dad laughed at me, I threw the dimes at him and cried out, "I hate you, I hate you. You're mean." I ran away, back to my bedroom.

This time when he came he didn't make me feel better at all.

He said he was sorry. He said, "Honey, I just got such a kick out of winning all those dimes that I forgot what I was doing—" Before he went back out to Peg, he said, "You can have more dimes in the morning. As many as you want. Okay, Ev? Okay?"

I said okay, but I had made up my mind not to take anything from him or Peg ever again. They couldn't make me. Dimes, a coffee table full of them. Big deal. A dime is nothing these days—I'd heard Aunt Lily say that when we were shopping one day.

I was shivering. Bets slept, sighing, in the crib that Vicky had outgrown. Vicky slept peacefully, warm as an oven; but even though my teeth chattered with the cold, I stayed on my side of the imaginary line I'd drawn down the middle of the double bed we shared. I fell asleep thinking of my room in Aunt Lily's house. It was always warm there. In the morning the sun shone on the yellow walls and made them look like melted butter.

Why couldn't I be hers? Especially when Peg had Vicky and Bets and another baby coming, and Aunt Lily's babies kept on dying? Aunt Lily had been sick in the hospital a long time with the last one. When she came home and Peg took me to visit her, I was scared at first. Aunt Lily was so sad. She hugged me too hard, it hurt me. "You're my little one," she whispered. "My only little one now." It made Peg cry.

Not right then. Later, when I overheard Peg and Dad talking. I saw her put Dad's hand on her big stomach. "Feel her move," she said.

"Him," Dad said. He always teased Peg about wanting a boy.

She smiled at him. "It doesn't matter, does it?"

He shook his head. "You know it doesn't."

"Poor Lily," she said, and that was when she started crying. "She just clung to Evie this afternoon. Oh, Tom, to think she'll never have a baby now. Imagine us without our girls."

Never? Aunt Lily would never have a baby? It wasn't fair. Greedy Peg.

Why wouldn't she let Aunt Lily have me?

It was at night-time, when my sisters were asleep and Peg and Dad sat out in the living room alone, that I hated Peg the most. Sometimes in the day she tricked me by being nice and made me forget that I would never, ever like her. But at night, when she sat with Dad on the couch and he rubbed her back if she was tired and kissed her, I remembered. She wasn't my real mother and never would be. My real mother was as beautiful as a movie star. Nothing like skinny old Peg with her ugly red hair and freckles.

Spying on them through the keyhole of my bedroom door, I'd whisper, "My mother is dead."

Vicky was three years old when Anne was born. Bets was two. "The Queens of England," Dad called the three of them. He'd look at the new baby and roll his eyes, because he could tell already that she was the third of a matched set. Vicky and Bets were so much alike that, even though they were a year apart, people often mistook them for twins. They were like little stick girls. Their knobby knees looked like the knees of the hungry children I saw sometimes in magazine pictures. They had Peg's curly red hair. Her huge, watery blue eyes. Her white, white skin. If you saw them in their Sunday dresses and Mary Janes, you'd have thought them sweet and frail, but they weren't. They were wild. They wore everyone out. Especially Peg, who had to spend all day every day with them.

That was probably why, when Aunt Lily and Uncle Paul invited me to take a trip to Chicago with them that summer, Peg said yes. In any case, I remember the trip because it was the first of many I'd take with Aunt Lily and Uncle Paul all through my childhood. Also because, on that trip, I saw the wall of babies.

It was at the Museum of Science and Industry, just beyond the huge model of the human heart. I walked slowly along the wall of windows, where unborn babies floated in yellowish liquid. The tiniest one was just a curled-up seed. The next few reminded me of the tadpoles we'd grown in school. Then parts started to look people-ish. Great, cartoonish foreheads grew into whole heads with mouths and noses. The bodies got longer, sprouting arms and legs. They had tiny hands and feet, with skin so thin you could see a blue scribbling of veins beneath it. The last baby was perfectly formed, a long cord coiling out of its belly. It had fuzzy black hair on its head. The others had seemed so small, like little dolls, but this one nearly filled the whole window—parts of its body were flattened, pressed against the glass. And I understood suddenly that it was a real baby. A dead baby. All the other babies behind the glass were real, dead babies, too.

Like Aunt Lily's babies were dead. I turned to her and saw that her face had gone pale, she was trembling. But she smiled, took my hand, and we moved on. We looked at the electric trains. We scared ourselves silly in the coal mine, marveled at the dollhouse that had real electric lights and furniture more beautiful than any we'd seen in a real house. That year, like every year after it, we strolled down the cobblestone street of the old-fashioned town. We had our picture taken in the Model T Ford outside the silent picture show.

We felt like a family there. People thought we were a family. In all the years we went to the museum, there wasn't once that someone didn't say to Aunt Lily, "What a lovely little girl you have."

"Thank you," she'd reply.

So far away from home, she allowed herself to pretend that I was hers. It made us all happy. She wanted a child more than anything; I wanted desperately to be her child. Uncle Paul was happy whenever Aunt Lily wasn't sad.

Every trip we took to the museum was exactly the same; we counted on it. We each had our favorite things. Mine was the model of the human heart. There was a tunnel cut through it; you walked up a little stairway, inside. I loved to stand in the center and trace the tangle of veins and arteries with my finger. "Ka-thunk, ka-thunk, ka-thunk," went the recorded heartbeat. But I started to feel creepy if I stood there too long. I hurried out then, and my own heart—safely inside me—would fill up with joy at the sight of Aunt Lily and Uncle Paul, waiting.

Not one of us ever said a word about the babies we had seen the first time; we simply never walked straight from the big heart toward that wall again. But I, for one, was always aware of them just beyond our sight. At night, in the motel bed, I dreamed them: curved baby-seeds growing like tadpoles, each one turning magically into myself as it swam into Aunt Lily's arms.

Chapter Three

*I*f I closed my eyes, I could imagine all the time after my life with Dad and Peg as a long line, perfectly straight except for two swerves. A big swerve, which was Florence more than twenty years ago. Then, I dropped everything to go help rescue the art that had been damaged in the flood. I met my friend, Ian, there—the person responsible for the second swerve, which had brought me here to London. I teased him sometimes. Two drastic things I've done in my life, I'd say. And there you are in both of them.

He had called me at the museum first thing one morning in early June. I'd just drunk my coffee, and was sitting at my desk, staring blankly at the work set out for the day.

"You know, I've been trying to get you to England for years," he said.

It had become a joke with us, the way I avoided a whole country just because my stepmother had been born in it. I laughed and waited for him to unreel the inevitable absurd scheme, the ritual preface to whatever his real business was.

"One of our Vermeers," he said. "You won't have heard about it yet, Evie, but there's been a terrible incident here. Just this morning. 'A Lady Standing at the Virginal.' It's been slashed."

"Slashed," I said. "Really, Ian. And the Queen's run off with Elton John."

"Evie, it's true. It's no joke." He explained exactly what had happened. The flat tone of his voice made me believe him.

"Will you come?" he asked. "You worked on that other Vermeer at the Rijksmuseum years ago. I want you to help us assess ours and make a plan. To stay and do the work on it if possible."

The logical response would have been, "Ian, I have a job. A life."

But something made me hesitate. In the days that followed, when I told friends what I'd decided to do, I laughed and said, "Who wouldn't jump at the chance to escape a miserable New York summer?" In fact, it was the chance to escape my life for a little while that made me say yes.

Not that it wasn't a good life, the life I'd chosen. Not that I wouldn't choose the same life, the same work if I had to choose all over again. It was just that, in the past months, I had begun to see myself in certain older women I noticed in the museum, at the ballet, on the street. Dressed in flowing black with wool paisley shawls thrown over their shoulders, or in expensive gypsy-like dresses, they wore soft leather boots, carried big soft leather bags to accommodate their bulging calendars, the books and magazines they kept handy to read over a solitary cup of tea. They were attractive, intelligent, white-haired women completely in charge of their own lives. Admirable women, obviously disproving the lonely old age that unmarried career women were always warned about. So why had the sight of them begun to unnerve me?

Working, I would glance down at my hands and notice the blue-green veins, or the way my loosening skin gathered at my bent wrist. I began to study myself in the mirror. Time had been kind to me, tricked me in a way. At first glance, I looked much as I always had: small and slim, olive-skinned, dark cropped hair with very little white. Even my face seemed unchanged, until I pressed back the skin beneath my earlobes and at my temples, erasing the still faint lines around my eyes and at the corners of my mouth and revealing a younger, nearly forgotten self: the thirty-year old person I was when, at last, my studies were completed and I came to work in New York. It surprised me how quickly those years had passed. I thought, in another fifteen years I'll be almost sixty. Old. I had never been one to worry about the passage of time, or to try to categorize it; but now the years to come seemed to take a shape in my mind, to be a palpable, nameable thing: what was left.

I told no one how I felt. Such self-absorption embarrassed me; it smacked of a mid-life crisis. Boring. I was tired, that was all. I needed a break. I'd been leafing through travel brochures for weeks. But what Ian offered was more alluring than any island paradise. A Vermeer all my own—nothing in the world to think about but that. I felt certain I'd come back to my real life in a few months, renewed.

By the end of the week, I'd made the necessary arrangements at the museum. Monday, I was on a plane to London. It was, by my watch, three in the morning when the taxi deposited me at the National Gallery in Trafalgar Square, my one suitcase in hand. The squawk of horns, the pigeons flapping around Nelson's Column, the red double-decker buses careening through Admiralty Arch: They were so utterly familiar from books and movies and from the stories that Peg had told when we were children that it seemed to me I'd been there before. In spite of myself, I imagined Peg and my father hurrying past the spot where I stood now, toward one of the clubs or dance halls she had loved to describe to us. Where was that theater they'd spent a whole night in once, during an air raid? It was near Trafalgar Square, she'd said. I shook my head to bring myself back to now.

Enter at the small staff door to the left of the main entry of the museum, Ian had told me. I opened it, reported to security, and was taken down a long, dark corridor to wait in a room that was furnished like a Victorian parlor. I sank into one of the long red sofas and stared at the antique tables, the grandfather clock, the paintings in gilt frames, the marble busts, startled by their unexpected beauty. Then there was Ian, exactly as he had always been. Still impossibly thin, his brown hair sticking up in places where he'd run his fingers through it. Was that the same shabby tweed jacket he wore when I saw him last, in Paris? The thought made me smile and embrace him, though neither of us was usually the embracing type.

"Well." He picked up my suitcase. "We'll go see it, shall we?"

I thought I had prepared myself. Immediately, when Ian spoke the name of the damaged picture on the telephone, I'd brought up its image in my mind's eye:

Just one figure, the lady, stands in the silver light that falls through Vermeer's familiar leaded window, her hands resting on the keys of a harpsichord. She gazes at the viewer through hooded eyes, smiles a secret smile. Her dress is the pale yellow of drying wheat. Her shawl, Madonna blue, the same color as the velvet on the upholstered chair in the lower right corner of the canvas. The pearls around her neck, the beads lacing her hair ornament and decorating her shawl, the upholstery tacks on the chair seem so real that you could pluck them from the surface; but when you look closely, you see that they are nothing but perfectly round stipples of paint.

There are three pictures within the painting. There is a vague Italianate landscape painted onto the upright lid of the harpsichord. Directly behind the woman, hung high on the wall, is a picture of Cupid in a wide black frame. The third picture, the smallest, hangs in the narrow space between the cupid and the window: another landscape— a stripe each of mountain, cloud and sky. Its ornately carved gilt frame is luminous; it glows. It is the only warm thing in the picture. Your eyes move away from it.

On the airplane, I'd stared at a print of "A Lady Standing at the Virginal" for a long time, imagining the damage Ian had described. Nevertheless, when I saw the real painting in the workshop, slashed, I had to lean against the heavy wooden table where it lay.

It shouldn't have hit me so hard. I'd seen willfully damaged pictures before, I knew there was never a rational explanation for such an act. Still, I burst out, "God, why would anyone do this?"

"Barmy," Ian said. "Some blooming fool with her knickers in a twist about art keeping women in their place. Clear case against educating the public, I'd say. Look here." He picked up a battered copy of the museum guide and leafed through it until he found the entry for the Vermeer.

"'The painting on the back wall of the room in which the lady is playing the virginal alludes to the subject matter of Vermeer's picture,'" he read in a clipped voice. "'It holds a cupid holding a playing card aloft, a gesture whose meaning is explained by one of the illustrations in Otto Vaenius's Amorum Emblemata (Antwerp, 1608). There Cupid holds a small tablet inscribed with the numbers two to ten. The verse accompanying this illustration praises fidelity to one as opposed to the love of many. Vermeer's painting is therefore probably intended to represent—' Here it is," he said, and sighed stagily, "'...a faithful woman.'"

"Ian," I began, "you don't really think—"

"Yes, I do," he said. "They found the guidebook in her bloody handbag, all marked up. That and a copy of *The Life and Loves of a She-Devil*. So you see it's me and Fay Weldon responsible for this." He smirked. "Fay writing those books about ladies putting poison in their hubbies' tea, wreaking havoc in Knightsbridge. Me writing the copy that got in that daft girl's hands. Faithful women, indeed. I say, Ev, it's all too much for me. I'm awfully glad you're here to fix it. You've arranged the time on your end?"

"I've taken the first few weeks as vacation, put in a request for a leave of absence—six months if I need it. I don't think there'll be any problem with it coming through."

"Brilliant." He raised his mug of tea to salute me, and left me alone to examine the damage more closely. We'd talk after lunch.

Alone, I looked at the pale face of Vermeer's woman, at her hands that had been poised in resonant silence above the keyboard for more than three hundred years. I allowed my fingertips to skim the line of her patrician nose, to touch lightly each stipple of paint that made her shining string of pearls.

I was in an odd, floating state of mind. Jet lag, I told myself. This beautiful, ruined painting I'd come so far to see. The foreignness of my surroundings. Surely all that explained why I seemed to have no sense of time at all; why, when I closed my eyes, I saw the other Vermeer I'd worked on years ago, "The Love Letter," as vivid and touchable as the one before me.

It is the same woman. In this painting, she is dressed in a yellow skirt, a yellow, ermine-trimmed jacket. Perhaps it is the same room, too, for the floor has the same black and white pattern of tiles; the light touching the overflowing laundry basket near her feet suggests the presence of the same tall mullioned window. The woman is seated, the fret of her mandolin in one hand, a letter in the other. She is looking up at her plain, white-kerchiefed maid with an almost fearful expression. Two black-framed paintings, a landscape and a seascape, take up most of the narrow stripe of white wall above her; a horizontal panel of gilded leather hangs beneath the paintings, directly behind her. A vertical slice of the tall fireplace is visible to the right. All these things are revealed by a pulled-back curtain in the dark foreground. It is easy to imagine the maid hurrying through the doorway, brushing against the vaguely rendered map on one side, the air from her movement causing the folio of music on the seat of the red velvet chair on the other side to rustle as she kicks off her slippers, rests her broom against the doorjamb, on her way to deliver the letter to her mistress.

It was so vivid in my mind's eye. I saw Joris in my mind's eye, too, standing before the damaged painting in the cluttered lab of the Rijksmuseum. The thief had sliced it from its frame, and Joris touched the rough fringe of canvas lightly, as one might touch a much-loved person who was in pain. "It is so much grief I feel to see this," he said. "But it is, as well, gratitude for the task we are given. These two things in equal measure."

"Yes," I said.

He was my teacher then, my mentor. No more. But that moment, when he turned from the painting to look at me and saw that I understood what he meant, saw that I felt exactly the same way he did, was the beginning of the larger, deeper, luminous thing between us.

I felt myself plummeting backwards to that time, but I did not dare allow it. I made myself remember, instead, something Joris had said to me earlier, not long after I'd arrived to study with him: "You have made the right choice to come here, Evie. You will do important work some day."

I turned on the raking light, an oblique beam which made every deviation in the surface of the painting clearly visible. Then I circled the table where the painting lay, observing it from all angles. It had been slashed in three places. The biggest cut, made from the upper right corner toward the center of the canvas at a forty-five degree angle, just missed the woman's face. It sliced across Cupid's left ankle, across the puffed sleeve of the woman's blouse and a fraction of her pale gold skirt, all the way down to the black and white tessellated floor. Another, shorter, cut ran parallel to the first one, crossing the lower right corner of Cupid's black frame, passing just above the woman's arm, and finishing in her skirt. The last cut was a small one in her blue shawl. Ian told me that the museum guard had grabbed the slasher's arm just as the knife punctured the canvas the third time. Now, using a magnifying glass to look closely, I saw that what I'd feared was true: The surprised twisting of her hand had caused the threads alongside either side of the gash to stretch and fray. Though this last cut was the smallest one, it would be the most difficult to repair.

The conservation file Ian had left me showed that the painting had been re-lined; that was standard procedure these days. Cleaned. The X-rays revealed no secrets beneath the surface of the paint. All these facts added up in my favor. In time, it would be possible to repair the Vermeer so that only the educated eye would pick out the flaw.

I'd forgotten the pleasures of a truly simple existence. In my real life, I was accustomed to juggling a dozen projects of my own as well as overseeing the work of others in the lab. Phones had to be answered, paperwork attended to, directors and donors appeased. Now there was the luxury of this one task.

In the beginning, I worked on assessing the full extent of the damage. I ran tests to establish the condition of the ground, the support lining, and the paint and varnish layers, so that I might formulate the best possible plan for the repair. Often, I simply stood and looked. Again, I thought of Joris, who had taught me to believe that what pictures revealed to my appreciative eye was as valuable as anything I'd learn from books or from technical analysis.

As always, with Vermeer, it was composition that I admired. Looking at other seventeenth century genre painters—masters, like Jan Steen, Pieter DeHoogh, Nicholas Maes—there is always the awareness of the moral message their work conveys. There's always a story. As Ian illustrated in the museum guide, Vermeer's work can be interpreted in those terms. Certainly, he was affected—consciously or subconsciously—by the moral construct of his time. But it is not the moral sense of Vermeer's work, the meaning of it, that stops viewers cold.

Art historians cite Vermeer's elegant spatial relationships, his remarkable treatment of light on a variety of textures in explaining why his paintings command our attention. But I have always thought that what rivets us is more simple, more amazing than that. It is that Vermeer saw as a child sees: purely, shocked by wonder. Like all great artists, he grew backwards and forwards all at once, brought every moment of his life, every aspect of his intelligence to bear in every single brush stroke. From the sad turbulence, from the deep, disturbing pleasure inside him, he made his perfect still lifes, so real, so impossibly idealistic that the objects within them seem to be suspended in a palpable web of tension.

"A Lady Standing at the Virginal" is not considered to be one of his greatest accomplishments. The light and shadow aren't treated as delicately as they were in earlier works—look at the left arm, for instance, and you'll see that it has a completely flat surface. And the woman's formal pose gives the painting a cold feeling; she lacks the lovely unselfconsciousness of "The Milkmaid" or "Woman Weighing Gold." Nonetheless, you can see Vermeer's genius for composition in the way the strong verticals are softened by a few elegant curves. In the way light holds all the elements in perfect balance and creates a stillness so complete, so satisfying, that you feel you could stand there and look at it forever.

I believe that the stillness of the painting was at least partly responsible for the uncharacteristic stillness I felt inside me those first weeks I was in London, before I met Cliff. It didn't take long to make a place for myself in a corner of the huge basement lab, I felt at home amidst the familiar clutter of equipment and supplies. There were a half dozen big heat tables that looked like billiard tables with steel tops. There were scarred wooden work tables, too; weighted clamps that looked like organ pipes were hung from the ceiling above them. There were pegboards hung with screwdrivers, hammers, vises, scissors, knives, funnels—tools that might normally be found in a kitchen or a garage. There were file cabinets. Wall cabinets stocked with chemicals and a variety of microscopes. Stools and ladders. And light: fluorescent tubing suspended from the ceiling, high intensity lamps clamped to the tables, standing lamps with movable necks, ultraviolet lights, X-ray machines, raking lights. Amidst all this, paintings lay on tables or balanced on easels, startlingly lovely.

Yes, I thought of Joris. When I worked, it was as if he were with me, instructing me. I remembered his voice: slow and determined, with that lovely sing-song quality that English takes on when it's spoken by the Dutch. In the evenings, alone in the flat the museum had rented for me, I could close my eyes and make his face appear before me: thin and sharp-featured. His watery blue eyes, the cracquelature of wrinkles around them.

How good he was. How truly he had loved me.

But he had loved Anneke, his wife, too. And Meip and Erika, their daughters. He had known what was not possible between us, what was not right. He knew, too, what was necessary, and so he carved a time and place where we could be safely together, a kind of alcove in our real lives. In this way, also, he had taught me.

Those first weeks in London, I sifted through my memories of that other time as one might leaf through an old book of photographs. The cluttered lab, a dark café on the Prinsengracht. The two of us traveling by train together toward some museum where there was a painting he said I must see: him smoking in the seat beside me, watching me watch the Dutch landscape fly by. Green polder, black and white cows grazing, windmills turning underneath the ever-changing sky. I was grateful to be able to think of those times without pain. It was a bonus, just another thing about this unexpected interlude that pleased me.

I was perfectly content in my little flat in Dolphin Square. The furnishings there were shabby, but serviceable: a sofa-bed, a comfortable arm chair, a work table. If I leaned out of the one window just-so I could see a silver slice of the Thames in the distance. I bought a big print of "A Lady Standing at the Virginal" at the museum gift shop and tacked it on the wall so that it would be the first thing I saw every morning. I felt like a student again, young and full of purpose. Sometimes I'd glance in a shop window as I passed and catch a glimpse of the person I was long ago, with Joris, my real life still before me.

I walked to work most mornings. Sometimes I followed the Thames along Millbank, to the Tate, then past Victoria Gardens, Westminster Abbey, and the Houses of Parliament, into Whitehall. Sometimes I took the back way, walking the perimeter of St. James Park to the Mall. I'd stand and look a long moment up the glistening surface of road that rolled out like a pink carpet from Buckingham Palace before I turned and walked the last bit of it through Admiralty Arch and into the chaos of Trafalgar Square.

I had seen all the great cities of Europe; I'd lived in several of them. Yet I had stubbornly resisted London because I'd thought of it as Peg's city. Ian was right; such a stance had been absurd. But I didn't even try to explain to him why I wasn't sorry I hadn't come before now. I couldn't explain to myself the way the city rushed into some clean, open space inside me and left me breathless with joy. It had something to do with that unfamiliar calmness I felt at my center, rather like the sudden absence of a noise so pervasive that your awareness of it registers only after it is gone.

Working, I'd lose all sense of time. The painting so beautiful, the feel of it beneath my fingers; I'd surface, stunned, and have to stop awhile because I knew it wasn't safe to trust my hand. I was in that vulnerable state on the morning Cliff appeared in the doorway of the lab. I was a week into the real work by then, securing the loose paint to the ground. I glanced up, stretching my neck muscles, and saw him. He was wearing jeans and an old blue chambray workshirt. And boots—hiking boots, the kind university students wore in the seventies: big, clunky cartoon boots. He was sunburned, his nose was peeling. His unruly blond hair, pulled back in a short pony tail, was streaked from the sun.

"The woman in the white hat," he'd said when Ian introduced us at a museum reception the night before.

I said, "I beg your pardon?"

"The good guy," he'd said. "The one who comes in for the rescue." He grinned at me. "Ian tells me you have the situation with the Vermeer quite in hand."

Was I supposed to have said, thank you? I didn't; I was annoyed.

"Cliff's a good chap," Ian said after he'd gone. "You've just got to get accustomed to him. You know who he is, don't you?"

I didn't. I shrugged as if to say, why should I care?

"Inspector Giles Bardon—" Ian paused and raised an eyebrow, as if to prod my memory. "People magazine. 'The Sherlock Holmes of the dig'."

"That Clifford Mills," I said. "Really." He was the archaeologist making the amazing Roman finds near St. Paul, beneath buildings that were going to be razed soon for development. He'd written half a dozen or so volumes of popular history. And in his spare time, he tossed off quirky detective novels with plots that hinged on some object a thousand years old.

I glanced over to where he stood, the center of a circle of admirers: dowdy women balancing hors d'oeuvres plates, effete men chain-smoking thin brown cigarettes. He saw me and waved cheerily, which annoyed me all over again and, worse, made me blush like a teenager.

Now he'd caught me off-guard again. He stood in the doorway of the lab, amused. "You remind me of my daughter, Monica," he said. "When she was little, she read her picture books just the way you're going at that." He nodded toward the Vermeer. "One day, I caught her standing on one of them, crouching on it, really. I'd taught my kids to be careful with books, you know. I was just about to scold her when she looked up and saw me. 'I'm trying to go inside, Daddy,' she said. Then burst into tears. I felt quite the ogre then." He grinned at me, just as he had the night before. "Think you'll make it inside?"

I'll just go back to work, I thought. If I ignore him, he'll leave. I stared at the canvas, as if assessing my next move. But strangely, unbidden, what came to me was the memory of standing before Vermeer's "View of Delft" for the first time, years ago.

I saw it in my mind's eye as clearly as if it were there on the easel before me: a world defined by light, gold at the center, gleaming, beading on brick and along the blue hull of a boat, the geometry of turrets, gables, chimneys all repeated in hazy shadow on the water. The peasant ladies strolling on the yellow quay.

I had wanted to walk into it. I would enter through the arched bridge, walk a red brick sidewalk along one canal, cross another arched bridge to the next, the next. The streets would be clean and empty. There would be white lace curtains in the windows. The deep silence of souls sleeping. I had stood before the picture a long time, memorizing it. Drinking it in.

It completely unnerved me that morning, the way Cliff had hit upon something about me that was absolutely true. The way he had brought a piece of my life back to me so vividly. It was as if I'd traveled backwards and become, for an instant, a person I once was. When he said matter-of-factly, "You could use a cup of tea," I said, without even thinking, "Yes." An hour later, I found myself beneath the basement of a building near the Barbican, drinking tea with the diggers, examining shards of Roman kitchenware.

That's the way things go with him. He says, "You could use a cup of tea," and we end up at an archaeological dig. A few days afterwards, he took me to the Museum of London to show me the Roman exhibit there, and we ended up in the Jesus Chapel at St. Paul's. Standing in front of the glass case that held the book listing all the Americans killed in Britain during World War II, he told me about his mother falling in love with a handsome GI—his father, who died when his plane was shot down over France.

Once over dessert, he demonstrated the technique of excavation—

"It's like dismantling our sponge cake, right? First the icing goes, then the first layer of sponge, then the layer of cream, then the filling, finally exposing the sponge base. You see, if you were to dig down recklessly to get at the strawberries first, the whole cake would collapse."

He laughed. Then, suddenly, he was talking about his childhood on a sheep farm in the north of England, the stepfather who endured him, and how he'd escaped by spending every spare moment watching diggers work the excavations along Hadrian's Wall. There, his unhappiness dissolved. Imagining the lives of the soldiers had made him feel connected. They were like his own father had been, he told me: lonely, far away from home. Each shard of pottery, each fragment of a weapon, each stone laid on the wall had been touched by real men. He'd become obsessed with knowing how they lived, as if every discovery he made added substance to his own life.

"And you?" he'd say after each offering, tricking me every time, drawing from me some long-buried shard of my own childhood.

"History is what's left," he said fiercely, again and again. "Ah, people are so careless, Evie. They keep secrets. Destroy things. They lie. What do they care about our whole lives spent collecting the poor little pieces they've left? We fit them together so carefully, we say this is how it was; but we know that every picture we make falls short in the end. We're guessing. Guessing. We know what we found. But how can we know what we haven't found yet, what's been forever lost?"

Some things are better lost, I wanted to tell him. Not necessarily bad things: Those, I agreed, you could learn from. But it was dangerous, sifting through old happiness. Each time you remembered it, there was a moment you believed in it again, lived in it. Then, again, it was taken away.

Chapter Four

I was nine the summer Angel was born.

"Your ma's P.G.," the kids in the neighborhood said. They leered at Peg. We were all old enough by then to have figured out that babies came from something messy and embarrassing that our parents did in bed.

"She's not my real mother," I said. That was what I always said when anyone mentioned Peg. But I was still mortified by the way she looked, the obviousness of what she'd done with my father. Her stomach was huge, her skinny arms and legs looked like pick-up sticks. For weeks before the baby was born, she sat out in the back yard in a lawn chair listening to the radio, her feet stuck in the little wading pool where Vicky, Bets, and Anne played. Her hair frizzed in the heat. Her skin was bright red between her freckles.

I read constantly, grateful for books that gave me entry to worlds other than my own. I spent whole days at the library, where—browsing one day—I had discovered a long shelf of big, unwieldy art books. Usually I loved to look at them in that quiet place, alone. But all that summer, I was so upset about the new baby coming that I just sat staring blankly at the pictures. Uncle Paul and Aunt Lily rented a lake cottage for two weeks in Michigan and took me with them, and all I did was float on my rubber raft for hours at a time, feeling sorry for myself. It was going to start all over again. A dumb baby crying all the time, the smell of dirty diapers and spit-up. Pretty soon, another little pest spoiling my few things.

When I saw the lady who owned the cottages hurrying along the gravel path under the trees one evening, I knew it had happened. Aunt Lily and I were playing Scrabble at the kitchen table. Uncle Paul was listening to a baseball game. The lady knocked on the screen door, then burst in without waiting to be asked.

"It's a girl!" She beamed at me. "Honey, you have a brand new little sister. Your dad called with the message. And your mom's doing just fine."

The lady was about to give me an excited hug, but when I said, "She's not my real mother," she stopped short, her arms flung out awkwardly.

"Evelyn Anne," Aunt Lily said.

Just my name. I dreaded her disapproval so much that that was all I needed to jolt me back into my good manners and thank the landlady for bringing me the good news.

Mary Angela was her name. Peg brought her home from the hospital right after we got back from Michigan. I was in my bedroom when I heard them come in. I heard my father thank the babysitter, heard Vicky, Bets, and Anne squabbling over who'd get to hold the new baby first. Then Dad called out for me. I ignored him, stared at my book, not reading. Soon, he appeared in my doorway. "Evie," he said. "Come on! Don't you want to see your new sister?"

No, I thought. But I didn't dare say so. I stuck my finger in the book, as if holding my place. I carried it into the living room with me so that Peg would see I'd been interrupted. She sat on the couch, cradling the baby in her arms. Dad stood beside me, smiling. His fingers on my shoulder pressed me forward, but I stood my ground. Peg tilted the baby up so I could see her.

I couldn't have been more surprised. This baby looked nothing like the other ones had; she had dark skin and dark hair that stuck out all over her head.

"I think she looks like you, Evie," Peg smiled at me. "Do you want to hold her?" She gestured toward the empty space beside her. I nodded. I sat down, let my book close on the sofa cushion, opened my arms.

My whole life changed in that moment.

The baby did look like me. And she was quiet, calm. When I touched her cheek, she made a small, happy sound in her throat, like a kitten purring. Before then, the only person I had ever truly loved was my Aunt Lily, but whatever happiness that love had brought me, I'd paid for again and again in longing and in grief. It had in no way prepared me for the love that welled up inside me that day, holding my sister. "She doesn't look like a Mary," I said to Peg, forgetting myself. "I'm going to call her Angel."

"Well," said Peg, "I think that's lovely."

She was mine. Peg was thrilled that the new baby had pleased me. The Queens had no interest in her. They ran in and out of the house, grabbing this toy or that treat. They were like one person, inseparable. I had always shared a bedroom with Vicky, but half the time she sneaked over to Bets and Anne's room in the middle of the night to sleep, tangled with them, in their double bed. So it was only natural that Peg and Dad would move Vicky there permanently and put Angel in with me. She slept in the crib that I had slept in. And I remembered, then, for the first time, the moon in the window, the smell of the shoe polish on my little white shoes, myself lying in the very crib Angel lay in, sensing the comforting presence of Aunt Lily somewhere near. I would be Angel's Aunt Lily, I decided. She would love me more than anyone.

Before, I had been a dawdler, wandering home from school in my own sweet time, now I rushed home every afternoon to take care of her. I lived for the moment that Angel would see me and smile. I was the first person she really knew. Even Peg said so. I was the first person she called by name. She walked, clinging to my fingers.

While other girls in my class suffered their first crushes on boys and gossiped on the telephone, I read Dr. Seuss to my sister. I had no interest in make-up or clothes or records. I used all my money to buy things for Angel: tiny purses, barrettes, mittens with faces embroidered on each finger.

Even through high school, she was my favorite companion. I had few friends of my own age; nobody in my life, not even Aunt Lily, understood the intensity with which I studied and planned toward the moment when, finally, I could step into the beautiful world that I knew now only in books. Angel required no explanation; she just wanted to be with me. Together we looked at the pictures in the big art books I checked out from the library. Saturdays, we'd take the bus to the little museum on the art school campus, near downtown. She'd stand before the paintings solemnly. She didn't talk much, but when she did speak, she always had something interesting to say. "Evie," she once said, looking at a very modern one, "Is it done?"

I loved to tell my sister stories about how it would be someday, just the two of us. We'd have an apartment in New York filled with wonderful things. We'd visit Paris and Rome. When Angel said, "But I'll miss Mom and Dad," I said fiercely, "No, you won't." And I believed it. I loved Angel more than anything, I was happy loving her—happy with my simple dreams for our future.

But I left home for college when the time came and I met Rob and a whole new life with new dreams opened up for me. I'd noticed him in my art appreciation class right off. It met in the lecture hall of the fine arts building at eight o'clock in the morning and once the lights went off and the slide projector clicked on, most of the students slumped in their seats, sleeping. The rest stared mindlessly at the flickering images on the screen. Across the room, one boy scribbled in his notebook as relentlessly as I scribbled in mine. Sometimes he sat five minutes after the lights went on, still scribbling. Sometimes, after class, he'd go up to the podium, where the professor was collecting his slides and lecture notes, and the two of them would talk intensely as the rest of us filed out of the room.

He was tall and lean and dark-haired. He was always dressed in sharply pressed khakis and an oxford shirt, blue or yellow. He wore shiny cordovan loafers. On cool days, he wore a navy London Fog jacket, like the ones all the fraternity boys wore.

It was late in October when we finally spoke. Or when he spoke to me, I should say: I'd never have had the nerve to speak to him first. Though I'd been on campus since September, I'd met only a few people. I'd explored very little. I was a scholarship student, scared to death that I might mortify myself by falling short of everyone's expectations, so I studied constantly. And, too, I had lucked upon a single room in the dorm. The privacy, the silence, were so wonderfully luxurious to me that I hated to waste a moment of it. I knew the girls in the dorm thought I was odd, stand-offish, and I was a little sorry—I meant no harm by my seclusion. But I was happy alone, really happy for the first time since I'd left Aunt Lily. Angel was the only person I missed at all. She missed me, too, Peg said. She often cried at bedtime. That was why Peg and Dad drove her down to spend a weekend with me.

She was nine, the image of the little girl I was when she was born. Even the girls in the dorm, who'd largely ignored me after the first few weeks of the semester, couldn't resist commenting on how much we looked alike, how sweet we looked together.

Angel loved the huge Union Building with its comfortable chairs and sofas, where we sat a long time and listened to a student play the piano. In the book store, I bought her a red and white spiral-bound notebook with INDIANA on the front, just like the ones I used to take notes in. I also bought her a special IU pen. That, I explained, was for writing the poems I was going to teach her to write. I had been introduced to William Carlos Williams's cycle of Brueghel poems in my literature class and was entranced by the idea of painting a picture with words. It was a way of owning a painting, I thought. Experimenting, writing little poems of my own about the paintings in my art history book turned out to be a good way of studying them, as well. I was curious to discover what Angel might see in a painting that I had missed.

I took her to the Commons, bought her a Coke and French fries. Then we sat down at one of the tables and I opened my art history book to Brueghel's painting, "The Fall of Icarus." I told her the story about Icarus, the boy whose wings melted when he flew too close to the sun.

"Can you find him in the painting?" I asked her. She leaned toward the book and studied the painting intensely for a long moment. Then she laughed out loud.

"Here!" she said. "By the boat. Just his leg sticking up in the water."

"Okay, now keep looking," I said. "And listen." I read her the poem that described the painting. "Want to try one of our own?" I asked.

"Sure," she said.

She leafed through the fat volume of art history, stopping finally at Masaccio's "Saints Jerome and John the Baptist." It surprised me. I thought she'd choose something larger, with more action in it. It wasn't even a painting that I'd have chosen myself, which made it all the more pleasurable to look at it with her, to see it through her eyes and help her sequence what she saw into a little poem.

It's all gold behind them.
The man with the red hat looks mean.
he holds a little house in one hand
and in his other hand an open book
with letters I can't understand.

His dog has sharp teeth.
Maybe he's going to bite
the sad man in the pink robe
who's barefoot
holding a pointy gold cross
with a twirling ribbon on it
pointing his finger
to tell which way to go.

"This is fun," Angel said. "Can we do another one, Evie?"

"As many as you want," I said.

I don't know how long we sat there, making poems from the paintings in the book. Later, Rob said he'd watched and eavesdropped on us for ages before he finally spoke.

All I remember is being startled when he said, "Hi," and sat down beside me. I guess it showed because he added, "You're in my art apprec class?" as if he thought I had no idea who he was.

"Oh," I said, like an idiot. "Yes."

Angel looked at him and said, "Are you Evie's friend?"

I was mortified, but he just smiled. "Not yet, but I'd like to be. Is that okay with you?"

She regarded him solemnly. "Sure," she said, and went back to making her poems.

"So, Evie," he said. "Evie what?"

"Slade."

"Evie Slade." He held out his hand, and we shook. "Rob Bonham."

I was surprised at how easy it was to talk to him. He was a freshman, too, an SAE pledge. He envied my single dorm room, he said, when I described it to him. He didn't really like living at the fraternity house all that well, but his father and two older brothers had been SAEs and they'd have been really disappointed if he hadn't joined.

He grinned. "I figure if I do this, maybe they won't disown me when I break the news that I'm not doing business school, definitely not law school. I'm not joining the family firm. I want to study art history," he said. "Taking the art apprec class made me decide for sure. I want to get a PhD and teach someday. Can you imagine how great that would be? I mean, living in a place like Bloomington all your life, doing nothing but thinking about pictures?"

"It's what I want to do, too," I said. "I've always wanted to, ever since I was nine years old and I found this whole big shelf of art books in the library."

"Well, we should study together then," he said. "I've noticed you in class. I mean, you're awake. " He laughed. "Can you believe those jerks in there, sleeping? Jesus. We *should* study together. It would be great to have someone to talk to. Do you want to? Sunday night, maybe? After your sister goes home?"

I said yes.

The two of us helped Angel make a few more poems, then we all walked up Kirkwood Avenue for ice cream cones. Eating them, we wandered through the old, wooded part of campus to Jordan Hall, where Rob gave Angel a tour of the steamy greenhouse with its huge flowering plants. He was charmed by her, just like everyone else was. She reminded him of a Renoir he'd seen at the Metropolitan Museum in New York.

"You've been there?" I asked.

"Oh, yeah. My mom loves museums. I'm the only one in the family who'll go with her without complaining, so I've seen them all. Well, hardly all—but a lot. I've seen the ones in New York and Washington, D.C. In Chicago—I live near there, in Winnetka. And once the Bar Association had meetings in London, so my whole family went there. For a long time, I had no idea what it was all about, then somewhere along the line I really got into it."

"I've been to the museum in Indianapolis," I said, abashed. "Where I grew up. My aunt and uncle used to take me to the Museum of Science and Industry in Chicago every summer when I was little. But we never went to the Art Institute. I doubt they even knew it was there."

"Well, it'll be great when you finally do get to travel then," he said. "You'll be able to go straight to the good stuff instead of dragging around for years like I did, with no clue at all about what I was seeing. Hey, who knows, maybe we can travel together someday, do some obscure, academic study."

"Me, too?" asked Angel, and Rob and I laughed.

"You bet," he said.

Looking back, it amazes me how suddenly my life merged with Rob's. How utterly safe and familiar he seemed to me just hours after we'd met. He was my best friend, I said when the girls in the dorm asked.

"Oh, too bad," they'd say, assuming that I wished he was my boyfriend. But I cherished the relationship we had. I'd never had a best friend before. The girls I'd gone to high school with were concerned with clothes and hairstyles and who would take whom to whatever party was coming up the next weekend. They were nice enough, but pretty quickly we ran out of things to say to one another. The girls I'd met in the dorm so far were no different. Before I met Rob, boys simply seemed like another species. I'd dated now and then, mainly because I was too embarrassed to say no when I was asked. I'd gone to the senior prom to please Aunt Lily. "Every girl should go to her senior prom," she said.

Poor Mike Barth. He showed up looking as miserable in his rented tuxedo as I felt in the dress Aunt Lily had made for me. Less than a year afterwards, I remembered little of prom night. Just the gym not quite transformed by the crepe paper decorations and that dress: a full-length pink satin construction, strapless, with long bone stays that dug into my skin and left dents that hurt to the touch a week after the dance.

Rob laughed when I told him about it and agreed that such events were very nearly unendurable. Thank God he'd found me, he said. If I'd go with him to the fraternity parties he was required to attend, he'd do anything I asked in return. Anything. But I didn't mind going to the parties. We'd find a quiet corner somewhere and talk. Then when everyone had had so much to drink that they'd be unlikely to notice us, we'd slip away. We'd put the top down on his red convertible and drive the Beanblossom Road out to a place we knew in the woods, where we'd sit and talk some more. We talked about pictures we loved, books we read. We talked about our families and how we did not want our lives to be anything like theirs.

He called me nearly every day over Christmas break.

"Who is this boy?" Aunt Lily asked.

"Evie's friend," Angel said. "I told you she had a friend. He's my friend, too, isn't he, Evie?"

"He is," I said, blushing.

"He gave me a present," Angel said, and Aunt Lily grilled me while

Angel ran off to get the beautiful edition of *The Little Prince* that Rob had sent her for Christmas.

"He's just my friend," I said. "Really. He's wonderful; you'd like him. But he really is just my friend, Aunt Lily. I've told you a million times, I'm not going to get married. Ever. Just because I have a male friend—"

She smiled and raised her eyebrows. "Well," she said. "We'll see."

I was right about Aunt Lily liking him. Rob drove me home for spring break and she immediately adored him. He was exactly the kind of boy she hoped I would find, she told me. And it was obvious that we were so close! She did not believe for a minute that we would not wake up someday and realize that our friendship was love. His mother had the same reaction when I visited there that summer. "You're so alike," she told Rob. "You're perfect for one another!"

We laughed and went on the way we were. Now and then, I'd look at him and feel a twinge of something that made me wonder if, someday, we might turn out to be more than friends. But I truly didn't want to marry, and it wasn't worth risking what Rob and I had together just to explore what that twinge might turn out to be.

Two years passed and, still, we were friends. We arrived in Bloomington the fall of our senior year, happy to see each other, more than ready to take up our familiar routines. Those first weeks, though, Rob was too busy to spend much time with me. He'd stayed active in the fraternity to appease his father, and was elected pledge trainer for the fall semester, which meant he had to spend quite a lot of time and effort helping the new pledges settle in. One of them, Terry Callahan, was driving him crazy.

He had appeared dressed in old blue jeans and a tab-collared shirt and he didn't give a damn when it was pointed out to him that he was the only person in the house dressed that way. He refused to help clean the actives' rooms on Saturdays, refused to do the push-ups demanded by drunk brothers in the middle of the night, refused to go out and throw the football on the front lawn at his scheduled time. He offered to fight anyone who wanted to try to make him do something he didn't want to do.

"The thing is," Rob said, "you've got to like him. He's so damn cheerful that only the real creeps in the house can stay mad at him for long. Plus, every male Callahan that he's related to–dead or alive–was or is an SAE somewhere on the planet. All of them loaded. We got the word straight from National. These people give us so much money that there's no way we can dump Terry, no matter what he does. So I keep telling everyone, lighten up. He's not a bad guy, just weird as hell. We're stuck with him. We might as well enjoy him."

He laughed. "They got back at me, though. Last night at chapter meeting we were assigning fraternity sons. Usually the pledge trainer doesn't have one, but everyone agreed that since I thought Terry Callahan was such a swell person, we could make an exception this time. Jesus," he said. "A kid. Just what I need."

But I could tell he wasn't really sorry.

I liked Terry just fine. He was a tall, red-haired goofy-looking guy, clumsy and oddly endearing. He clearly worshiped Rob, who may have been the first person who'd ever treated him with respect, and he was happy to tag along whenever and wherever Rob would let him. The three of us spent a lot of time together that fall. I didn't mind. He was as smart and well-read and as interesting as anyone I'd ever met. He was one of the few people who was perfectly comfortable with the way Rob and I were together. And God, he was funny.

When I think of that time now, I still think of the Terry stories that became house legends even as he lived them. Terry running the hose through Bo Baker's window, stuffing the space between the floor and door with towels on the inside, and turning on the water full blast so that when big dumb Bo came home from class and opened his door, water gushed out, various fraternity dance favors floating into the hallway like little boats. Terry dumping five boxes of Ex-Lax into the big pot of chili the cook had left for Saturday night dinner. Terry drilling a hole through the wall between his and Mike Preston's room and selling tickets to the other pledges for the spectacle of the pompous, uptight Mike making out with his prissy Kappa girlfriend.

"Why do you do it?" I'd ask him, weak with laughter.

"Well," he'd drawl, "because I can."

Rob would shake his head. "I'm supposed to shape him up, you know. His father calls me all the time and wants to know how he's coming along. How am I supposed to tell the guy his kid is hopeless? He'll do anything!"

Terry would give him this maddening, serene smile and Rob would laugh and say, "The truth is, I half wish I had the nerve to do that stuff myself."

What would we do next year? When we weren't trying to keep Terry out of trouble, that was what Rob and I talked about. We were both applying to graduate programs and we spent hours that winter working on our applications, boning up for the graduate exam that would determine our eligibility for fellowships. I needed the money to continue my studies. Rob didn't; his parents could easily pay his tuition, and were willing to do so now that they'd adjusted to his decision not to pursue a career in law. But the prestige of a fellowship mattered; we were both still dead-set on academic careers.

Sometimes we fantasized about getting accepted to the same program. It would be wonderful to be able to continue as we were now. Chicago was our first choice. Rob had always loved living near there, and I liked the idea of being close enough to Indianapolis that Angel might come to visit sometimes. But we wouldn't know until late spring what options would be open to us.

Rob became distracted and edgy for the first time since I'd known him. "Stress," he'd say if I asked him what was wrong. "I hate this not knowing."

So did I. All either of us knew to do after we'd sent off all the applications was to keep busy and try not to think about what lay ahead. We went to movies, put in long hours studying. One day in March, the first almost-warm day, we drove out to Beanblossom with the top down and the heater blasting. The sun shone on the lake, breaking the surface into thousands of tiny mirrors. The sky was blue as a plate. We sat a long time without words, just letting the beautiful day soak into our winter-white skin.

Maybe I dozed, because I remember being surprised by Rob's voice speaking my name. I turned to him and he lifted his hand to my face, ran his fingers lightly along my jawline, brushing my collar bone as he drew them away. In all the time I'd known him, he had never looked at me as he was looking at me now.

"Are you all right?" I said. "Rob?"

"I want to marry you, Evie," he said in a rush. "Let's get married. I've been thinking about this a long time now and I think we should—"

"Marry?"

"Yes," he said. "We'd have a good life. We want the same things, we'd be happy. We're happy together now. I swear, I must know a dozen guys getting married this summer and not one of them gets along with his girlfriend the way I get along with you—"

"I love you," he said, and I began to cry.

We both sat there in stunned silence for a long time. Then finally, miserably, Rob said, "Evie, don't. Please. I'm sorry. I shouldn't have . . . I know you don't want—"

"No," I sobbed. "No. It's what I want, too. I just didn't know it until now."

That night we made love for the first time, spent the night wrapped in each other's arms. We woke the next morning, looked at each other, and started to laugh. It was absurd not to have realized earlier how right this would be.

I had meant it when I said I'd never marry, but it had never occurred to me until now that marriage could be whatever two people wanted it to be. Rob and I didn't have to have children; we didn't have to have small, crushing lives like Dad and Peg; we didn't have to have suburban, country club lives like Rob's parents, either. We didn't have to change any of our plans. We'd simply choose the best graduate school that admitted both of us, and when we were finished we'd make a life that would be exactly what we wanted, our own. We'd teach, write, travel. We'd have a small house full of beautiful, beautiful things.

That weekend, we drove to Winnetka to tell Rob's parents our plans. I'd visited there a number of times, and I felt comfortable and welcome in their home, so I was not surprised that they were pleased about the engagement. What did surprise me—and it touched me deeply—was the delighted way that they introduced me to their friends at the country club that evening as their new daughter. I was touched, too, by the engagement ring that Rob's mother insisted I should have: her own mother's diamond. Rob had always been her soulmate, she confided to me. She had saved it all this time for his bride.

This is right, I thought. This was the family I was meant to have all along. They knew me, they understood what mattered to me as my own family never had.

Not that my family wasn't happy for us, too. They were. On our way back to Bloomington, we stopped first at Dad and Peg's. Vicky, Bets, and Anne grinned and said, "We knew you guys would end up getting married." Angel flew at me and would not let go.

"I can still come visit you, can't I?" she cried. "Whenever I want?"

"Absolutely," I said.

"We'll have a special room for you wherever we live," Rob said. "Your very own. What do you think about that?"

Dad kissed me and shook Rob's hand. Peg did what she always did at any kind of surprise, good or bad: she burst into tears.

When everyone had calmed down, we went on to Aunt Lily's. She hugged me hard and made me promise to let her make my wedding dress. She took both of Rob's hands in hers, stood on her tip-toes, and kissed his cheek. "I knew it the first time I met you," she said. "I just knew you were the one for my Evie."

At school, no one seemed surprised but Terry; but then, he was the only one who had actually believed us when we said that we were only friends.

I found out quickly that planning a wedding was no simple task. Even though it would be small, in the pretty little chapel on campus, we still had to plan the service, make decisions about flowers and music, where to hold the reception afterwards, and what the refreshments would be. We had to plan our honeymoon, too. It would be a trip to Europe, Rob's parents' wedding gift to us. Two weeks, they said. Italy, France, whatever you want! So in the muddle of picking out china, silver, linens, and dozens of other items a newly married couple apparently could not live without, there were guidebooks, brochures, and possible itineraries to consider.

Not to mention papers to write, finals, commencement looming. Life became one huge list. "At least we get to sleep together," I said to

Rob late one night. "It's the only time we have together anymore. It's like we've had to give each other up, give up everything that has to do with why we're getting married in the first place so we can get married."

"It's only time," he said. "We have plenty of time, our whole lives."

"I hate it, though. I feel like I've lost my best friend."

I turned and burrowed my head into the place just above his collarbone, where it fit perfectly. His skin smelled of soap, so familiar. His arms felt heavy encircling me, and I felt that odd burning sensation that seemed to dissolve the edges of my body, to make me press myself against Rob as if it were the only way to stay in the physical world—and, oh, I wanted to stay in the world now that I had discovered this feeling and given it a name: desire.

Rob murmured, "Tired, really tired," and sighed. He stroked my hair, cupped the back of my head in his hand, which felt lighter and lighter and finally fell away to the pillow when he drifted off to sleep.

I lay there, breathing deeply, evenly, until my body gathered itself and became just a body again, no more than the necessary receptacle of my mind. But I couldn't sleep. I got up and pored over the travel books I'd left on the kitchen table. Italy, we'd decided. I looked at the pictures and felt as I had always felt looking at a painting I loved. But I would enter these pictures, and soon. Rob and I would enter them together. It was only weeks away now, days really. I counted them on the calendar: twenty-seven.

Only time, I reminded myself. You just have to get through it. When Terry's dad invited Rob to spend Memorial Day weekend at their lake cottage, I said, "Go. Relax. I'll take the car and drive up to Aunt Lily's so she can do the last fitting of my dress. I'll finish up the last few things on our list. Everything's ready, really." I smiled and hugged him. "All we have to do now is walk down the aisle two weeks from now and get it over with. Then we can have our life back. I've missed you," I said.

He drew me to him, held me a long time. "Maybe I shouldn't go," he said. "Maybe we should spend the weekend together."

"Go," I said again. "It'll do you good."

I expected him home late Sunday afternoon. We'd go out for good meal, I decided, then he could stay the night. It had been well over a week since the last time we'd slept together. I tidied the apartment, changed the sheets on the bed. When I was finished, I took a long bath, then dressed in one of the pretty sundresses Mrs. Bonham had sent me. For Italy, the note she sent with them had said.

I waited, reading. When I heard Rob's footsteps on the stairs, I stood up and began to move toward the door. He opened it just as my hand touched the doorknob, and I stepped back quickly, a bit out of balance.

"Evie!" he said, as if astonished to see me in my own apartment.

"I heard you on the stairs. I was—"

"Evie, we have to talk. I have to talk to you."

"Sure," I said. "I thought we'd have dinner at—"

"No, here. Now. Evie, listen to me," he said. "Please."

His voice frightened me, so flat. And the way he wouldn't look at me.

"Evie, I can't do this," he said.

I sat down on the couch, and he sat beside me, not touching me. "What?" I whispered, even though I knew. "You can't do what, Rob?"

"Marry you," he said. "I can't marry you. I never should have said I would."

"You can't marry me," I said. "You don't want to marry me, you mean? You don't love me?"

"No," he said. "I love you. It's not that. I love you, but I don't love you that way—"

And I saw, quite suddenly, what I should have seen all along. "It's Terry, isn't it. It's Terry you—"

"I don't love him," Rob said miserably. "I—"

"How long?" I asked. "Since the beginning?"

"Since semester break, when I went up to his place in Michigan. To ski, that's what he said when he invited me. And he really wanted me to meet his dad. Then I got there, and it was just the two of us. I knew what he wanted, I should've left—not that it would have made any difference in the long run, I suppose. I'm queer, Evie," he said. "Queer. I should have told you long ago, when we first met."

Now I was the one who looked away. I'd have gotten up, walked right out of the apartment and away from him if I could have. But his words poured into me like lead, and I must sit there and listen to him try to make me understand him.

"Terry wasn't the first," he said. "At camp, when I was thirteen, that was the first time. In high school, there were a couple of—oh, who cares how many times, who or when? Or that I knew long before anything happened that I wasn't like my brothers. Like any other boys I knew. It's just that until Terry there hadn't been anyone for a long time and I had begun to think that maybe I would be all right after all. I did love you, Evie. I do love you. And I stopped with Terry in the spring because I thought—

"But then he talked me into going with him this weekend—" Rob put his hands to his face, as if covering it might make what he had to tell me easier to say. "I hate what we do together," he said. "But I'll do it again. I know I will. If not with Terry, with someone else. Evie—"

He look my hand, lifted it to his lips, and his breath on his fingers felt like short, cool kisses. The way it had felt on the back of my neck in the middle of the night sometimes, stirring me deliciously, half-awake into desire.

"I'm so sorry," he whispered. "There's nobody in the world I care more about than you, nobody who's ever been so good to me—for me. And I've ruined that, I've ruined everything. And the wedding—what are we going to do about that?"

In the end, I was the one who did everything. I dialed his parents' number, handed him the receiver, and listened to him tell the lie: that we had decided too hastily, that both of us had had second thoughts about the marriage and we thought it best to call the wedding off. We were sorry for any pain we'd caused, for the expense. We were sorry for everything. But, no, we could not be dissuaded. We really had made up our minds.

I told the same lie to my family. I was too humiliated to tell them the truth. Peg and Dad tried to be kind. Aunt Lily pretended to be understanding, but I could tell she was angry at me for throwing away the kind of life she'd always wanted me to have.

Only Angel could comfort me. She was nearing thirteen, and when I looked at her it was like looking at a memory of myself at the end of childhood, a time when I couldn't have imagined what I was now. It seemed to me that if I could just remember how I'd felt then, I might go back to that place and start again. When I was accepted at the University of Ohio and got the fellowship there, I took Angel with me to look for an apartment and to help me furnish it. I depended on her instincts for bright colors, her way of finding objects and images that made their own sunshine in the tiny, dark rooms. I imagined the two of us living there together someday: the old fantasy. I should never have let it go in the first place. I remembered, knew for certain now: Angel was the only person in the whole world that it was safe for me to love.

Chapter Five

*T*his couldn't be good for me, this digging and probing. It was Cliff's fault. It was his voice that carried me back. I had begun to hear it even when he was nowhere near. I thought of the two of us at Silchester just yesterday, another life. Teaching me ancient history, he had cracked my own life open like an egg. Then, driving back, he said, "I want to show you my flat."

It was lovely, which surprised me, unbalanced me right off. There were deep corduroy couches piled high with pillows. Restored fragments of mosaics that looked like puzzles missing half their pieces. An ancient leather shoe—a child's shoe—under glass.

"Look," he said again and again. "Look," taking my hand.

An oak shelf hung on the wall of the library, and on it was a series of miniature Roman deities. A household shrine, he told me. Every Roman family had one to house the *lares familiaris*, or favorable spirits—figures of dancing youths that were used to toast the gods. His home was so orderly, nothing like his mind. Even his dark, shuttered bedroom. There, one book lay on his bedside table, beside it a stack of magazines as perfectly aligned as a deck of cards. The coverlet was smooth, except for the curve of pillows under it, each side falling to exactly the same height, just above the floor. When he opened his closet, there were his starched blue workshirts like a row of soldiers. His jeans and khaki pants were folded over wooden hangers, his shoes lined up on the floor.

I knew what was going to happen. I had known it since the moment Cliff told me about the secret life beneath the field. I thought, I shouldn't do this. I'll be sorry. I'm too old for this; I don't need this. I decided against this years ago. But I was like a person anaesthetized, floating.

He placed his hands on my shoulders and they held me there, collected me. His thumbs found my collar bone and traveled along it, met in the hollow of my neck and rose to tip my face toward him. Yes, he asked without words. And without words, I answered. I let his patient, sturdy hands unearth me, search the depths of me until it seemed my very heart was revealed.

That night I dreamed of Joris. First his house: tall and narrow, red-shutters, red window-boxes, flowers spilling out against the brick. So clean inside. And quiet, as I walked through the familiar rooms. The parlor with its heavy draperies pulled back to show the mullioned windows. Heavy, claw-footed chairs and settees, end tables covered with lovely little Persian rugs. The dining room: its big table shining with hundreds of years of polish. The kitchen: all blue and white and yellow. In my dream, I opened the door to the back staircase and wound up to the second story, to the bedroom. There were crisp white sheets on the old-fashioned cupboard bed, its blue velvet curtains were parted, and Joris was there, waiting. Now, after all this time, yes.

But after we had made love and I cupped his face in my hands, joyful, released, the dream shifted and it was Cliff's face I saw. We were back on the green hill again, at Silchester. Beneath us, the ancient city had dreamed itself alive, and I was shocked awake by it, vulnerable. I was disoriented by my strange surroundings, by the way the real, sleeping Cliff turned and drew me to him, settling the shape of his body against my own, as if to comfort me. As if he had been dreaming with me. The press of him against my back, the weight of his arm across my shoulder, the feel of his breath in my hair kept me awake, but could not keep me from dreaming of Joris—although now I dreamed him in my mind's eye. I remembered the way it actually had been: the two of us climbing the stairs late one winter afternoon to my small, spare room in the Jordaan. The window darkening as we lay together, still as the circles of lamplight on the white walls.

"Ah, no," he had said, finally. "Evie, I cannot." And when he took me in his arms, it was only to console me.

Now I was bent over the binocular microscope, as I had been most of the morning, aligning the threads of the long clean tear, applying almost invisible beads of glue with the hot needle, tamping them ever so gently. The work was slow and tedious, but comforting. There was nothing but the feel of my fingers, sensitive as a blind person's. The eye of the microscope revealed all I needed to know. I was surprised when I looked up and saw Ian tipped back in a chair, his feet resting on the open drawer of a file cabinet. He nodded toward the cup of tea he'd brought me, sipped from his own mug.

"You've forgotten to eat, I suppose."

I had. At the sight of the sandwiches he'd brought, I was ravenous.

"You'll stay late again tonight?" he asked.

"I want to finish the gluing on this cut before I go. Then there's just the small one left, but the way it's all stretched out, it'll take longer. I'd hoped to be ready for the cleaning by the end of this week—"

"There's no deadline, Evie. Better the work is done well. And everyone here knows you're doing it well. Don't hurry and run off because of Cliff."

I turned and examined what I'd been working on, smoothed the re-joined section of the tear lightly with one finger to avoid acknowledging Ian's words.

"Ah, you'd have laughed at the two of us at university together," he said when some time had passed. "Both odd ducks, we were. You can imagine it. Me rhapsodizing about dead painters. Cliff going on about his Romans, mucking about in the dirt. We went on that way a long while after we left school. We shared a flat until my mother became ill and needed me to be there with her.

"We weren't alike, though, Evie. I was happy to go back and care for Mother. Since she died, I've been happy living on my own. I'm not a passionate person, you know. Like Cliff is. Like you. I really don't need anybody but myself."

"Me, " I said. "Passionate?"

"You don't like to think of yourself that way, I know. Except about your work. But I saw it right off, when we were in Florence together. I saw you'd lost something, I saw you deciding that what you'd found there was going to replace it. You've had to teach yourself to be happy alone, Evie. Cliff's still trying to teach himself that—

"Loneliness is the only possible explanation for his taking up with Metta," he went on. "I'm sure of that. I never could bear her. One of those dreadful women who goes about with brambles in her jumper. Earthy, you know. She weaves. Cliff sank into domestic torpor. The house in the country. Dogs and horses. And then they married and had those ghastly children—" He looked as if he'd just been given a dose of ill-tasting medicine.

"Ian, you don't like *any* children," I said.

"Trust me, Evie. Robin and Monica are ghastly. Metta's a great believer in the innate goodness of children, all that rot. If left to their own innocent devices, they'll naturally do what's right." He snorted. "Like the feminists who say the world would be a kinder, happier place if women ran it—forgetting all about our Mrs. Thatcher. In any case, if you should continue in this—relationship with Cliff, you must definitely press for an agreement about how little time you'll be obliged to spend with those children."

"Cliff and I do not have a relationship." I said this with more conviction than I felt.

"Really. What is it you have then?" Ian smiled his owlish smile, and I saw I'd laid myself open for the question he'd meant to ask me all along.

I had to admit that I had no idea. "But whatever it is, I don't need it," I said. "I hate feeling this way. I told you, Ian, coming over here to work on the Vermeer was perfect for me: a nice break, the chance of a lifetime. What I don't need is suddenly feeling as if I'm sixteen again. No, it's worse than that. At sixteen, I knew what I wanted: to get as far away from my family as I could. To have my own life."

"And now you want?"

"Now I want not to have gotten myself into this—thing I've gotten myself into with Cliff. Well, that's lame, isn't it? You see the problem. I don't know what I'm doing. I can't even think straight enough to say what I feel, let alone do the sensible thing—"

"Out of control, then?"

"You say that like wanting to be in control of my own life is some kind of crime," I said. "Tell me, who doesn't want that? For God's sake, you can't just fall in love at my age and drop everything." I stopped short.

"Ah, so you're in love," he said, lighting a cigarette, maddeningly calm. "You're considering dropping everything."

"That's not what I said, Ian. Don't be ridiculous."

He raised an eyebrow at me. "Unclench your teeth, Evie," he said. "I'm just trying to bully you into figuring out how you feel. I say something, you react. You'll recall, we've done this for years. Since Florence, when you finally told me about Rob."

Suddenly, I was exhausted. I'd been a wreck for days. I was behind schedule with the Vermeer and it was my own fault. I'd sit and stare at the print of it pinned on the wall above my work table for hours on end. It seemed different to me. When I had started working on it, what I loved was the beautiful, cool surface. The look on the woman's face, as if she saw right through me. Now I had begun to look at her and think, who is she waiting for?

I might as well face it. Even before Silchester, I'd begun to wait for Cliff's calls. Then when he did call, I didn't know what to say. I longed to see him, I was afraid to see him. I lay awake at night thinking, what will I do?

"Evie?" Ian repeated.

"Okay, Ian," I said. "Okay. Cliff and I spent last night together."

"Oh," he said.

His obvious shock at this piece of information gave me a moment of unworthy satisfaction. "I told you we were going to Silchester," I said. "Well, afterwards, we went back to his flat and—"

"Please," he interrupted, recovering his aplomb, "spare me the details."

But I was too distracted to laugh. "What does he want?" I said. "You know him, you know me. What does he want?"

"I'll wager he doesn't have a clue himself," Ian said. "But he's happier than I've seen him in a long while. You are, too—aren't you Evie? If a bit off-center. Enjoy it, can't you? There's time enough later to sort out what it means."

I ran my finger again along the tear I'd been mending. I thought of the woman lunging for the canvas, the blade of her knife slicing through the world Vermeer had created there. No matter how carefully I mended the torn place, traces of her hateful act would remain beneath the surface. It would never be perfect again. Why had I come here?

"Evie?" Ian said.

"But there's not time," I said miserably. "It's not like we're twenty, with everything before us. There's my job to think about. My life. I can't just walk away from it. And Cliff has a life, too—those children. Ian, you do see this is impossible—"

"Really," he said. "Well, then. You'll break off this impossible thing right away, will you? Before it gets even more out of hand?"

That was exactly what I'd been telling myself I was going to do since I'd left Cliff's flat that morning. But as soon as Ian spoke the words, I knew I wouldn't do it. "It's your fault," I said, determined to revert to our usual teasing exchange. "If you hadn't dragged me over here—"

"Perhaps," he said. "But then if you hadn't dropped everything that other time and bolted for Florence, you'd never have known me."

I thought of Cliff's own personal domino theory then, another of those odd ideas of his that had a way of bringing the world suddenly into focus.

"The universe is perfect, Evie," he had said. "Don't you see? Everything was set in motion ages ago and we're like dominoes, waiting patiently for our moment in time. Falling is inevitable. It's in righting ourselves that choice and chance enter and give us a shot at making some sense of the muddle—at defining who we are."

Ian had been joking, but I knew that if Cliff were with us he'd have regarded Ian's observation about Florence as proof that this theory was true.

I learned about the flood on the television news. Riveted, I watched volunteers carrying huge canvases through the ravaged streets of Florence, three on each side, like pall bearers. They loaded sculptures and objects of brass and silver and gold into the beds of trucks. They made a human chain to hand priceless rare books from the collapsed shelves of libraries to the hands of monks who would try to save them. I've never been an impulsive person; I still can't say exactly what it was that made me decide that I would go to help. But within a day I'd made arrangements for another graduate student to teach my classes at the university through Christmas break. I flew from Cincinnati to New York and on to Milan; I stood the whole way to Florence on the train.

It was on the train that I met Ian. I noticed him first. He was tall and as gangly as an adolescent, wearing round wire-rimmed glasses. There was about him an extraordinary tension, which to this day I've never named to my satisfaction. Intense patience? I've never met another person who can sit as still as he can, who can focus all his energies on one thing, however small, for as long as he decides is necessary. On the crowded train to Florence, he sat on his bedroll reading a collection of essays on seventeenth century Dutch art, his eyes glued to the page despite the fact that the space between the railway cars where we had gathered swayed wildly, despite the people who stumbled over his long legs coming and going. I was curious about what he read; it was my own area of expertise, and I wondered if his interest was professional. I couldn't resist the temptation to ask him; and when I did, he focused on my face—on me—as intensely as, moments before, he had focused on his book.

Yes, it was a professional interest, he told me. He was a doctoral student himself, an intern at the National Gallery in London. By the time the train arrived in Florence, we were friends. He'd made plans to meet some of his colleagues at a pensione they knew, near the Uffizi. Since I'd made no arrangements, he invited me to join them.

We made our way there together in silence, sobered by what we saw. The raging river had dislodged paving stones, uprooted iron poles and chains, snapped the stems of street signs, and carried them, along with automobiles, household debris, and ruined shop wares, through the streets. And small personal objects, too, each speaking of its own private tragedy: a child's stuffed toy, a tortoise shell hairbrush, a pair of broken eyeglasses, a nightgown trimmed in delicate lace. Now all of it lay piled up in the piazzas, covered in a residue of mud.

Fango, we learned to call it, spitting the word out with disgust, as the Florentines did. Palaces and shops gaped empty, the long stretches of muddy building fronts looked as if fire had left them charred and sooted. On the marble steps of churches, mud swirled like thick fudge icing on a cake. In every building, in every street there hung a dank humidity, the stench of rotting refuse, spoiled foodstuffs, and sewage.

There was the acrid tang of the fuel oil that had burst from the heating plants of the big buildings and ridden the tide of the floodwaters, its sludge blotching statues, marking the flood level on the walls of churches and palaces with ugly black lines.

Everywhere, I saw lovely ruined faces that I had known in books—painted faces, stone and marble faces, wood faces full of anguish. In the church, Santa Croce, I watched friars sift through the mud, using vegetable strainers to search for tiny paint fragments of the Cimabue "crucifix," which lay, ravaged, on a scaffolding. I stared at the thirteenth century Christ—the very beginning of Renaissance art—now lost forever. A corpse. A relic. Nothing recognizable but one closed eye, the halo, the red blood falling in droplets from the savior's outstretched hands. I grieved as if these art works had been human, I grieved for the artists' souls. It would take years to restore the art that had been damaged. Ten years, the conservators predicted. Maybe fifteen, twenty. There were so few people qualified for the task.

Bisogna fare la bella figura. The people kept face. There was among them little hair-tearing, no harshness; rather a grave restraint, a quiet masking of private pain. They worked night and day, and we worked with them. Ian and I were sent out with a team to clean the oil and muck from stone sculptures. We worked methodically, retrieving sculptures from under tumbled pews and altars, searching cellars, ankle-deep in slime, often to find a dozen or so sculptures deposited in one spot like stranded travelers huddling together. The work was tedious and slow. Masked against the fumes, we sprayed solvents on the oil-coated stone. We swabbed the folds and crevices with Q-tips.

I had been so certain about my decision to study art history until then, so fervent in my desire to teach others to love what I loved. But the first time I touched a real work of art—my own hands responsible for saving it—I knew that teaching would not be enough for me. How completely different this rescue work was from the click of slides falling from a carousel into the light, the drone of my own voice lecturing about the flat images on the screen. In Florence, I stood again and again before a carved face, my hands poised, so close to the sculpture in the moment before my fingertips touched it that I could no longer see the features, only the grain of the stone, ancient and enduring. Then there was the cool surface: my fingers where the artist's had been. Sometimes

I believed that I was touching the artist himself, far beyond time.

To work on paintings like this, I thought. A Rembrandt. A Vermeer. My whole life swung open at the thought!

Any time we had a spare moment, Ian and I walked across the Arno to the Pitti Palace, where a huge masonry shelter built to house a collection of lemon trees had been made into the picture hospital. There, in oppressive humidity, conservators worked at large tables, dampening panel paintings with water to soften the mud that was caked on them. Others pressed wax coatings to the backs of canvases using scavenged household irons. There were hundreds of paintings laid out on the sawdust floor awaiting repair, made ghostly by the transparent tissue facings that had been applied to support the paint layer. Some were tinted blue from the Kleenex and toilet tissue the restorers had used those first days, not daring to wait for new supplies of the more desirable rice paper to arrive. Beside each painting lay a piece of paper holding tiny bits of paint that had become detached from it. It was strange sometimes, the form the damage had taken. I was haunted by a Pontecorma I saw one day: A woman fleeing in alarm, moving toward what had been a Christ figure—now completely effaced, except for one beckoning hand. In the background, a city set on the hills had almost vanished.

I should have been thinking about going home. As Christmas neared, the ranks of volunteers thinned considerably. Ian and his colleagues left, and I was alone in the pensione during those few days before the holiday. On Christmas Eve morning, while all of Florence made final preparations for the Pope's arrival in the city, I went to the *limonaia*. Ian had a friend there, a conservator on loan from the National Gallery. I'd gotten to know him a little, and I went to find him that day, to ask his advice.

"If I wanted to do the kind of work you do," I said, "where would I start?"

"School," he told me, and named the best ones. The Courtauld Institute in London. New York University. A school in Rome, one in Stuttgart.

"How much school? How many years?"

"Three," he said. "Perhaps four. Perhaps an apprenticeship somewhere after that. Depends on what you want. It's a major undertaking, in any case. You'd want to be sure. Could you stay on here a while?" he asked. "They'd train you to do the most basic kind of work now. They'd even pay you a stipend. Small, mind you. But it might help you decide—"

All day I walked the streets, trying to make up my mind what to do. I was twenty-four years old, a year into a doctoral program in art history, my future set. If I stayed in Florence, failed to fulfill my teaching obligations this semester, I'd lose my fellowship. I could never go back. To change my mind about what I wanted to do would mean years and years more of struggling to make ends meet.

And there was Angel. Living in Columbus, I still saw her a lot. Adolescence had made her gawky and shy, but after we'd been together a few hours, the old Angel always emerged. She still said wonderful things about paintings, things I often found myself working into my lectures. I had such high hopes for her. She needed me.

That night, I went to midnight mass. The Duomo was full, overflowing, so I stood in the cold crisp night surrounded by thousands of Florentines who had come to hear the Pope's message to the city. Reverent, waiting, they looked toward the vast doorway filled with light. At the first crackling of the speakers, they bowed their heads. Silence fell upon them like a cloak. When the Pope began to speak, there was a palpable lifting, as if everyone present had taken a deep breath at exactly the same moment.

I am not a religious person. I went to the Duomo that night because I believed I had earned the right to stand among the Florentines, if only for that one solitary midnight. But the sound of the Pope's voice made thin and reedy, unearthly, by the poor amplification, the chanting response echoing in the piazza like a memory: thousands of voices merging with all the voices from all time—this changelessness spoke to me. It made me tremble.

No, I was not "saved" that night. I did not fall to my knees. But I believed for the first time since I'd abandoned the provincial religion of my childhood that there was something more in this world than ourselves. Something beneath and above us, running through us. A force. God, if you will. The name of this changelessness did not matter. My own hands where the artist's hands had been would put me in touch with it, would teach me all I need ever hope to know.

Chapter Six

"*A*nd you think it was your sister who paid the price for that joy?"

That's what Cliff asked me. We were in his Land Rover, barreling north across rich, rolling farm land and pastures, on our way to Hadrian's Wall. I was trying to explain to him how finding my work and losing Angel had always seemed like part of the same thing to me.

"I was a mess," I said. I told him the long story about Rob and the canceled wedding. "Angel was the one who kept me the least bit sane that whole time. She was only fifteen when I left for Italy. She'd been with me in Columbus the weekend before; she used to come visit whenever Peg and Dad would let her. And I just left. Like she didn't even matter. By the time I saw her again, she and Matt were married, a baby coming. God, at seventeen. If I just hadn't stayed away so long."

"You could have saved her."

"I'd have seen what was happening. Peg and Dad were so stupid. I would have—"

"What? Done what?"

"I don't know, I don't know. Reminded her there was more—" I turned from him and stared out the car window. A glider circled above the wheat fields like a great bird. But all I could think of was Angel. The way she had offered her baby, Jenny, to me that first time. Proud and anxious simultaneously, the look on her face saying please. "She's beautiful," I said. And she was. But I did not take her. If I had, I'd have remembered the feel of Angel in my arms that day so long ago, how everything had changed because of it. I'd have remembered how much I had loved her, and I knew I did not dare risk loving her or anyone that much again.

A long time passed before Cliff asked, "So how did it all turn out for her? What's her life like now?"

"Perfectly ordinary," I said. "She and Matt went to night school. She teaches second grade; he coaches high school football. They live maybe two miles from Dad and Peg."

"Is she happy?"

"Happy?" I asked.

"Yes," he said. "They're still together after all this time. These days, that means a lot."

"Inertia?" I shrugged, tried to ignore my mind's eye's review of the progression of family photographs that Angel had sent me religiously over the years: she and Matt, smiling; Jenny growing into a girl as pretty and full of life as Angel had been.

"Ah, Evie—"

And, damn it, my eyes filled up with tears. I was ashamed of my mean spirit, ashamed that I hadn't told the whole truth about Angel, the part that hurt me the most: she *was* happy. Stupidly, stupidly happy. That's what I couldn't accept.

"You can't imagine it, can you?" Cliff said. "Just falling in love— bam. So hard nothing else matters. Not the smartest thing, maybe. But it happens." He touched my hand. "I've heard sometimes it even lasts." Then he smiled, directing my attention to some pretty black and white cows lying on a hillside. "They're not real; they're ceramic," he said. "They cart them out in the early morning and set them in their places so the tourists passing by can ogle them."

I knew what he was up to. He'd make me laugh, then I'd feel better. Yes, I'd say. Okay, Angel is happy. I'd see that he was right: it's love that matters, after all. But I couldn't laugh. I couldn't stop the ugly chatter in my head. I was sorry I had agreed to come on this trip with him.

We'd made the plans for it during our picnic at Silchester, before what happened that night—and every night since, in his flat. "Why not come up and see the Wall with me," he had said. "I've got to go up next weekend with some things from the lab. We can stay at the farm. You can meet my mum, see the countryside there. It's lovely."

I hesitated even then. An outing to Silchester was one thing, a weekend with his family quite another. But he so earnestly tried to persuade me, promising a landscape so beautiful that I would think he'd driven me directly into a work of art.

"All right," I said, laughing. "All right, I'll go."

The sky *was* a Constable sky, alive. Patches of French blue—thin-glazed, delicate as bone china—showed through fluffy white clouds that looked as if they'd been drawn by a child. Huge turbulent clouds scudded beneath the prettiness, constantly shifting the pattern of blue and white, shifting the pattern of light and shadow in the valley below. The low clouds were the color of weathered stone.

I had never seen country like this before, so large and lush. Shaggy green hills rose and crested as far as I could see, crisscrossed with the white lines of stone fences. It had rained recently, and everything was shining. Cliff had grown up here, in the ancient farmhouse that seemed to have sprouted from the rocky terrain. Purple lobelias cascaded from its window boxes, vivid against the red shutters. The house was shaded by sycamores, their dark leaves the size of hands. Its lawn was as green as a golf course, rimmed in flowers: phlox, foxglove, lupine, lilies, Canterbury bells. The blue delphinium lining the picket fence stood taller than either one of us. Giant sunflowers bobbed their yellow heads. I suddenly understood Cliff's sense of space, the reason he moved as he did—widely, boldly—not at all like Londoners, who were accustomed to a lifetime of cramped quarters. Every morning, he had awakened and walked into this scene.

We stood and watched three little boys in slickers and wellies, playing in the muddy farmyard. Their black and white soccer ball was splotched brown. They ran and kicked, their slickers flying out behind them, their wellies flopping against their sturdy legs. They shouted and wrestled good-naturedly with each other, sliding, ducking. Their cheeks were flushed, partly from the damp chill of early evening, partly from over-exertion.

Beyond them, on the other side of the rickety bar, men were shearing sheep. They took them one by one, removing each coat deftly, all in one piece, like a little woolly rug. Released, the poor, bald mama sheep gathered at the far fence line and cried for their babies penned up on the other side. The babies bleated back, thin, miserable bleats, and huddled as near the mothers as they could. All this desperate bleating and the boys' shouting and the men calling back and forth blended and rose with the wind that whipped up suddenly, and just as suddenly was gone again. For a moment, in the stillness, the bleating sounded human.

"Like the little children crying in the railway stations when they were evacuated during the war," Cliff said. "That's what my mum used to say. For years, she wore earplugs at shearing time. Couldn't bear it. She'd work right alongside my step-dad. Castrate the lambs and never blink. But it was a long time before she got used to that crying."

He was the one feeling uneasy now. I watched him glance at the boys, his nephews, who kept playing. At the men, one of them his half-brother, who kept working. No one had noticed us yet. We could have gotten back into the car and driven to a bed-and-breakfast in a nearby village. Or back to London. We could have been there by midnight, perhaps in our own separate beds.

Then a woman opened the red door of the farmhouse, and beckoned us inside. "I'm Mrs. Murray, dear," she said, smiling, and held out her hand to me. She was probably near seventy, but her eyes were bright and she looked as sturdy as the boys playing out in the yard. "So pleased to meet you. Do come in. And Clifford—" She tilted her face toward his kiss.

"Mum," he said.

She settled us into our places. Cliff went to the room he'd had as a boy, one of the little boy's rooms now. "They'll double up tonight," she said. My room, the guest room, had pink sprigged wallpaper, a pink satin comforter. There was a white-tiled fireplace with a spray of cut flowers on the hearth and pretty pink-and-white knickknacks arranged on the mantel. The long narrow window was hung with white lace curtains.

When we had unpacked and freshened up, there was tea waiting for us in the kitchen. It was steamy there; Mrs. Murray and Ivy, Cliff's sister-in-law, had been cooking all day.

"Shearing time," Mrs. Murray said cheerily. "It's dreadful. You feed the men in the morning, then send them off and start in cooking the midday meal. Then tea." All the while she was talking she was loading the table with plates of sandwiches, quiches, pork pies, beans, and a half-dozen kinds of salads. "You call those boys now," she said to Ivy. "All of them."

The three little boys and the men tromped in, bringing the dank smell of wool mingled with the smell of their own bodies, the smell of mud and damp.

"Uncle Cliff!" The littlest of the boys threw himself into Cliff's arms. "Where's Robin and Monica? Did you bring them?"

"Not this time, mate. I brought my friend, Evie."

"Mind your manners," Ivy said before the boy could express the disappointment we all saw in his face. "William, Charles, and Stephen," she said, turning to me, reciting the boys' names in stair-step order. They looked away shyly. "Thomas," she said, gesturing toward her husband.

He was large and raw-boned. His face was chiseled. He nodded toward me, shy as the boys. Bob and Glen—one a friend, one a worker hired for the shearing—nodded similarly. They all shook Cliff's hand. Then, relieved that the social amenities had been attended to, they crowded around the table to eat. When they'd devoured the meal and drunk at least a gallon of tea among them, Mrs. Murray brought out the desserts—cream cakes, flans, and tarts—and they devoured those as well. Then they were gone again, back to the barn to work until it was too dark to see. Cliff went along to help them. The little boys had to stay in, though, Ivy said, and ordered them upstairs to take a bath.

"Go on, now," she said when they complained. "You sound like those poor sheep, bleating."

I helped Ivy and Mrs. Murray with the washing-up, which I could tell pleased them. I thought of Aunt Lily. "Always help, wherever you are," she used to tell me. "There's never an excuse not to." It had been a long time since I'd heard her voice inside my head like that, directing me, and I missed her suddenly. It had been ages since I'd written to her. She didn't even know I'd come to England. I promised myself I'd send her a postcard the very next day, a pretty one that showed the countryside. When I got back to London, I'd write her a long letter.

"When Clifford rang up about coming, he told me that you'd come to London to do some work," Mrs. Murray said.

"Yes. A special project at the National Gallery." I told her a little about the Vermeer, and she expressed polite interest; but I could tell that she and Ivy both thought it was strange for the museum to bring a person all the way from America just to mend a few tears.

"Is it your first trip to England?" Mrs. Murray asked.

"It is. Although my work keeps me mostly in London, I love seeing the countryside when I can. I appreciate your having me here.
Having the chance to see Hadrian's Wall—"

"Oh, yes," Mrs. Murray said. "You must take a good look at the
Wall tomorrow. It's quite remarkable. Vast."

From the floor above us, we heard thumps and bumps, an occasional howl of pain that dissolved into laughter. Ivy excused herself to
go settle the boys down and get them ready for bed.

Mrs. Murray and I retired to the lounge. It was cozy there. The
walls were the color of cream; the old woodwork, the ceiling beams
were stained a rich brown. The draperies were red and green and white:
a large flower print, full-blown roses. In the fireplace, a gas fire glowed.

Mrs. Murray settled in a worn green armchair and picked up her
knitting. I was content to sit and gaze out the window at the landscape
purpling with dusk.

"Lovely, isn't it?" Mrs. Murray said.

"It's so—large. Somehow I hadn't expected that."

"It is. I must say, even after forty years it can still surprise me. Grew
up in London, I did. The war, you know." Her voice was wistful. "People
ended up in the most unlikely places because of it."

"Yes, I know," I said, thinking of Peg. It was only when I saw Mrs.
Murray peering curiously over her glasses at me that I realized I'd spoken in an authoritative tone.

"My stepmother is English," I explained. "She met my father
during the war."

"Your mum, you say?"

"No. She's not my real mother. My stepmother." Speaking the
words brought a sense of *deja-vu;* I had said them so many times all
through my childhood. They brought the ripple of anger they'd always
brought, but it was more like a memory of anger than anger itself. In
any case, Mrs. Murray didn't seem to have noticed it. There was a far-
away look on her face, a shadow of a smile.

"It was the times," she said. "I fell in love with a Yank myself during
the war. Clifford's father, you know. Oh, he was handsome. Blond, like
Clifford. Clever, too. It's where Clifford got his cleverness, I'm sure.
We'd have had a good life together, I suppose. But I lost him—

"I don't regret a bit of it, though," she went on resolutely. "Nor do I regret settling here, with Angus Murray, when he offered to take the both of us on. Your stepmum, dear, what part of England was she from?"

I told her that Peg was from London.

"Ah, my home, too, as I said. South London, near Wandsworth. Not much left of my old neighborhood when the war was over. Just the stories—

"For us younger ones, you know, so much of it was a lark. We didn't have a lifetime of furniture and crockery to lose, like our mums and dads did. No children to worry about. We were too foolish to be afraid for ourselves. We couldn't wait to join up and put on those smart uniforms. Cocky, we were. The war meant finagling a leave to sneak off to London with a boy you fancied, dancing at the Hammersmith Palais till all hours." She laughed. "One of the boys I knew, a flier, had a parrot he'd trained to recite all the great lines from Mr. Churchill's speeches. He kept it in the window of the barracks. His Nibs, he called it. We girls would pass by and it'd squawk, 'Blood, sweat, toil, and tears!'" Mrs. Murray laughed. "I'll bet your stepmum has her stories, too, doesn't she?"

Because she was Cliff's mother, I told her the story about the Christmas goose. "My father got it trading whisky and cigarettes," I said. "But he was so excited about the prospect of surprising Peg's family with it that he didn't notice the farmer hadn't wrapped it properly. He went straight from the farmer's to the railway station, got on the train for London, and put the goose on the luggage rack. By the time he noticed blood leaking down the wall, it was too late to do anything. The train was crowded with servicemen on leave—"

"Oh, yes, the trains were dreadful," Mrs. Murray said. "Packed."

"And military police pacing up and down the aisles."

"Yes, that, too." She shuddered.

"Anyway," I continued, "my father didn't know whether the MPs had seen the blood or not. Maybe they had and were watching to see who claimed the package. If he got caught with black market goods, he'd be in real trouble. On the other hand, he was going to meet Peg's parents for the first time, and surprising them with a goose when they thought their Christmas dinner was going to be Spam and beans was bound to put him in their good graces. He argued with himself the whole way to London.

"He chanced it in the end. He got away with it. But Peg always used to tell us, 'Your dad very nearly had his goose cooked for the sake of one!'"

This made Mrs. Murray laugh so hard she had to take a tissue to wipe her eyes.

"Peg told stories all the time," I said. "My little sisters—my half-sisters—begged for them. For the longest time they thought England was a made-up place, like in a book."

"Ah." Mrs. Murray's eyes went teary. "Has she ever come back, your stepmum?"

"No," I said.

For the first time, this struck me as strange. Had she wanted to? Of course, for so many years there wouldn't have been the money for her to make the trip, no matter how homesick she was. And who would've looked after us children? But once we were grown and on our own, surely she could have made a visit. Her parents had come to visit us one time, not long after we'd moved into the new house. I didn't remember much about them, though. Only that Angel, who was just beginning to talk, picked up a bit of an English accent, which everyone found amusing. And I remember Peg's father refusing to eat corn on the cob when Aunt Lily served it.

"Peasant food!" he growled, and Aunt Lily hadn't known whether to be mortified or insulted.

Had it been after that summer visit that the Christmas packages from England had stopped coming? Even I had come to look forward to the big boxes wrapped in brown paper, tied with heavy twine. The crinkly wrappings inside smelled different from our Christmas wrappings, foreign. There were books with pictures of English children, sturdy and rosy-cheeked, like Ivy and Thomas's boys. Pretty handkerchiefs. Rolls of buttery toffees in bright red packages. Hand-knit sweaters. Scots kilts one year, even for the baby.

Come to think of it, when had the postman quit delivering their letters written on thin blue paper? "Peg lost touch with her family at some point," I told Cliff's mother.

She nodded sympathetically. "A lot of those girls never really knew what they were getting themselves into, going off the way they did after the war. There were terrible rows, you know. Many a father was unhappy about his daughter marrying a Yank. Cut her off right then. Other families just drifted apart over time. It's so far away, America. Another world. She's been happy, though, your stepmum?"

The truth was, I'd never thought about whether or not Peg was happy in America. I'd only thought of her as happy to have stolen my dad away from my mother. Now I remembered the way her eyes shone when she talked about England, the way she always called it "home." I had a sudden memory of spying on her one day when she stood at the kitchen sink doing the breakfast dishes. My father had left for work, we girls were supposed to be outside playing. Peg was up to her elbows in bubbles, the damp dish towel slung across one shoulder. "Fools Rush In" came on the radio and she stood stock-still and sang along, tears rolling down her cheeks and falling into the dishwater. But she had looked radiant, as if transported to another place.

"I guess she was happy," I said to Mrs. Murray. "She never did become an American citizen, though. My dad used to tease her about being an alien; every year he'd threaten to forget to drive her to the post office in time to fill out that card she had to fill out. She'd laugh—"

"A lot of them did come home, you know," Mrs. Murray said. "The war brides. Babies and all. America was not like they thought it would be was all they'd say. Myself, I still wonder now and then how it would've been. My life there with Clifford's father—"

I had a strange thought then: How easily Peg could have ended up just like Mrs. Murray had. One thing I knew from years of eavesdropping was that Peg had been surprised when Dad came back to get her. And he'd been surprised, too. Peg hadn't told him she was pregnant. If he hadn't come, if Peg had stayed in England, my sister Vicky would have been like Cliff, never knowing her real father. I couldn't fathom where that turn of events would have left me. But it was easy to imagine Peg there in Mrs. Murray's parlor, her cup of tea before her, her knitting on her lap. Whole lives had hinged on things much more unlikely than a man making the kind of choice my father had made. My own life, for instance. A natural disaster in Florence years ago, the crazy woman who'd slashed the Vermeer had brought me to this night.

"You should get your mother to write those stories of hers down," I said to Cliff later. "Tape her or something. The way you love history."

"Not bloody likely," he said. "Her idea of history is like what you'd see on American television. Cleaned up. Viewer safe." He fell quiet.

It was long past midnight. He had crept across the hall to the pink room, where we'd made love. Now we were lying in the double bed together, the slippery satin duvet covering our bare skin. It was cold for July, even for the north. Stars glittered in the black sky that was framed by Mrs. Murray's white lace curtains.

"You know, for years, when I begged her to, she wouldn't talk about the war at all. Her whole family lost in the Blitz. Then losing my father. I guess you couldn't blame her. But, since Angus died, she talks about the war all the time. I think it's more real to her than the life she has now, without him. But she's polished away all the pain. These stories she tells: they're just that, stories. They're not real. I'd rather know nothing at all."

I thought of Peg telling the story of the day Dad appeared in the doorway of her mother's kitchen—months after he'd been shipped home and she'd accepted the fact that she'd never see him again. "Marry me," were his first words. Her tea cup clattered into its saucer and she stood up, huge with the baby she'd kept a secret from him.

"Tom didn't miss a beat," Peg said when she told the story. "Both of you marry me!" he said.

She never told the story if she thought I was listening, of course. But, eavesdropping, I wondered why she'd tell *anyone* that Vicky was very nearly illegitimate? And tell it laughing! Why wasn't she ashamed?

"Because it had become a story," Cliff said when I told him what I remembered. "Polished up, you know—like my mum's stories. That's why what most people tell you is no help when you try to puzzle out the way things really were.

"I tell myself it's pointless to be angry when Mum does it. I tell myself the world can be divided into two categories of people: those who think about their lives and want to understand them, and those who don't. It's not a moral issue, just the way you're made. Mum's a good woman, you can see that. She drew a tough lot in life, she did the best she could by me. I know that."

"But?"

He sighed. "I've spent years reminding myself about her good intentions."

"You're here, though," I said. "You keep coming home."

"Have to, sometimes—or take some kind of stand. What for? I've failed my own children enough these past few years to understand the need to be forgiven."

"Oh, please," I said. "You sound just like my sister. Last time I was home, I said something to her—I don't even remember what. Something about Peg, probably. Some complaint. And Angel said, 'You don't have kids, Evie. When people do, they realize how hard it was for their own parents. It changes the way they feel.' I thought it was absurd when she said it. I still think it's absurd. As if giving in, settling for less is what makes you a real adult—"

"You think I should make a scene, then?" Cliff asked in a flat voice. "Lay out all the ways Mum hurt me? Demand she make them right? As if she could bring my father back from the grave."

"You know that's not what I mean," I said. "Just don't act as if parenthood is some kind of secret club. I hate that. And don't act as if you've got everything so well in hand all the time, either. I mean, you brought me along as a kind of buffer, didn't you? I'm the one who spent the evening talking to your mother."

"True." He paused. "Does that make you angry?"

"Actually, no," I said. "Not that."

"But you're angry about something."

"I was. Upset, anyway."

"Because I brought up the children."

"I guess," I said. "I don't want to think about them, I don't know how."

"Nor do I," he said. "I love them. But I don't have a clue what to do about them. It's true that I've made terrible mistakes with them, Evie. All the while I was growing up, I told myself that if I ever had children of my own I'd be the perfect father. I comforted myself with that. And look what a mess I've made—

"Though, I must say, it makes its own odd sense when I think it through. Starting out, I thought the obvious thing to do, raising them, was to provide the direct opposite of whatever made me unhappy when

I was a child. I felt deprived, so I spoiled them. I longed for a father, so I put myself at their beck and call. Then, when I saw what a mess I'd made of everything, I left."

"You left Metta, Cliff. Not them."

"I doubt they see it that way," he said. "And the truth is, they're right to be angry. I know that what I've done—leaving them—is far worse than my father's absence was for me. He never chose to be dead. He never chose not to be with me. I didn't have to live with that."

"You think you should go back, then?"

"No," he said. "But I don't see how I can live with what I've done, either. And to be happy without them, well—"

I knew what he was thinking: to be happy without them, especially to be happy with someone else, would make things even worse.

"It *is* funny what comes to you as you grow older, though," he said after a while. "I used to get so mad at my mum for being happy when I was a kid. Ending up on this godforsaken farm, working her fingers to the bone—and singing while she was at it. Now sometimes I find myself wishing I could be more like her. Just *go on* as she does. I think I'm really bats then."

"You could do worse," I said. "In any case, you're not nearly as different from her as you think. She has a big heart, doesn't she. She's curious, in her own way—and every bit as good as you are at getting to the bottom of things. I'm still not sure exactly why I suddenly found myself matching her, war story for war story."

"Peg's stories." In the darkness, I could sense him smiling.

I said, "My Aunt Lily taught me to be charming." But as I spoke, I thought about the way I'd always acted toward Peg. I thought about Cliff's children, how likely it was that they would hate me on first sight.

We were quiet for a while. Then Cliff said, "Evie, do you really think there are things we're better off not to know?"

"I used to," I said. "Now I wonder."

"I found a snapshot," he said. "Long ago. I was twelve, maybe. Snooping in my mum's bureau. It was a picture of her and a man, dancing. Both in uniform. 'Happy New Year' strung across the background. 'Alice Mills & Roy Clifford, 1943,' was written on the back in my mother's hand. The man was my father, I knew right off. I looked like him.

"She'd never told me anything about him. Not even his name. She said it would be disloyal to Angus, who loved me like a son. But when I found that photograph, I took it, stomped down to the garden where she was working, and thrust it right into her face.

"'So, Clifford was *his* name,' I said to her. 'His surname.'"

"She looked up at me, perfectly calm. Said, 'Clifford was his surname, yes. So, will you call yourself Clifford Clifford now?'

"I'd never heard her voice so bitter. Still, I pressed her. I thought I had the right to know. He was from Houston, Texas, she told me. He died when his plane was shot down over France. That she held to. She swore she knew nothing about his family. She took the photograph from me, and I never saw it again. But I had memorized his face. When I grew to be the age he was in the picture—twenty-five, maybe—I looked exactly like him. Now I probably look as he would have if he'd lived. I often wonder if seeing that picture, seeing myself in him, made never knowing him worse—

"Evie, I've never told this to anyone. Not even Metta." There was just Cliff's voice in the darkness, his breath mingling with my own. "When I went to America a few years ago, to New York, I went to the public library and found the telephone directory for Houston. I looked up 'Clifford'. There was a full page of them. No Roys. I sat and thought a long while. I believed that my father was dead. My mum often avoided the truth, especially if it was painful, but I'd never known her to actually lie. Still, as a boy I'd fantasized about presenting myself to my father's parents one day—my grandparents. I imagined they'd be ever so happy to see me: a replica of the son they'd lost. And I thought I'd love them instantly, too. And be like them. Finally, I'd belong. That day, in the library, I saw it was clearly too late for that. If they were alive, they'd be in their eighties, in no shape for a long-lost grandson to appear. More likely, they were dead.

"Sitting there, I finally accepted that I'd never know any more than what my mum had told me about my father. And, though I'd built a career on the idea of how history can fail us, I saw that I hadn't really understood before exactly what that meant. Its randomness. This business of things getting lost, for all kinds of reasons.

"It should've pitched me right into the future. Instead, I've gone backwards, deconstructing my family's life as if I'm on a kind of dig.

When I left Metta, she said she felt as if she and the children were artifacts, tagged and numbered, shelved safely until I finally decided it was the right time to figure out where—or if—they fit into the big picture of my life. It's self-indulgent, Metta says, mucking about in people's lives the way I do. Now I've been doing it to you. Taking you off, teaching you lessons. Like I know anything at all—"

"Hush," I said, turning to hold him. And I understood for the first time how my sister might have felt all those years, turning in utter darkness to the man she loved.

Chapter Seven

In the morning, Cliff was himself again. Exuberant. He reminded
me to wear comfortable shoes. We were going to see Vindolanda first,
then hike to Houseteads from there, along the wall.

"Hike?" I said. "I don't know. How far?"

"Oh, a few kilometers. A lovely walk. I used to do it all the time
when I was a kid. I'd fancy myself a Roman soldier coming home to
the fort after the battle—"

Mrs. Murray waved from the garden as we drove down the gravel
road lined with trees. "Look." Cliff pointed north. "If you look hard,
you can see a patch of the wall there along the horizon."

I looked, but all I saw was a wild patchwork of green, the bound-
less sky. It wasn't long before I had my first glimpse of it, though, and
of Vindolanda. The settlement there predated Hadrian's Wall, Cliff
explained; it had been a civilian settlement as well as a fort. Nearly
twenty years ago, he had been a part of the team that discovered the
clay writing tablets which made the site famous.

"An excavation that resolved a number of crucial questions about
Roman culture," he said, his voice dry. "Did the Romans wear under-
pants, for instance? Yes, they did. We know because a soldier's letter
from his mum said she'd sent him two pair in a parcel."

It was still early, the car park was empty. It would be another hour
or so before the onslaught of tourists and schoolchildren. Cliff hailed
the person at the ticket booth, gestured to the carton of artifacts he
had hoisted onto one shoulder—things that had been sent to the university labs for analysis. The man waved us on.

"I'll take these up to the museum. Will you come, or have a look
around here yourself?"

"Look around, I think." I wasn't ready to meet his colleagues yet.

I bought a guidebook at the information stand and wandered. It
was eerie the way everything was laid out so neatly, I thought. Like a
map of itself. It reminded me somehow of the subdivision we'd moved
to when I was twelve. Ours had been the first block finished; when we
moved in, there were streets and sidewalks laid out behind our house
and, all along them, concrete slabs waiting for houses to be built on
them. The slabs were the same size as the slab our house had been built

on, I knew. But they seemed so small. Sometimes near dusk, after the workers had gone home, I'd go out and walk slab to slab, standing on each one, trying to imagine it with walls and rooms. I'd imagine the people—children my own age, perhaps—who'd soon be living there.

Now I tried to imagine the houses that once set on the carefully spaced rectangles of stones that defined their foundations: sturdy Roman houses with sandstone tiles and real glass windows like the ones the guidebook described. The houses of former soldiers, perhaps. Had the men who lived in them adapted to civilian life, found it any more or less strange than the men of my father's generation did, trading bombers for lawnmowers, K-rations for steaks on the grill?

I was still standing there, gazing at the ghosts of houses, when Cliff reappeared on the path. As we walked to enter the fort through the ruins of the stone gates, I told him about the concrete slabs I remembered.

"Funny the way foundations of things reduce lives to their proper perspective, isn't it?" he said. "Whether they're yet to be built on, like yours were, or like these." He gestured toward where the line of barracks had been, now no more than a neat pattern of stone and grass dotted with flowers. "All the ruins I've looked at in my life, and my first thought is always the same. They're so *small*. But they're lovely, aren't they? And there's so much to be learned from them just the way they are—"

He laughed, and took my hand. "I'm about to lecture you again," he said. "Do stop me. But I marvel sometimes that there are people who think it would be a capital idea to build the fort back up, into some kind of game park. What a shame it would be to spoil what time's made here. The way the ruins fit perfectly into the landscape. The way you see it's the land itself that owns them."

"Some would say the same about paintings," I said. "They'd say the repair I'm doing on the Vermeer is wrong. The damage is part of what the painting is now. The Vermeer that I worked on years ago, in Amsterdam, the one that had been sliced out of its frame—there was actually a group of conservators that believed the picture shouldn't be restored at all. Or if it was restored, the damaged areas should be painted in some neutral color, so they'd be perfectly obvious."

"But that's not the same at all." Cliff said. A work of art isn't like a building or an artifact. It's someone's idea: that idea in material form. Your Vermeer, for instance, it explains nothing but itself. Ruined, it doesn't become something different, it becomes something less."

My Vermeer. Yes, mine. For a moment, I missed it fiercely. I wanted to be alone, in the quiet lab, where that one thing was enough for me. But at the same time I was grateful that Cliff understood such a crucial thing about my work, and I felt a dangerous, singing happiness to be with him here, now. I'd felt this way before in the time we'd been together, and I waited for the dull weight to settle near my heart as it always did, for the knowledge to assert itself that none of this had anything at all to do with my real life. But for once it did not.

We watched some diggers, young men, who were working way down in a big hole that was partially filled with water. A gasoline-powered pump rattled, sending water coursing out through a fat hose. Two of the men were shoveling, tossing the dirt into a pile above them. Another was breaking up pieces of rotten timber, sifting the slivers carefully through his fingers, then tossing them back onto the pile of dirt when he was satisfied that there was nothing valuable hidden in them. It was a hot morning. There was no shade. The diggers were shirtless, dressed only in cut-off jeans and battered work boots. They wore American-style bandannas tied around their heads like sweatbands.

"Glamorous work, eh?" the sifter said, grinning up at us.

"Quite," Cliff answered.

Later, the same young man tromped into the staff room of the museum, where we were having tea with the director. He looked mortified when he was introduced to Cliff and realized who he was. He bumbled, speaking.

"Odd," said the director, watching him hurry out. "Usually John is so personable. And curious. I'd have thought he'd like a chance to chat with you."

Cliff just smiled. "Will you send someone after us at Housesteads, Cyril? Say, half past one? We'll have had a good hike then, and a chance to see the fort."

"What? Oh, yes, certainly," the director said, still looking confused. "Happy to."

Just outside the Vindolanda gates, we passed a Roman mile marker, then a sign that read, "Public Footpath" and pointed us toward a stile. We climbed over it, but the only evidence of a path I saw was some slightly beaten grass. Nonetheless, trusting that Cliff knew where we were going, I relaxed and enjoyed the blue sky and sunshine. I followed him up a steep hill, where Canterbury bells and buttercups grew wild. Sheep grazed in the distance. I saw tangles of their wool caught in the brambles as we drew closer to them. At the crest of the hill we rested a moment, turned, and there was Vindolanda neatly laid out below us like a *papier maché* model of a fort.

The grass was waist-high as we went down the other side. Insects buzzed around us. I could see a ribbon of asphalt at the bottom of the hill. Beyond it, high at the crest of another hill, I saw the wall. I stopped, breathing hard, my heart pounding. It seemed a vast distance from us. It looked no larger than a farmer's stone fence from where we stood.

"It's not as far as it looks. And well worth the walk, in any case—I promise," Cliff added when I looked skeptical.

Still, it seemed forever before we got there, the last bit a sheer incline. The muscles in my calves burned. I felt my heart beating all through my body. But Cliff had been right. The wall was magnificent. Where we stood, on the inside, it was chest-high; but looking side-to-side, I could see that it was built along a formidably steep slope, so that—from the outside—the wall seemed to rise straight up from the farmland far below. Looking straight out, north, was like looking out of an airplane window. A yellow-green checkerboard of fields gave way to wild, open country, then the darker green of forests. And light fell from the clouds onto it all, in ever-changing patterns. It *was* like a painting, just as Cliff had promised it would be. And I felt the way I felt looking at a painting I loved: willing to spend my whole life looking, at the same time I knew that I would never, ever be able to take it all in.

"I love that about you," Cliff said, breaking my reverie. "The way, every now and then, I see exactly what you feel in your face. Willing and awestruck, in this case. That's my test, in case you wondered."

"What test?" I blushed beneath his affectionate gaze.

"It's new," he said. "I only just made it up, watching you now. Willing and awestruck: I saw it was exactly what I need a person to be."

"And happy?" I asked. "Because I am right now. Happier than I've been since—maybe ever."

"Happy, definitely." He took my hand then, and we walked on into the day.

We were alone a long while, hiking wordlessly up and down the steep terrain. Parts of the wall were wide enough to walk along, and Cliff hopped up and walked them; but I stayed on the ground. Once, stopping to rest, he recited mournfully, "'Over the heather the wet wind blows/I've lice in my tunic and a cold in my nose/The rain comes pattering out of the sky/I'm a Wall soldier, I don't know why.'

"Auden," he said. "I'll wager you never learned that in school."

"True," I said, laughing, and we hiked on. The wall meandered through fields, through shady wooded places. I was jarred when I saw one person, then clusters of people, and then the fort, Housteads, spread out on the hill to the south.

The tourists were out in full force by then, meandering about, consulting their maps, snapping photographs. School children searched earnestly, matching the drawings on their worksheets to the various outlines of stone before them, scribbling, drawing, counting. They clustered at the latrines, giggling, and at the murder house, reading aloud about the mysterious skeleton that had been found with a knife point lodged between its ribs. In the National Trust Shop below, they jostled at the postcard racks, trying to decide among the various views of the wall and the artists' reconstructions of Roman life: standard bearers in sandals and fur helmets, soldiers hobnobbing in the latrine, carpenters at work on a lathe, market day at the south gate of the fort.

I bought Aunt Lily a postcard, a view that showed the section of wall we'd walked and the view of the country beyond. "Dear Aunt Lily," I wrote, "Sometimes my own life amazes me. Today I found myself here, walking along this wall where Roman soldiers walked more than a thousand years ago. I'm in England to do some work at the National Gallery, which I'll write and tell you about soon. I've been busy trying to do all I have to do and see as much as I can, as well. It's been a good time, an interesting time. Hope you are well and happy. Love, Evie."

"What's she like?" Cliff asked when I'd finished writing it. "Your Aunt Lily. Now."

"It's been ages since I've seen her," I said. "Though I suppose she's the same as she's always been: neat and proper, determined to do things her own way. Older, but then so am I. In fact, it's strange. I'm the age she was when I left home to go to college, and that's how I always think of her—I guess, because it was the last time in my life we ever spent much time together. Once I left home, I came back only when I had to. And then there was the thing with Rob. I don't think she ever quite forgave me for that. She never knew the truth, so why wouldn't she have thought I was crazy not to go through with the marriage, when Rob and I had been so close until then and it seemed our life together would've been perfectly wonderful? God help her, her own life turned out to be so full of disappointments—

"She's had a hard time in a lot of ways. My Uncle Paul never got over whatever happened to him during the war. He fought in the Pacific, the worst of it. His health was never right again. He drank. He tried to make Aunt Lily happy, he loved her. And things might have been all right if she hadn't lost the babies, even if they'd been able to adopt a child; but the unhappier she was, the more he withdrew into himself. All she had in the end was the dressmaking, the success she made of that. Which she's rightly proud of. And she's always had her good friend, Lois. I really should go visit her when I get home," I said. "I will. It's been too long since I've been there. Several years—"

"Why haven't you gone?" Cliff asked.

"Because I can't go see Aunt Lily without seeing Dad and Peg and Angel, too. And my other sisters. I think I've got everything in my life in order. It *is* in order. It's the life I want. Then I see them and I'm sucked right back into being the unhappy child I was. Seeing Aunt Lily when I have to deal with all that is even worse than not seeing her at all. Every time, it's as if I lose her all over. So I don't go. It's stupid, I know. To be angry after all these years—"

"I'd go back with you," he said. "Would it help, do you think? Would your Aunt Lily like me?"

For a moment, I could imagine the two of us on Aunt Lily's front porch, hear the rap-rap of her brass knocker, see her face light up when she opened the door. But if I took Cliff to see her, I'd have to explain who he was, what he meant to me.

The car from Vindolanda pulled up just then, and Cliff rose and pulled me up to stand beside him. He held my hand an instant too long, held me there beside him. "We're off," he said, letting me go. "Back to London in lieu of America. Dash Aunt Lily." His voice was light, but measured.

"We'll go sometime," I said. "I promise. I'll hire you on: chief archaeologist. We'll dig up all the artifacts of my youth and put them in their proper places, once and for all."

"Will we?" he said, but turned and began walking toward the car before I could answer him.

Chapter Eight

A brand-new house in a brand-new neighborhood, Peg and Dad said, as if that were so exciting. But I hated it there. The houses were like little game pieces set down in long rows: you knew yours by its color or number, or because your father's car was parked in the driveway. Dozens of similar low-cost housing developments had sprung up all over Indianapolis during the Fifties, as returning veterans settled into family life. Ours was on the west side of town, near the Allison factory, where both my father and Uncle Paul worked. The Indianapolis Motor Speedway loomed at the far edge of it, a long expanse of bleachers and chain-link fence.

When we moved in, the development hadn't been landscaped yet. We all had to stay indoors on the day the big earth machines drove the length of our block, back and forth, spreading the black soil, sowing the seed for all the lawns at once. We watched men plant spindly trees, two to each house, in the grassy rectangles between the sidewalk and the street. Then the shrubs: four at the front of each house, under the bedroom windows. That first summer, before people built fences and planted their own trees and bushes to define their space, it was as if there were one vast backyard behind all the houses. The kids ran wild. They played tag, running and shouting. They played fort in the mountains of left-over black dirt that the contractors had dumped at the ends of each block, infuriating their mothers, the women Peg had coffee with each morning, when they tramped through the houses leaving footprints.

They frightened me, they were so loud and wild. There were so many of them. I wanted to go back to the old neighborhood, where there were old people and spinster ladies and the children played proper games in the schoolyard down the street. In my old neighborhood, there was a library within walking distance and a drugstore with a soda fountain and big jars of penny candies. Now if I wanted to go anywhere I had to wait for my father to take me in the car on Saturdays, or hope that Aunt Lily would have time to drive over and get me.

She and Uncle Paul had moved, too; but their "new" house was an old one in a lovely neighborhood on the north side of town: brick, two stories, with a fireplace in the living room. When she wasn't too busy with her dressmaking business, Aunt Lily would call Peg and ask if I could come spend the night. She'd take me to the library first and I'd get six books, the limit; then we'd spend the afternoon together, lounging on wicker chaises on the screened-in porch, reading and drinking iced tea. When Uncle Paul came home, we ate in her pretty dining room. We always used the beautiful, breakable dishes I loved: Spode china, white with pink roses. They'd been her mother's, Aunt Lily always told me. My grandmother's. Someday they'd be mine. She let me carry them into the kitchen, rinse the food from them and stack them by the sink. She never warned me to be careful the way Peg did any time she was at Aunt Lily's with me. Aunt Lily's fancy things made her nervous; I'd heard her say that. Never to Dad. He still thought Aunt Lily and Peg were going to get together some day and be friends. But I'd heard her say it plenty of times to her girlfriends when they were all gathered around the table in the dinette, drinking coffee. That and, "Lily thinks she's better."

Peg sent me out the back door to play with the other children every morning; she had no idea that I often sneaked back in the front and sat just around the corner in the dark living room pretending to read a book.

Aunt Lily *is* better, I'd think.

I longed to be transported to my room in her new house. She'd made it exactly like my room in her old house so I'd feel at home there: yellow, with white curtains at the windows. There were always fresh daisies in a milk-glass vase. There was a photograph that Uncle Paul had taken with his Brownie camera, framed, on the bedside table: Aunt Lily and I reading on the porch. I loved that picture because, in it, we looked enough alike to be mother and daughter. We were small, but not skinny like Peg and the Queens were. We were dark. We had the same wavy brown hair, the same eyes: brown and serious.

Back in Cliff's flat the next morning, I woke, smiling. I had dreamed of Aunt Lily's house, dreamed her in it. In my dream, she was young again, as young as she had been when I was a child. I saw her, plain as day. She was sitting at the kitchen table in her flowery robe, her cup of coffee before her, a dreamy look on her face. But propped against the sugar bowl was the postcard I'd sent her from Hadrian's Wall the day before. I lay beside Cliff, imagining the real postcard now flying toward her. I imagined it sailing through the brass mail chute on her front door, landing face-up in the foyer. Aunt Lily finding it.

The scene was so vivid in my mind's eye, Aunt Lily so real, that I felt the impulse to move my arms, as if to embrace her. Vermeer must have seen his woman in his mind's eye just this way long after the painting was done, felt in his fingers the brushstrokes that had made her. Just as, sometime in the future, I would see myself in Cliff's bed this morning, fresh from dreaming. I would feel again as I felt now, watching him, waiting for the day to begin.

Tonight, I'd write the letter I'd promised myself I'd write to Aunt Lily. I'd be on my own because Cliff planned to leave this morning to visit a dig in Wales and wouldn't be back until late. I'd stay in my own flat, I decided. I'd take a hot bath, make myself a pot of tea. I'd tell her all about Vermeer's woman, about Cliff. Maybe I'd even tell her about how I hadn't been able to imagine the two of us beyond this time and place until yesterday, when I'd imagined us on her doorstep. Maybe, writing, I'd say something about us that I didn't know I knew.

Later that morning, when I arrived at the museum and read the first words of the letter from Angel that I found waiting there, the thought of what I might have written to Aunt Lily, the image of the postcard I'd written the day before, right that second flying toward her, made me feel worse than anything.

"Dear Evie," I read again and again. "I've been sitting here a long time trying to figure out a way to tell you that our Aunt Lily is dead—

"When it happened—three days ago now, it happened really fast, without too much pain. I was with her. I think she was at peace. One of the last things she said to me was, 'Evie knows how much I love her, how proud I am of her. She knows that, doesn't she?' I said, yes. I knew it was true.

"It was cancer. She hadn't seemed like herself to me for a while. She'd lost weight, and she had that pinched look sick people get sometimes. But you know Aunt Lily. Just tired, she'd say if I mentioned it. Her these-old-bones number. She wasn't about to go to the doctor.

"Then Lois called me one morning last month from the hospital. Aunt Lily had called her in the middle of the night with chest pains, and Lois had taken her to the emergency room, thinking it was a heart attack. They were running tests at that point. Later, she called me back and said they'd found a shadow on Aunt Lily's lung. But the doctor said they'd need the results of all the tests to know what it meant. That would take a week or so. Then they'd look at everything.

"'Thank God, they're letting her go this morning.' That's what Lois said to me. Like Aunt Lily was going home cured.

"As far as Aunt Lily was concerned, she was. That's how she played it, anyway. And she did seem better. She sewed in the mornings. She and Lois went to the movies. Every time I went to visit, she'd send me home with a cake or cookies she'd made for Matt and Jenny. Aunt Lily didn't want to talk about how she felt, she put me off if I tried. In fact, she was aggravated with me when the time came to go back to the doctor for the test results and I said I was going with her. Then the first thing she said when it was over, when we knew, was "Angel, don't you dare tell Evie till it's absolutely necessary. There's no sense in her worrying all the way in New York. Promise me, now." She meant it, Evie. So I promised.

"Then she said, 'Honey, I want to run over to the shopping center. I've been meaning to pick up a summer handbag. If we stop now, it'll save me a trip later. You don't mind, do you?' Honest to God, we stood at the purse counter at Ayres forever, Aunt Lily checking out twenty bags to find the one bag in the universe that would do. Chatting with the salesgirl. Then she wanted to buy one for me.

"You know, it was crazy. I did fine in the doctor's office. I listened to the two of them chat forever about the damn weather and baseball and Aunt Lily's garden; then he cleared his throat and gave her the news—the tumor was inoperable, it wouldn't respond to chemotherapy.

I felt sick inside. Aunt Lily looked terrible for one second, she knew exactly what he meant.

"I mean, I got through all that. But then, when Aunt Lily made me buy a purse, I wanted to shake her and scream at her, 'Jesus, Aunt Lily, what do either one of us need a goddamn purse for right now?' I didn't, though. I calmed down. I let her buy me the purse she thought I ought to have. You know how she always thinks my things are tacky.

"Evie, I didn't think it would happen so fast. The doctor had told her he wanted to see her again in a month, and my plan was to wait until then before deciding what to tell you. I stopped by every few days; we had her over for dinner. Like I said, she seemed okay, better than she'd been for a while. The only weird thing was, she kept giving me things. Knickknacks she knew I'd always liked. That Delft lamp, those antique plates with birds on them. She cleaned out the linen closet and gave me a whole armload of sheets. She gave me the Royal Doulton balloon lady for Jenny; she'd never forgotten how Jenny loved it when she was a little girl. She was in some pain, I could tell. She still had that drawn look. But even Lois says that that her last few weeks were good ones.

"What happened was, she caught this flu that was going around, a respiratory thing, and in a few days it was over. The doctor said it happens that way sometimes, especially with older people. A blessing, he said. She didn't suffer like she might have. But I miss her so much. I still can't believe she's gone.

"My poor Jenny, though—I think she took it the hardest of all. She just loved Aunt Lily, you know. She's never forgotten all those times Aunt Lily used to keep her, when Matt and I were still trying to get ourselves through college. I tell her that Aunt Lily got to see her graduate from high school last month, and was so proud of her. I know Jenny's glad of that. Still, she worries me. Sometimes, lately, she seems so lost. But then, I feel kind of lost myself when I think that in another month she'll be off to college, no longer our little girl. Time goes by.

"I am so sorry, Evie. When I realized that Aunt Lily wasn't going to make it, I did try to call you. But there was no answer at your apartment, and it was the weekend—so no one answered at the museum either. By the time I got through Monday morning and found out where you were, I knew you wouldn't be able to get here in time. Then I couldn't just call and tell you. You were so far away, and I didn't trust myself to be able to tell you all I needed to tell you just the right way. I hope I did the right thing, by writing instead and by sending you this little book. I found it, cleaning out Aunt Lily's desk drawers. The note inside said, for Evie, so I didn't read it. In any case, I'm sending it with this letter and hoping that, whatever it is, it will make you feel better."

Aunt Lily, gone. Impossible. I turned from Angel's package and looked a long time at the Vermeer. My Vermeer, Cliff had called it just yesterday. Today the woman's face looked sad, resigned. "I'm sorry you didn't know better than to interrupt me," it seemed to say. As if I were the one responsible for the absence of music, for freezing her forever in silence.

Still, I made myself keep looking, as if continuing to look at the woman could make me forget Aunt Lily's death. Work, I told myself. A good painting has many layers of meaning, and they emerge slowly. What does this painting mean?

Here, think of this: Seventeenth century thought was metaphorical. Reality was controlled by a formal system of knowledge and belief, and most paintings of that time can be "translated" by anyone familiar with the moralistic sayings and proverbs that people lived by in those times, and with the puns and symbols that were familiar to them. According to this school of thought, Ian had decoded the painting correctly—Vermeer had meant the figure to represent a faithful woman, just as the museum guidebook said.

But why the cool, detached colors? Why that one warm spot: the gilt frame that resonates so disconcertingly out of her line of sight? And why had Vermeer chosen this woman, this moment in a lifetime of moments, real and contrived? Who was she?

Oh, who was my Aunt Lily?

I opened the pretty, cloth-covered book that she had left me, and read the first page—

"I'm going to start at what seems to be the beginning of my real life and try to write it as well as I can. I say real life because I separate it in my mind from the life I always thought I'd lead, the life I believed so hard in and was so stubborn about letting go of that I caused the people I loved most in this world terrible hurt. You most of all. Evie, forgive me. For all I wasn't brave enough to tell you before. For lacking the courage, even now, to say it anywhere but here."

Chapter Nine

I was twenty-three years old when your Uncle Paul left for the Navy. The two of us had been together every day of our lives since grade school, and the idea of being on my own scared me to death. The only thing that scared me more was thinking that if Paul got distracted worrying over me he might do something careless, something that could get him hurt or dead.

So I made up my mind to write him cheerful, newsy letters, but keep a diary of how I really felt. The war would be no more than an intermission in our marriage, I thought. When he came home, Paul would tell me everything that had happened to him, and I'd give him my diary to read so he'd know everything about how it was for me while he was gone. Then real life would start up again.

But the war had changed him. Those first months after he was discharged, it was all he could do to get from day to day. For a long time, I told myself that if I was patient, he'd get better. After all, other men did. They quit having nightmares, quit waking up in the dead of night soaked with sweat. Their eyes lost that blank look. But your Uncle Paul just coiled deeper and deeper into himself. I never understood it. I tried—but either he just didn't believe I could understand what had happened to him, or he couldn't bring himself to tell me what I would need to know to help him. To the day he died, Paul just went quiet any time the war was mentioned.

Now they talk about those boys who went to Vietnam and how their whole lives have been a mess because of what they did there, what they saw. Delayed shock, they call it. It seems like every time I turn on the television, someone's talking about it. I wonder what Paul would have to say about such a thing. Not much, I suppose. But I sit and listen, and for the first time the way he ended up makes some sense to me.

As I wrote that last, a nasty little voice in my head said, "Too late. Isn't that just par for the course?" If I listen to that voice, I'll sit here the rest of the afternoon brooding, asking myself, what good does it do to figure these things out when Paul's dead and there's not the first thing I can do to make things right? The truth is, Evie, I wouldn't *want* your Uncle Paul with me now. He wouldn't be able to help me, and I'd be worse off than I already am, worrying about what in the world he'd do when I was gone. It's still hard for me to admit, even to myself, that one of the things I found out during the war was that I could get along just fine on my own. In fact, I liked being on my own. I like it now.

I do what I want to do, when I want to do it. If I feel like getting out of bed at two in the morning to read the diary I kept forty-odd years ago, who's to know or care? That's what I did last night when I couldn't sleep. I lay in bed thinking, how am I going to tell Evie that I'm sick? I knew I had to, or I had to agree to let Angel tell you soon. But I wanted to think about some things first. There are things I need to tell you, Evie—about your mother and father, about myself. I had to figure out the best way.

I remembered that old diary then, and it occurred to me that it might help you understand the way it was during the war, how our two lives came to be so tangled up together. So I went up to the attic and dug through the boxes of things left from that time. I got side-tracked any number of times, looking at pictures and old ration books and reading Paul's letters. I found a coat I'd made for you from an old one of your mother's. A little red wool coat. I remembered as clear as crystal taking you to an Armistice Day Parade the first time you wore it. A lady standing near us said how cute you were and what a pretty coat you had on, and Lois took it upon herself to tell the lady I'd made it for you. She said I'd made lots of other things from old clothes, too. You know Lois. The lady asked me if I was a professional seamstress. I laughed and said, heaven's no. And she said, "Well, you could be."

Lois got all excited. After the lady walked away, she said, "Lily, I'll give you my two cents worth whether you want it or not. There are plenty of girls at work who'd love to have you make over their old clothes for them. I can't believe we've never thought of it."

We were both working at Allison's then, six days a week, second shift. I said, "Okay, Lois. Just for you, I'll do it. When God makes an eighth day every week so I can fit it in."

But back to the diary. When I found it, I tried to find what I'd written on the day of the parade and, guess what? I hadn't written a single word. I could hardly believe it. What that lady said planted an idea in my head that led me to the one thing in my life I know I did right. But at the time, what she said must not have seemed important to me at all.

I went back to the beginning and read the whole diary then, but I already knew what I'd find. Not one of my most vivid memories of that time was written there. I had thought I could give you the diary, Evie, and when you read it, you'd understand some things about how it was during the war. You'd see why I had come to believe—wrongly, I know now—that I was your true mother. Then you could forgive me for all the hurt I caused everyone when I couldn't let you go.

But I found nothing there but anger and complaint. All during the war, I got up first thing in the morning and wrote my cheerful letters to Paul. Most nights, I wrote in my diary. The truth, I thought. But it turns out that the diary was no more true than the letters were. Especially what I wrote there about your mother. She wasn't the glamorous fantasy mother I let you believe in after she died, that's part of what I need to tell you. But she wasn't the bad person my diary made her out to be either.

She was just so young. I should have seen what was happening between Carol and your dad that Christmas and tried to put a stop to it, but it was such a terrible time for me. I'd just had my first miscarriage a few weeks before, and I was still grieving. Your Uncle Paul had bought a little tree and decorated it, so that I would have it to come home to from the hospital. He'd shopped for me, piled my presents underneath. He'd hung a wreath on our door. He did everything he could to comfort me. I couldn't tell him that every kindness just made my heart crack deeper.

When I was alone, I'd take out the little red and green striped bootie I'd knitted right after Thanksgiving. I'd meant to hang it on the bedpost on Christmas Eve to make Paul laugh. I couldn't keep it now, I knew. It would upset Paul if he saw it. So one day, bawling like a baby myself, I bent my finger and slid it inside the bootie like a skinny little foot. Then with my free hand, I snipped a stitch near the ruffled top and pulled it. The yarn unraveled onto my lap, kinky—like your hair used to be when I undid your braids. I sat there the longest time, not even crying, just rocking and rocking in the pretty antique chair I'd bought the very day I'd gone to the doctor and found out that Paul and I were finally going to have the child we'd been waiting for so long. You see, Evie, what kind of shape I was in. You can see why I was happy to have the romance blooming between Tom and Carol to distract me.

I'd always been crazy about my sister, and mothered her—just like you did Angel. And I'd always had a soft spot for your dad. By that time, he was as much my brother as he was Paul's. He hadn't expected to get a leave, so I was thrilled when he showed up that Christmas day and surprised us. We all thought it was so funny when he didn't even recognize Carol. They were five years apart, and she'd had a terrible crush on him from the time she was a little girl. Now there he was, blushing and acting a fool—exactly like Carol used to do when he was the star of the football team.

She'd grown up since he'd left for boot camp in the summer. She was still in high school, but she looked twenty. She'd had her long blond hair cut in a pageboy. Her cheeks were rouged. I was astonished in the change in her myself. She seemed like a completely different person to me.

Tom must have felt the same way, because he couldn't keep his eyes off her all through Christmas dinner. You could tell Carol was getting a kick out of it. She'd smile and lean toward him, batting her eyelashes. It was romantic, like a scene in a movie.

Tom had gotten orders for England, he told us; that's how he finagled the leave. In a week, he'd go to New York. The week after that, they'd sail. Those days, "overseas" was a magic word. It got soldiers most anything they wanted. Girls used it to justify every kind of wildness. People were stumbling through that Christmas right after Pearl Harbor overwrought. Nobody could really know what the war would bring, but we knew our lives were bound to change because of it. And soon. As for me, I knew that this Christmas might be the last one Paul and I would spend together for a long time. It might be the last one we would *ever* spend together. Wrapped up in my own misery, I guess I didn't see what was really happening between Tom and Carol. Or maybe I saw it and let it happen because their pleasure in each other was the only thing that gave me a shred of hope. I was selfish, that I do know. Three days later, when they eloped and ran off to New York for the rest of Tom's leave, I thought, if Carol's married, she can't go back to high school. Now I won't have to live alone.

I'm still selfish, I guess. Even now, even knowing how wrong that marriage was and how much pain it caused—knowing that it ended in my own sister's death, I'd let it happen all over again, because you came from it, Evie, and I loved you more than anything or anyone. You brought me so much joy.

Just writing that makes me feel weepy and sentimental, like the old lady I am. Lately, the littlest thing can reduce me to tears. And I've gone way off track. Here it is practically evening, and I still haven't told you what I started off to tell you. I burned that wartime diary. Then I went to the shopping mall today and bought this book. I mean to write all that I remember from that time in it, the things that have stayed with me and that I see now were what really mattered. I guess you could call it a kind of diary-after-the-fact.

Your dad told me about Peg a few weeks after your mother's funeral, and he told me that he was going back to England to marry her. He said, "She doesn't expect me. I broke it off before I left. Lily, I really meant to make a go of it with Carol."

I didn't believe him. Or maybe it was just that if I didn't believe him, it meant that he had had not been as sorry as he should have been about her death. From there, it was easy to twist it around and blame him for the accident that killed her.

The truth is, if anyone was to blame, I was. None of us had really wanted to go to the party that night, but I insisted. People were expecting us, I said. And so we went.

Tom and Carol had been quarreling in their room before we left. Then, at the party, there was a lot of drinking, and that made it worse. I don't remember what they were arguing about, but I remember being so embarrassed at the way they were shouting at each other right in front of everyone that, finally, I went over to them and said, "For heaven's sake, if you're going to do this, can't you do it outside so everyone doesn't have to listen to you?"

Carol stalked out. Tom went after her.

But it was nobody's fault what happened, really. I know that. Carol had on those ridiculous high heels she always wore, the street was slick. She ran out the door of the union hall where the party was being held. She was halfway down the block, no coat in the freezing rain, when she looked back and saw Tom coming after her. I guess she meant to get clean away from him, because she darted into the street. But she turned her ankle, stumbled, and fell. She was run over by a cab that came too fast around the corner. It happened so fast, Tom said. There was nothing anyone could do.

All of a sudden, Carol was gone. She was my baby sister, my only sister. I loved her. When you're young and someone dies, you believe that the deep love you feel for that person is what makes the loss so hard. It's true: to lose someone you love is a terrible thing. But there's a worse kind of grief than that, and it comes when there's been trouble between you and the person who's died, and the trouble is left unsettled. Now I see why Carol's death hit me so hard, why the only way I could bear to think of her was to freeze her forever in my memory as the beautiful blond girl who fell in love with your father that first Christmas of the war.

Your father seemed to understand that, to accept it. When he came back from England, he tried every way he knew to heal the rift your mother's death had caused. He was more than generous, allowing me to spend all the time I wanted to spend with you. He thanked me for coming to get you first thing every morning, even though we both knew it made it harder for you to get used to your new life. It made things harder for Peg, too. But she thanked me, just like he did, and acted as if my taking you was a big help, giving her all that extra time to spend with Vicky.

When I look back on it now, it seems that—as hard as they tried—*I* could have tried harder to accept your dad's marriage to Peg. If only she hadn't had those three babies right in a row, one for each one I lost, maybe that would have been possible. If your dad hadn't been so head-over-heels in love with her, constantly reminding me of the way Paul had felt about me before the war. If I hadn't missed you so much some days that it seemed to me like you'd died. If, if, if. None of those things excuse the way I acted toward Peg, mind you. But maybe they help explain it.

I used to watch her with you girls—with her girls, especially—and I was shocked by her easy ways. She'd let you kids spread your toys all over the living room. The television was always blaring. Mealtime was whenever anyone was hungry. When she and your dad moved to the new house in Speedway, the whole neighborhood was a mess. Mud everywhere, and Vicky, Bets, and Anne tromping in and out of the house, never even bothering to take off their shoes. Any nice thing Peg ever had got broken or ruined. She didn't care, though—or she didn't seem to, anyway. As long as everyone was happy.

Once I said to your father, "Tom, don't you think Peg ought to be a little more strict with the children? They run around like wild Indians sometimes."

He didn't say anything; but the way he looked at me, I knew he thought I was out of bounds. Which I was, of course. Time has proved this to be true. Peg's girls have grown up to be perfectly fine. Maybe not as ambitious for themselves as they might have been, but happy. And they are devoted to Peg, every single one of them, which in this day and age is nothing to make light of.

Yes, the bad feeling between Peg and me was my fault, and I'm sorry. But it's worse than that. Evie, I loved you more than anything. I can say that without a shade of doubt, even now, knowing as I do that I twisted so many other things in my life into what I wanted to believe.

I loved you. And that makes the fact that I used you to hurt Peg all the more disgraceful.

Oh, I'd never have admitted that that was what I was doing at the time. I convinced myself I had a responsibility toward you. After all, you were my sister's child. I let myself believe Carol would have wanted certain things for you that Tom and Peg couldn't give you, or didn't think were important. I made you beautiful clothes and told myself it was okay not to make them for the other girls, because I knew they'd get your things when you grew out of them. I took you places. I taught you what I believed was correct—civilized—behavior. A lot of the time, I did it in a way that made Peg feel small and made your father feel that what he was able to give you was not enough.

I am embarrassed to say that, by then, I thought I was an expert on the subject of good taste. My dress business was a big success; my clients were the richest ladies in town, and they were willing to pay whatever I asked to have me copy the clothes they'd seen in fashion magazines.

I ignored the fact that what I was doing made your Uncle Paul uncomfortable. These were not his kind of people, and it pained him to have to make polite small talk with the ladies who came for fittings. Later, it pained him to use my money to buy the house on North New Jersey Street, a nicer house than we ever dreamed we'd have. He was just plain embarrassed, living there. None of the men in our neighborhood worked at Chrysler, like he did. I'd try to get him to be friendlier; once I even called him a snob when he told me for the hundredth time that he didn't belong there. I couldn't see what I was doing. My nice house and my business were the only things that made me forget how sad I was, how cheated I felt at the way my life was turning out. I listened too much to those ladies, my customers, who were the only people in my life then who made me feel worthwhile.

"Oh, Lily," they'd say, "you're so wonderful. You're a genius with a needle." They'd tell me about the parties they'd worn my dresses to, repeat the compliments they'd gotten.

I guess that's how I got to thinking that I was better than people like Peg and Tom in their dinky little house full of noisy children. But in the middle of the night, when I couldn't sleep, I had to face the fact that I'd trade places with Peg in a minute if I could. I'd lie there for hours sometimes, turning the hurt over and over in my mind the way you worry a cracked tooth with your tongue. I'd think, if only the war hadn't happened. I'd go back to the day my life started to go wrong.

I was mending your Uncle Paul's work clothes when I first felt it: an odd, dipping shudder inside me. I sat still until I felt it again. It was the kind of feeling you get when a roller coaster begins its descent. Gentler though. A tickle. I remember thinking about the rolling country roads near our hometown, a particular place with three thank-you-ma'ams that made your stomach float and turn if you drove over them too fast. The baby moved again. There, I thought. That's how I'll tell

Paul what it's like.

I've never been as happy in my life as I was that moment, when our baby moved for the first time. I still feel happy when I think of those few months I carried it. Every morning I'd wake up, and the first thing I'd see was the pretty white eyelet curtains I'd made, so full of light they couldn't hold it all. Light shone through the pattern of holes, and made the glass knickknacks on the bureau sparkle. I had to turn to Paul beside me and shade my eyes against his back. Then I'd rub his shoulders until he woke up.

Every morning, I'd say, "I'll get up and fix breakfast while you get dressed." Every morning, he'd say, "No, Lily. You sleep."

He pulled the shade then. The room got all shadowy. I'd lie on my back, taking deep breaths, my hands on my belly, and I'd listen to the sounds of the house as Paul moved through it: the water running, the toilet flushing, the thunk of the ice box door. I knew just when he would tip-toe back into the room and stand beside me. I pretended to sleep, but I could feel him there, his energy and gladness mixing with my own. He'd brush my hair back, kiss my forehead. I'd sigh like I was dreaming.

But I couldn't stay in bed. As soon as Paul closed the door, I got up. I made the bed. I ate a good breakfast. I cleaned. I thought of my mother, who'd died not long before, and I missed her. I remembered the home she'd made for us, and tried to give the little house I lived in with Paul the same feeling. I was finished by noon and sat a while, happy and sad at the same time, everything we owned shining around me.

After lunch, I took a nap. Then I drifted into the late afternoon listening to the radio, reading magazines, looking out the kitchen window at the children playing on the sidewalk. When I heard Paul's footstep on the porch, I ran out to meet him. We sat down to supper, two parents just waiting for our family. Each empty chair between us seemed like a promise.

And then the baby moved! That day the sun was shining so hard, the sky was so blue that I could almost believe it was spring. When we got up, Paul and I had dressed in our church clothes; but the minute we stepped onto the front porch, Paul had said, "It's too nice to be inside. We won't see another day like this for months! Come on, Lil. Oh, come on, Lily. Let's don't go." He was like a little boy, he pestered me until I gave in. It was such a beautiful day, so warm for December. I couldn't resist.

We took my favorite walk, north from our neighborhood of bungalows, past the grand houses lining Meridian Street, then across Pennsylvania Street and Washington Boulevard to wander through my dream neighborhood, where more modest versions of Tudors, Colonials, and Cape Cods lined the streets—the neighborhood I live in now.

Paul teased me. "The next time we see a day like this, we'll probably be buried in diapers and bottles, at our wits end, with a howling baby."

I had tried to imagine it, but even that morning the baby still didn't seem real. Then, in the time it took for Paul to run out for a newspaper, I felt it move.

When I heard him coming up the front steps, I sat, serene as a Madonna, waiting to tell my news. I sat with my hands on my belly, knowing it would make him tease me again. Nearly five months pregnant, I was as slim as a girl. I had to stand up, stand sideways for him to see the little bulge the baby made.

He rushed into the living room and stood before me. The peculiar look on his face made me think for a minute that he'd guessed what I was about to tell him. I smiled at him, but he didn't smile back. He didn't say anything to me. Just hurried past and turned on the radio.

". . . ships, aircraft destroyed," a voice said. "Naval and air forces of the Empire of Japan have attacked the American fleet at Pearl Harbor. The full extent of damages is not yet known—"

Paul paced the floor, listening. On his face, I saw his love for me. I saw fear and sadness. And an awful excitement that scared me. The Sunday paper he'd bought lay on the coffee table, still folded. It was old news now. I sat there, paralyzed. What I was feeling inside me was nothing like what I'd felt an hour before. I held my hands on my belly now to try to calm myself. Paul noticed finally, and asked if I was all right. He made me rest.

Hours later, the pain woke me up, and I knew right away what was happening. I knew it was far too soon. The pain felt like steel inside me, cooling and hardening. I whispered to the baby, "Stay. Oh, please stay with us." But I knew it would not.

The miscarriage had nothing to do with the shock of learning about Pearl Harbor, the doctor told me. It was bound to happen: God fixing his own mistake. Maybe that was the truth, it probably was. But it didn't make me feel one bit better. All that night I lay in the hospital bed, empty and grieving for my child. I imagined it, a tiny thing in the palm of the doctor's hand. Had it been alive in the world even one second? Was it a boy or a girl? Oh, where was it?

Afterwards, I thought it might have been easier if only I could have buried it properly, like a real child, even though I'd only known it in my heart. But I didn't even ask to see it. Women didn't ask for such things in those days. I didn't ask for anything at all.

I tell myself that at my age, knowing what I know, it's natural to be thinking about my life: to let the old sadnesses out, to cry over them and put them, at last, to rest. It's good. But this bitterness—

I try to understand it, and to understand the anger I feel—even after all these years—when I think about what my life might have been like if that baby hadn't died, if the war hadn't happened, if Paul had stayed the way he was on that Sunday morning so long ago. I try not to dwell on it, but no matter what I do or what I tell myself, sometimes I wake up in the middle of the night full of bitter rage. Evie, it scares me. When that happens, I believe the bitterness is my punishment for all the hurt I've caused. All I can see is that I sinned, claiming you when you weren't mine to claim. I see the terrible hurt I caused trying to keep you. It seems simple then, just like the Bible warned: the wages of sin is death. Losing you, the miscarriages after the war, Paul's poor health and drinking, my own death now, a kind of living death, can be traced right back to that sin.

Of course, that's ridiculous. That's what I tell myself when I go downstairs and turn on all the lights and fix myself a cup of tea. I tell myself: Lillian, the good Lord just did not want you to have children, and that's that. But lately, I've been thinking about Angel's Jenny getting so fascinated with reincarnation when she studied it in school last year. She said to me, "Aunt Lily, if it's true, it means that every soul has every single experience a human being can possibly have. Then when it's had them all, it's perfect and it gets to go to God. So all the poor people will be rich, or they already have been. All the ugly girls will eventually get to be pretty."

And every soul will know the grief of being barren. Like I said, I think about it. If what Jenny described is true, it means there's an answer to the question that has haunted me nearly all my life. The answer is that it was my turn.

I'm feeling more myself today. Lois was here all morning. We watched TV for a while, but the program was about reformed smokers.

"Reformed smokers are boring," Lois said, and turned it off.

"You're a reformed smoker," I reminded her.

You probably don't even remember that about her, do you, Evie? She quit, cold turkey, ages ago. She doesn't like to make a big thing of it, though. Anyway, just seeing a little bit of that show got me to thinking about how, during the war, the two of us used to sit in the car after work, smoking and talking. We worked second shift, you know. We'd get home at midnight, but sometimes we'd sit out there yakking till one or two in the morning.

I thought of when I started smoking, too: the day your Uncle Paul left to go overseas.

All during his last leave, it seemed to me like time was going backwards instead of forward. In his uniform, Paul looked as young as he'd looked in high school. I could hardly remember the time just a few months before when I'd catch sight of him walking up the sidewalk after work, carrying a newspaper, swinging his lunchbox and I'd feel like a wife, almost a mother. Now I felt like a teen-age girl again, daydreaming about the two of us together, but with no common-sense idea of real life beyond the dream.

I felt lonelier waking up to find Paul sleeping beside me than I had felt waking up alone all the time he was at boot camp. Go, I thought. Just please go. I felt almost sick when I was with him. I felt weak, like my very bones were crumbling inside me. I wouldn't have admitted it to anyone alive, but when he finally hiked his duffel bag over his shoulder and kissed me that last time, what I felt, mainly, was relief. I watched him out of sight, heard the trolley stop at the end of the street to carry him downtown to the train station. The porch swing we had sat in together a few minutes before still swung from our rising.

Paul had left his cigarettes. The half-filled pack of Lucky Strikes lay on the kitchen table beside his empty coffee cup. I held it, felt the crinkle of the cellophane, the shape of the package in my hands—the same as all the other cigarette packages he'd left on that table, on the bedside table, the radio table.

I didn't cry. I took a cigarette out, tapped it on the table-top like I'd seen Paul do. I lit it and inhaled. The rush of smoke brought tears to my eyes. My lungs hurt. Good, I thought. Good. The little pieces of tobacco on my tongue tasted bitter. Paul would not have liked this, I knew. But I finished the first cigarette and lit another one.

I sat all morning in Paul's chair in the living room, smoking. The radio was on, and the war news seemed no more real to me than it ever had. Music played. It was as if I had never in my whole life heard any of it. My eyes burned from the smoke. I felt sick from the tobacco. But if I closed my eyes the smell tricked me, and I could believe Paul was nearby. Later, when I went out to do the marketing, I bought a fresh pack of cigarettes, my own.

This morning, when I told this story to Lois, I said, "That little act of independence. Isn't it strange the way it was probably the beginning of this?"

The cancer, I meant. I didn't have to explain. Lois always knows exactly what I mean. When she laughed, like I knew she would, I realized there was no one else in the world I could have said that to. Anyone else would've been thinking, she should've quit long ago. She should quit now. Though they probably wouldn't have had the nerve to say so. But Lois took what I said at face value, like she always does. *Isn't it strange?* Well, it is, isn't it? Life is strange. If only you could foresee the consequences of what seem like such little things.

Like the coincidence of Lois and me being neighbors in the first place—and on top of that, the fact that even though we'd lived next door to each other for over a year, we'd said no more than a friendly hello now and then from porch to porch until the war took both of our husbands away. Who'd have thought we'd end up as close as sisters?

We got to talking about that, about how working at Allison's during the war was when we'd really gotten to know each other. She'd been working there as a grinder for a month or so by the time Paul left.

Just in passing one day, she mentioned that she was pretty sure she could get me on, too, if I was interested.

At first I said no. I knew Paul wouldn't like it. But you know Lois, she can talk you into anything. It was what she said about working the swing shift that made me decide to give it a try.

"Evenings are the worst, right? The empty place at the dinner table, listening to the war news, going up to bed all alone. Kid, if you work the swing shift, you spend all those lonely hours in the factory. Believe me, when you get home you're bushed. Out like a light. When you get up, it's time to think about going to work again. Whole weeks go by in a blur.

"It's darn good money, too. When Paul comes back and sees the head start you have on a house—or a business, if that's what he wants— he'll be glad you did it." There was no need to tell Paul now, she said. Why upset him? She hadn't told her husband.

That first afternoon, I got dressed in the work shoes and coveralls that Lois had taken me to buy. I tied a bandanna in my hair the way she'd taught me: the knotted ends stuck up on top of my head like little ears. Walking out to Lois's car to leave for work, carrying Paul's lunchbox, I felt like a kid in a Halloween costume.

"Don't you worry," Lois ordered as we pulled away. "I've told you a hundred times, if I can run a machine, anyone can."

Sure enough, by the end of the evening, I'd learned to read the specifications and set the controls. I could feed the stock into the grinding wheel. I knew how to pick out the little shift in sound that the machine made the moment when the gear was perfectly ground. I was exhausted when the shift ended; my feet were killing me, my lower back throbbed. But I felt tingly inside, excited, kind of. Like I'd drunk too many cups of coffee.

"You did great, Lil!" Lois said, starting the car. She turned up the radio as we pulled away.

The announcer said, "Broadcasting from the ballroom of your dreams—" and "Racing with the Moon" came on. I remember that because I remember laughing and saying to Lois, "Me, working in a factory. There was a time I'd have said that that was about as likely as racing to the moon."

"Oh boy, those were the days, weren't they?" Lois said. "Remember how dumb we were when the war started? Good Lord, right after Joe left for boot camp, the car went on the blink and I drew a diagram of the dashboard and sent it to him in a panic with a note, 'Does it need oil?' By the end of the war, we were checking oil like pros. And changing fuses and fixing plumbing."

Then she got this funny look on her face and said, "Gosh, I hardly even remember Joe. Sometimes that seems like another life." When I saw she had tears in her eyes, I knew she was remembering the two of us on her front porch the day we found out that his plane had gone down.

I was the one who saw the messenger first. When he started up her walk, I swear my heart stopped beating. When it started up again, it rattled so hard inside me that my hand flew up to calm it. When Lois saw him, she grabbed my arm.

"Mrs. Joseph Harper?" the man said.

I'll never forget it: the way his voice sounded, that yellow piece of paper in his hand.

Honestly, the death of my own mother did not hit me as hard as the death of Joe Harper. Poor Lois. There was no body. No funeral. Nothing to help her let him go. Just that awful yellow telegram. Nothing really changed, that was the hard part. Lois's day-to-day life was no different from what it had been before the telegram came. She went to the market, she went to work, she ate and slept. On Sundays, we went to the movies. But there was Joe's death, the fact of it. I could actually see it in her face when, in the middle of doing or saying something, she remembered he was dead.

Lois never has been able to hide the way she feels. Sometimes, now, she looks at me and I can see that she's remembering I won't be here much longer. It's the opposite of Joe Harper dying when he was already gone, but somehow the same. Our lives haven't changed at all since we found out about my cancer. We go shopping, we trade books, we play cards in the afternoons. Most of the time I feel fine. Then, at the most unlikely times, it hits me. It's really crazy, Evie. I'll wake up in the night thinking I need to write down the recipe for a chicken casserole—as if there's anyone who's going to be left behind, hungry, because I'm not there to cook for them. I'll be out weeding the chrysanthemums and realize that when they bloom in the fall, I'll be gone. Or, worse, I'll picture myself in the hospital, all shrunk up, suffering—the tubes and needles, the pain that will surely come.

The only thing that comforts me then is knowing Lois will be with me. She'll know what to do. I hope you have a friend like her, Evie. For nearly fifty years now, Lois and I have pulled each other through, the balance always shifting as each one sees what the other needs, like two people rowing.

Here's a happy memory, completely happy.

You are just a year old, toddling around. Such a funny little thing, determined as you can be, yet patient in your way. You'll look at a book for the longest time, sometimes chattering and poking at the puppies and kittens and children in the pictures like you're trying to make them come alive. You're so bright! I can see that already. I'm so proud of you when I take you out for a walk in the buggy and people stop and say, "What a beautiful child."

I can't wait until the day of the Allison picnic because your mother has agreed to let Lois and me take you with us. I can't believe our luck when the day dawns and it's perfect. I dress you in one of the pretty little sunsuits I've made for you, and tie on a lacy bonnet. Of course, all the girls from work fuss over you just like I knew they would. The older children swing you in the baby swings and take turns holding you going down the slide. It gets so that you hold out your arms and squeal with delight each time you see one of them coming. They entertain themselves saying words over and over, trying to make you repeat them.

You say, "Lo," when Lois brings you a cookie, getting into the spirit of the game. "Lo-lo." Lois beams. It's the first time you've ever said her name. We all laugh when she goes back to the table and returns with a whole handful of treats.

"Here," she says, holding a piece of cupcake just out of your reach. "Say Lo."

"Lo," says a deep voice from behind us. Hank, our foreman.

Lois blushes. "Oh," she says. "Stop that, Hank." But she isn't as embarrassed as I'd have thought she'd be. Later, when the band starts up, he asks her to dance, and she says, yes.

I was thrilled when the two of them started seeing each other now and then. I thought the world of Hank, and everyone knew he was crazy about Lois. Joe had been dead more than a year then, and I'd been thinking for a while that it was time for Lois to start living again.

If the girls in the car pool asked her about him, she'd just say, "I've always liked Hank. He's a real nice fellow." But a lot of nights, after we'd dropped everyone off, we'd sit in the car, talking about how she felt.

In the kitchen, in bright daylight, we never talked the way we did those midnights in Lois's car. I've often thought, since then, that if you really wanted to get to the bottom of something, the way to do it would be to put the people involved in a dark car late at night and say, "Just talk." It's the way the world seems from there that tricks you. The houses all down the block look flat, like a child's drawing of houses. The lighted windows don't have anything to do with people at all. They're just bright squares, that's all. Nothing seems quite real, not even your own life. You'll say anything.

"I loved Joe so much," Lois would say over and over. "I still love him. But how can you love a person who—*isn't?*"

"People die," I told her. "Love doesn't."

"So what do you do with it then? It can't be fair to Hank the way I feel. Lil, sometimes I think what I feel about Joe is killing me."

I said, "I don't know, Lois. You don't want to not keep loving Joe, do you? That would erase everything you had together. So I guess all you can do is find someplace inside you, where the way you feel can be, and keep it there. Like you find a place in the attic to keep those things you loved and can't stand to part with, even though they're useless to whatever your life turned out to be.

I told her that sometimes I thought that all I felt was killing me, too. Unlike Joe, Paul was somewhere; but wherever it was seemed to

have nothing to do with me anymore. I didn't doubt that I loved him;
it was more like I didn't know anymore what loving him meant. It was
this blind thing, like faith. If I didn't keep loving Paul—

Finishing that sentence was what scared me. If I didn't keep loving Paul—what? Since grade school, Paul and I had been almost like
one person. We even looked alike. When we were kids, people had often
mistaken us for brother and sister. Lord, I missed him now. I thought
of him all the time and longed for the time we'd be together again, but
it was also true that I'd gotten used to his being gone. I was proud of
the way I'd been able to take charge and run our little household on
next to nothing. I liked buying war bonds with my own money. I missed
Paul, yes. But I wasn't exactly unhappy without him.

I remember saying to Lois, "He'd be shocked if he knew how much
I liked working."

She laughed and said, "Not to mention how he'd feel if he could
see you sitting out here at midnight, smoking and yakking with your
girlfriend."

"I didn't have girlfriends before."

"Yeah," Lois said. "Me either."

She took out another cigarette, offered me the pack, and I took
one, too. The cigarette lighter glowed bright orange. She lit hers, then
held the lighter for me. A gray swirl of smoke drifted between us and
out the open window, like fog.

I wish you were here with me now, Evie. I've been writing so long,
it's evening. The house is dark. If you appeared right now, I'd say, "Sit
there on the sofa, honey," and you would. From where I'm sitting at
my little desk, you'd be no more than a shadow. Just like Lois was in
the car all those years ago. And maybe I could tell you what I'm thinking.

I was wrong about so many things. Lois used to say sometimes,
"Lily, Peg isn't half as bad as you like to believe." My own best friend,
the one person in the world who understood what I'd gone through
with my sister, and I still wouldn't listen. Poor Lois. She was torn between being loyal to me and the truth of what she saw. Finally, she gave
up. It wasn't until you'd gone off to college, and your Uncle Paul died
not long afterwards that she started in on me again about Peg.

Lois said, "You know how absent-minded Tom is. Do you really think he'd come by all the time to see if anything around the house needed mending if Peg didn't remind him to do it? Do you really think those teenage girls are likely to go out in the garden and pick tomatoes for their lonely old aunt if their mother didn't say it would be a nice thing to do?"

But I was still stubborn. I said, "I'm not anybody's lonely old aunt; and even if I were, the last thing I'd need would be for Peg to feel sorry for me."

It took what happened to Angel and Matt to open my eyes. Lord. Seventeen years old and a baby coming. At first, I couldn't believe Peg and Tom were going to stand for Angel marrying. There were plenty of places a girl could go to have a baby, and then start over again. I'd had hopes for Angel, like I know you did. I knew, with a baby, she'd be stuck here forever, no better off than her sisters. All Peg said when I brought it up was, "You're right, Lily. They're so young, it breaks my heart. But those two love each other. If they give up that child, nothing for either one of them will ever be right again."

Lois told me, "Butt out, Lily."

Thank heavens, for once I listened.

Jenny became a kind of second chance for me, such a joy to me. No child could have replaced you, Evie; but maybe that was the reason I was able to love her the right way, the way I should have loved you. Maybe that was the reason, too, I was able to see that Peg allowed it. No, she more than allowed it. She took pleasure in my loving Jenny. I finally saw what she'd seen all along: if you just let love alone, it multiplies. There's plenty for everyone.

I could have let you love Peg, Evie. I should have. Which brings me right back to what I've been avoiding since I sat down the first time to write about the past. I made up my mind I was going to tell you the truth about your mother, and I mean to do it now.

She was so young. That, of course, you know. But I cannot impress it upon you enough. She was young and very, very pretty. She hadn't even finished high school when she ran off with your dad. Then, you couldn't go to school if you were married. So when Tom shipped out and she came back to Indiana, she moved in with me. The little bedroom that was going to have been our baby's room became a teenager's room instead: powder and lipstick and bobby pins all in a clutter on the dresser top, snapshots and ticket stubs stuck in the frame of the mirror. The radio blared songs from the *Hit Parade*. A picture of a gawky boyfriend suited up for basketball would have fit right in; but instead, there was Tom in his army uniform. I'd look at him and I'd think, I'll help her grow up for you. I believed I could.

I was heartsick when I found out she was pregnant. I thought, I can't stand this, Carol having a baby she doesn't even want and my own baby dead. But worse, I remembered the promise I'd made to my mother before she died. "Take care of your sister," she'd said. I'd been so romantic, so stupid about Carol and Tom. Now look what a mess things were.

The temptation was to mother Carol. Because of the difference in our ages, I'd mothered her from the day she was born. And, good grief, she was so distracted and dreamy it was hard to imagine her fending for herself now. But Lois said, "She has to grow up, Lil. Be practical. If you keep on taking care of her, why would she even try to take care of herself?"

I knew she was right. That was one of the reasons I decided to take the job at Allison's when I did. As long as I was at home all day with all that time on my hands, I knew I'd fuss over Carol. If I went to work, she'd begin to get used to pulling her own weight.

But she was too sick the first few months to get a job or help with the chores. Then she was too tired. She didn't want to go out to do the gardening or the marketing because being pregnant embarrassed her. No matter what I said or did, she spent most of her time alone in her room, reading movie magazines and listening to records. Sometimes when I came home at night, I'd hear her crying. I felt bad, but I didn't know what to do for her. By June, even Lois could see the situation was hopeless. She said, "Lil, let's just get her through this, get the baby born, and then, when things settle down, you can talk about who's going to do what to keep the household running."

We were all relieved when Carol went for her check-up the first of September and the doctor said, "Any time." Lois had heard about a place called The Victory Store, kind of like an on-going rummage sale where people bought and traded clothes and household goods that were getting harder and harder to find in the stores. It might be a good place to get things for the baby, she told Carol. Why spend money she didn't have to spend? If she could buy what she needed for the baby second-hand, there'd be enough money to buy some pretty new clothes for herself when she got back her figure. It sounded like a good idea, so Lois drove us there.

The store was in an old house, out near Plainfield. The paint was peeling, the porch sagging. The yard was a disgrace, junk everywhere: worn-out furniture, cracked mirrors, beat-up bicycles. I remember laughing at the sign in one of the windows that read: "Give your salvage, save your country." As if that mess could save anything!

Inside, it was bright and clean, though. The Red Cross ladies had organized the clothes onto dress-racks in what had been the living room. Tables held all kinds of household goods, costume jewelry, hats. And baby clothes. The lady in charge was thrilled to show those to Carol. But Carol made a bee-line past her for the racks of ladies' clothes, holding up dresses the size she soon hoped to be.

The saleslady said, "She's so young," excusing her rudeness.

"My sister," I said. I told her Carol was living with me because her husband was overseas.

"These poor little babies," the woman said. I didn't know whether she meant girls like Carol or the little ones that they were bearing.

Lois and I picked out the baby things: sleepers, undershirts, a bunting, two dozen diapers, soft from use. And real rubber pants, I remember that. There was no elastic in the new ones they were making. I'd heard mothers say they fell right off their babies' bottoms. When we were finished, the lady said, "I have a wonderful bargain on a crib."

She took us to the back of the house, where the maple crib was tucked away among easy chairs and sofas and end tables. A lady from the north side had brought it in the day before, the woman told us. She said it came from L.S. Ayres.

I knew. Day-dreaming in the baby department there, when I was pregnant myself, I'd looked at that crib a million times. It was rock solid, beautifully carved. It was a copy of an antique crib, a clerk had told me. I never could have afforded it. Now the Red Cross lady was saying that they had a flat price for used baby cribs, five dollars, and wouldn't it cheer my sister up to get something so lovely?

"Absolutely," I said. "In fact, I'll buy it for her." But the truth is,

I wanted the crib. We paid for the things we'd bought, took down the crib, and jerry-rigged it with ropes in the open trunk.

Poor Carol. She had to move the dressing table out of her bedroom to make room for it. Then when we got it in there it looked ridiculous. It was meant for a real nursery, not a tacky little old room like hers.

"Did I do wrong to buy it?" I asked Lois on the way to work.

"Oh, Lil," she said. "No. You want it for the baby you and Paul will have when he comes home. I know that."

It was true. But that night I dreamed my lost baby in that crib, so tiny that it slipped right through the pretty carved slats and disappeared into the darkness.

Angel came by today and brought me some bread she'd baked. We had a nice visit. She asked me again if she could call you, and I said no. She won't go behind my back. I know how she feels about people who treat their elderly relatives like children. But I know that not telling you troubles her. She feels like she's betraying you, and she's afraid you'll be angry at her when you find out. You know how she's always adored you.

So I'm asking you here and now, Evie, please don't be angry with your sister. She did exactly what I asked. And while I'm on the subject of what I want and don't want people to do, I might just as well say that I don't want you to feel bad for being out of touch with me now, for not somehow knowing that something was wrong.

I love you, I've always loved you, and I know that you love me. You did the right thing, making the kind of life you've made for yourself. When I think of all you've accomplished, I'm so proud. What I hope is that, by now, you've begun to see that as we get older time just doesn't mean much any more. What's the difference whether I saw you last month or last year or the year before? The times we've been together seem round and perfect to me, like pearls, and they are all strung together making one beautiful thing, so real that it is as if you are with me always. You are with me now, as I write these words to you. You have been with me since the day you were born.

Lord, that day seemed to go on forever. Carol's water broke first thing in the morning and we rushed her to the hospital. Of course, then they wouldn't let anyone stay with the mother in the labor room, so all we could do was wait.

Lois chattered a mile a minute to keep me distracted. After a few hours passed and we hadn't heard a word, she cornered a nurse who came out of the delivery area. "Mrs. Slade is coming along nicely," the nurse said, and then went on about her business.

It aggravated Lois, so she questioned the next nurse and the next one and the next so that it got to be a joke with us, and every time we saw a nurse we laughed out loud. We chain-smoked. At noon, she spread out the lunch she'd brought and made me eat.

She stayed with me until she had to leave for work. I passed the time looking through the magazines she'd left. I did parts of crossword puzzles, wrote half of a letter to Paul. I thought of him sitting in that very waiting room the night I lost our baby. I remembered lying in the labor room where Carol was now. I stood up like I meant to stretch, but I was really just trying to stop the train of thought that I knew would bring me nothing but heartache. Why I walked down the hallway to look at the babies in the nursery, I don't know. Maybe I thought it would somehow prepare me for the first sight of my sister's child.

I stood at the window a long time. There were so many of them. Tiny, bawling babies in beds that looked like shoe boxes for giants' shoes. Their arms and legs moved like they still remembered the drag of water in the womb. I made myself look at them, one by one: their froggy legs, thin as sticks; their blue eyes, cloudy to protect them against the sudden harshness of light. The veins on their eyelids, lavender, like scraps of thread. Their lovely perfect little fingers.

I knew what Lois would say if she saw me there. "For Pete's sake, Lillian, get ahold of yourself." When the doctor came near four o'clock, I was back in the waiting room, composed.

"Shouldn't be long now," he said.

Thankfully, he was right. Soon a nurse opened the door. "Mrs. Slade? You're an aunt! Come, look. Your sister has a beautiful little girl."

Evie, I still remember that moment just as if it were yesterday. I stood at the nursery window, and when the nurse held you up so I could see you, I knew I could've looked at all those other babies till kingdom come and I still wouldn't have been ready for the rush of love I felt for you. Your dark baby-hair went every which way, your little fists were clenched against your cheeks. I swear, even in the first hour of your life, you were curious. You couldn't see yet, I knew. Nonetheless, you seemed to be looking right at me, demanding, where am I? Who are you? Why?

I'm ashamed when I think of the diary I kept all through that time. I went on for pages and pages about your mother's irresponsibility, her childishness during those months after you were born. I was so sure about what kind of mother she should have been.

Things seem so clear to you when you're young. In any situation, there's a right way to behave and a wrong way. Good people always do what's right. As you get older, you see it's not that simple. Always tell the truth, we're taught. But what if the truth hurts someone you love? What if it hurts anyone, for that matter? It's only your truth, after all. Can you be so sure you're right? Can you be sure you won't look back someday and see that things weren't at all what they seemed?

As much as I loved you, Evie—as much as I love you now—I'd be lying if I said you were an easy baby. As if you knew right off that this world was full of sorrow, you started crying the day you were born and kept on for three months straight. Colic, the doctor said. But, aside from naming the problem, he didn't offer much help. An eyedropper of bourbon mixed with the formula was what one of our neighbors, an older lady, said was the only relief she'd found for colic. It didn't sound like a good idea to me; I knew our mother never would have have stood for such a thing. But we walked you, burped you, walked you some more, and you just wouldn't stop. I'd come home from the factory and find your mother with dark shadows under her eyes, punch-drunk for lack of sleep. Finally, we gave in and tried our neighbor's cure. Those few quiet hours between midnight and dawn were the only peace we had.

It was no wonder that Carol decided she didn't want to be cooped up in the house all the time, and decided to get a job. Now, looking back, I see her plan made sense. If she worked the day shift and I worked the swing shift, there would be only a few hours every afternoon when one of us wouldn't be able to take care of you. But then I was beside myself at the thought of leaving you with a stranger for any amount of time at all.

I took you to Mrs. Cox, the lady who watched you, at the last possible moment every day. I'd get you up in the morning, give you breakfast, take you to the park, and then on whatever errands I needed to run. I'd walk you down the street to Mrs. Cox's house when it was time for your afternoon nap. I felt a little better as time went by and I saw that you were happy there. But I found plenty of other things to nag Carol about. In my mind, she failed to take her responsibilities as a mother as seriously as she should.

She hadn't gotten any better about helping around the house either. Which was stubborn of her, true. And childish. But when I look back, keeping score the way I did seems so petty. After all, it was Carol's house, too. She was paying half the rent. If she didn't mind a mess, why should she have been expected to worry about the way the house looked every waking minute the way I did? And did I really have the right to tell her how to spend her time? I'd get so mad when she left you with a sitter to go out for the evening. It wasn't that I thought she was cheating on your father, or anything like that. I believed Carol when she told me that what she and her friend, Vera, did when they went out was perfectly innocent. I knew it was natural to want to go out and have some fun. But I couldn't help trying to impress upon her that you were the most important thing in her life now.

It got so that when I tried to talk to her, she'd say, "You're not my mother, Lily," and make me feel a hundred years old.

Between our bickering about the house and my nagging that you should be raised a certain way, the *right* way, things became awfully strained. It all came to a head the winter after your first birthday. Our church called for volunteers to help out at its Servicemen's Club during the holiday season, and Carol and Vera signed up to work three nights a week. Carol found an older lady down the block, a grandmotherly sort who liked earning a little extra money, to take care of you.

I didn't like the idea, but I didn't say anything. Those days, you sure didn't criticize anyone who wanted to help cheer up a bunch of homesick boys who were about to be shipped off to war. And at Christmas, to boot. But when the new year came around and Carol decided to keep on volunteering, I told her I thought it was a mistake.

She said, "You know, Lily, it won't hurt Evie to learn that the whole world doesn't revolve around her. Besides, Mrs. Archer is good for her. She loves her, but she doesn't spoil her."

It's true, Evie. I did spoil you. It became real obvious later, when you had such a hard time with Peg and your dad. But then I didn't see it. What your mother said to me that day hurt me so badly, all I could do was turn away and act like I was busy. I knew that if I tried to say any more about the babysitter, I'd start to cry.

I did cry the next morning. You woke me up and called me, like you always did, and I went to get you from your crib. The way your face lit up at the sight of me, the way you held your little arms out for me. Well, I sat on the edge of Carol's bed, holding you, crying my eyes out. You patted me on the back to comfort me.

I told myself: things have gone too far, Lillian. You've got to tell Carol it's time for her to find a place of her own. You're keeping her from growing up. If she's on her own, she'll settle down. She'll have to. She'll be tired doing everything she has to do for Evie and working on top of that, too tired to want to go out with Vera every night. There won't be so much extra money for babysitters, either. But there was a weakness in me, Evie, that wouldn't let me send you away.

I felt half-sick to my stomach at the factory that night. I couldn't keep my mind on my work. When I'd made scrap for the third time in an hour, Hank said, "Take a break, Lil. Go sit down and smoke a cigarette in my office. Everyone makes scrap now and then. Don't worry about it."

But I did worry about it. And about you and your mother. And your Uncle Paul. Well, I worked myself up into a terrible state there in Hank's office—an anxiety attack I guess you'd call it now. Hank's kindness, the girls fussing over me at lunch only made me feel worse. "I'm just so tired," I said, and covered my face with my hands.

In the car, on the way home, I couldn't stay awake. I rested my head on the car seat and drifted in and out of sleep. When we got home, and I heard Lois's car door open, I could barely raise myself. I felt dizzy.

Lois opened my door and took my arm. "Come on," she said. "I'm putting you to bed."

Later, she told me she decided to walk to the house with me because she'd noticed that it was completely dark. Usually, it was lit up like a Christmas tree. Carol was careless about such things, and Mrs.

Archer had a nervous streak and kept the lights blazing to scare off would-be intruders.

I didn't realize it myself until I stepped inside. Moonlight made the little room strange and shadowy. It fell across the clutter of magazines on the coffee table, cast the curved outline of the radio against the wall. Lois headed for the bedroom where you and your mother slept. It wasn't until she came out, stricken, and said, "Lil, they're not there," that all the pieces fell together, and I was afraid.

Lois turned on the light and rummaged around until she found Mrs. Archer's phone number in the drawer of the phone table. She dialed it and stood there tapping her foot, waiting, for what seemed forever while it rang. Lois got the poor woman out of bed, it turned out. You weren't with her.

She hung up and started pacing, talking a mile a minute, really to herself. "They're probably fine," she said. "I'm sure they're fine. Okay. What we have to do is try and figure out what Carol would be most likely to do." She thought about this awhile. "The other babysitter. The day babysitter. How about her?"

As she spoke, there was a banging on the front door that scared us both out of our wits. Lois opened it, and there stood Mrs. Cox, the day babysitter, as if she'd conjured her up with a magic wand. You were fast asleep in her arms.

She stepped inside. "I saw your lights go on," she said. "I've been waiting for someone to get home so I could go to sleep. Mrs. Slade, I'm sorry, but I won't be able to care for Evie any longer. Would you let your sister know that, as of this evening, she'll have to find someone else?"

I asked her if she would please stay for just a minute, while I put you to bed, and then tell me what had happened.

"Well, just a few minutes," she said, and came on into the living room.

You were still dressed in your corduroy overalls, but I didn't want to risk waking you to change you into your pajamas, so I laid you down just like you were. When I came back, Mrs. Cox told me that Carol had called around dinner time, which was already well past the time she was supposed to pick Evie up. She said she had to work late, and asked if you might stay there a bit longer. She went on to say that it wasn't the first time something like that had happened. Carol had been leaving you there longer and longer hours during the past weeks, and she'd asked Mrs. Cox not to mention the extra hours to me.

She was apologetic. She was fond of you, she said. But she just couldn't continue sitting for you. She was responsible for several other children, too; and of course, she had her own family to take care of. The long hours were just too much. When she got up to leave, she said, "I hope there aren't any hard feelings."

I assured her that there weren't, and paid her for the evening. Then I fixed Lois and myself a cup of tea. We were both so wound up by then that there was no way we'd have been able to sleep.

"Well?" Lois said.

I told her that for the first time, I knew exactly what to do. "I'm going to quit my job and take care of Evie myself," I said. "Don't ask me if I think it's the right thing to do, because I don't have any idea. I'm just going to do it. I'll take in sewing if I need the money. I've made up my mind."

Lois knew there was no use arguing. From then on, she helped me all she could, even though I'd look at her sometimes and know she was thinking how foolish I was. How I was doing things all wrong. Evie, I let you become my center. From that night until the end of the war, your growth, your small achievements were my only real measure of time.

Your mother allowed this, she even seemed relieved by it. In fact, it was when I took total responsibility for you that she learned to love you. She did love you, Evie. Please believe me. She played with you, bought you little presents.

I asked no questions about where she went or who she saw. I just prayed each night that she would fall in love with your father all over when he came back. I prayed that I would have the strength to give you up when it was time. I still believed then that I'd have children of my own to make up for losing you. I didn't know I was living what would turn out to be the happiest days of my life.

Chapter Ten

*T*here the writing stopped. The sections had been dated, the last entry written less than two weeks before. Aunt Lily must have begun to write soon after she came home from the hospital, written every day from then, until—

Until she got sick. I couldn't even make myself think the word "died" yet, let alone believe it. Still, the knowledge of her death rushed into me each time I looked at the book she'd left, each time I thought her name. When I'd thought of Aunt Lily just two nights ago, talking to Cliff's mother, she was already gone. When I mailed the postcard and imagined her in the foyer of her house, shuffling through her mail— her delight at finding it among the bills and flyers—she was gone. The world should have shifted the moment my Aunt Lily left it, but I hadn't felt a thing.

I was alone, in my flat. I vaguely remembered leaving the lab after reading Angel's letter, stumbling along the corridors of the museum, my head down, hoping that I would not encounter anyone who might expect a cordial exchange or, worse, might look at me too closely and ask, "Evie, are you all right?"

I was not all right at all. At that moment, I felt bereft of everything I had ever loved about my Aunt Lily, all I had believed my life with her might have been. I felt weak, the way I felt looking at the Vermeer that first morning in London—ruined, slashed.

I paced the tiny apartment. Angel should have called me, I thought. She should have called the minute she found out Aunt Lily was sick, no matter what. She had had no right to keep it from me and then write me a letter when it was too late to do anything. As if I were a distant relative to be notified. Oh, by the way, don't send birthday cards any more. Or Christmas gifts. Or postcards if you go on a trip—

109

Ian called, having learned of my abrupt departure. I told him what had happened, and made him promise not to tell Cliff yet. I was all right, I told him. I just needed to be alone. But the truth is, I was so angry that it was all I could do to keep from tearing the pages from the book Aunt Lily had left me. I wanted to burn them, as she had burned the other diary she described. The neatness of her handwriting, as perfect as a school teacher's, enraged me. I saw her at the antique desk in the little den, where she always did the bookwork for her business. Sitting there, day after day, writing steadily. She did everything so steadily. I stopped pacing then and stood looking out at the street. The red double-decker buses, the black taxis, the cars careening along Grosvenor Road. The pillared post box on the corner. The pub down the block. The scene framed by my window looked absolutely foreign to me at that moment.

I'm so far away from home, I thought. I've never been so far away from home. But it wasn't home I ached for: my apartment in New York, or that city.

Home was my Aunt Lily.

Then the grief roared in, fiercer, meaner than the anger that had, for a little while, kept it at bay. I read Aunt Lily's real life over and over that day and deep into the night, until I could stay awake no longer.

I would work. Yes. I would go to the Vermeer, lose myself working. Setting out for the museum the next morning, I felt as I might have felt talking myself down from a high place. Move this foot. Good, now the next. Don't think. See the painting before you in your mind's eye, because that's what matters. Enter its silence. I succeeded in this mental exercise to such an extent that I was surprised to look up and see the classical facade of the museum looming before me. The sudden thud as the staff door closed behind me was jarring. The sound of my name spoken.

"Miss Slade."

"Yes, good morning," I said to the guard. I signed in and started past him.

"Miss Slade, there's someone to see you in the waiting room. A young lady."

"But I'm not expecting anyone," I said. "There must be some mistake—"

"No, mum." He thrust the visitors' clipboard toward me. "No mistake. There's a young lady, all right, and she's quite anxious to see you." His blunt finger pointed to a name written in loopy girlish script. "Here."

It read, "Jennifer Parker." My niece, Angel's daughter. But Angel hadn't said a word in her letter about Jenny being in England this summer.

"She's been here about an hour," the guard said. "Got a bag with her. Come directly from the airport, she told me." He raised his eyebrow, directed me with a tilt of his head toward the room where I'd waited for Ian the morning I arrived in London.

I found her fast asleep. She'd obviously been sitting straight up, waiting for me, and had fallen sideways onto the plump upholstered arm of the sofa. A ratty day pack rested precariously on her knees. A brand new suitcase stood at her feet. She wore jeans and an old jeans jacket. A faded pink tee-shirt. Worn sneakers. Even in her disheveled state, she was lovely. I sat down on the edge of a chair across from where she slept, and studied her. The long brown hair tangled across her face. The dark skin, the long lashes. She looked exactly like my sister.

She had Angel's smile, too. Tentative, slow. "Aunt Evie?" she said, waking. "I hope it's all right I've come. I can go right back if you don't want me." And Angel's voice.

Jenny sat up, leaned toward me. "See, I just needed to get away from my mom and dad for a while. I'm not, like, running away or anything like that. I just needed to get away from them, so I decided to come and visit you."

"Me."

"Well, yeah. I need to think about some things. About what I'm going to do next? Like college. Everybody's so happy I'm going off to college, you know? Like it's such a big deal, going away. You know how my dad went to night school when I was a baby, and then my mom went a little at a time. Well, the two of them have this idea that going away to college is the be-all and end-all of the universe. My mom's always talking about how you got that big scholarship because you were so smart, how you even studied in Europe, all that. She wants me to be like you. So did Aunt Lily. My dad thinks I'm going down to Bloomington and I'm going to work my butt off and get into law school, so I never have to worry about money and stuff the way he and my mom did when they were young. He wants my life to be easy—

"I mean, I want to go to college," Jenny said. "It's not that. It's just, maybe I don't want to be a yuppie lawyer with some big office and a fancy car. And I hardly know you, so how do I know if I want to be like you? So—"

"So you came here."

"See, I had my passport because I went to France last summer. That honors program? My mom probably told you about it. She told everybody else. Anyway, I found out that Aunt Lily left me some money. Like a lot of money, enough for college, so I used my own money for the ticket, the money I've made, working—

"I guess I should call my mom and dad pretty soon. You know, let them know where I am? It's just I knew they'd say no if I asked," she rushed on. "They never want to bother anyone. But Aunt Lily would've thought it was a great idea. The way she was always talking about you—" Her voice trailed away. She blinked back tears.

Weird, I heard Peg's voice in my head, clear as a bell. "Listen, I've got my hands full here," she used to say if Dad phoned and I was acting up or she was in the middle of some ridiculous negotiation with the Queens. It was exactly how I felt now. I had no idea what I was supposed to do with Jenny, but I had to do something. We couldn't just sit there in the waiting room all day.

"Come on," I said finally. "We'll go up to my friend, Ian's, office. You can use his phone to call home, then we'll figure out what to do next."

There was that smile again, Angel's. Jenny stood up and hoisted her pack over her shoulder. I picked up her suitcase. It was a very nice one, brand new. I knew without asking that Aunt Lily had given it to her for her high school graduation. A suitcase was what she'd given me for mine.

"Well." Ian tipped back on his chair and blew three very careful smoke rings. "The plot thickens."

"Very funny," I said. "What am I going to do?"

It was too early to call yet, barely dawn in Indiana, so Jenny had gone to freshen up in the restroom down the hall. I moved a pile of prints and papers from the sofa in his office and set them on the floor so I could sit down. I'd stopped smoking a long time ago, but I reached across Ian's desk, shook a cigarette from his pack, and lit it. It tasted terrible. I stubbed it out.

"Seriously, what am I going to do with a teen-age girl? I don't even have any place to put her. That tiny flat—"

"Send her home if you must," Ian said. "Though she seems quite bearable, I must say. No pink hair. No ring in her nose. And curious. She must've asked me a dozen questions in five minute's time, jotting everything in that little notebook of hers. Imagine, a girl that age so earnest that she's afraid of what she might forget. I should think you'd be able to entertain her easily enough."

"But I have work to do. I can't just set that aside and go sightseeing. Especially not right now. Just this morning I was going to start—"

"Don't whine, Evie. Things happen. I say, don't look so woebegone, will you? What's a few days delay on the Vermeer, after all? You could do with a bit of a holiday, what with the bad news about your aunt. You're right, though. You will need help." He picked up the telephone and dialed, handing me the receiver before I could ask who he was calling.

"Department of Archaeological Studies, Clifford Mills."

I should have known. I glanced at Ian, half-aggravated, and he shrugged, as if to say, I knew you'd be silly about calling him.

"Hello?" Cliff said into the silence.

"Cliff, yes. It's Evie."

"Evie?" The pleasure I heard in his voice opened something inside me. In a rush, I told him all that had happened since yesterday morning. When he said, "Don't do anything until I get there. I'll get a taxi. I can be there in twenty minutes," I didn't argue.

Ian's secretary cleared a place on a table and set down a tray that held a little pot of tea, a plate of scones, strawberry jam, and a bowl of Devon cream. "There you go, dear," she said to Jenny, who had come back and now stood uncertainly in the doorway. "Here." Miss Smythe patted the chair. "You must be famished. All those hours on the plane.

That ghastly food! A cream tea is just the thing to set you right." She smiled kindly as Jenny settled herself.

"Thank you," Jenny said. "Thanks a lot." Then to me, anxiously, "Did you get my mom?"

"No," I said. "Drink your tea, now. A few more minutes won't make that much difference, will it? In any case, you *know* the first thing she'll ask you once she finds out you're all right is whether or not you've had anything to eat."

She smiled, her first real smile, and polished off the plate of scones as if she hadn't eaten for days, licking the cream from the sides of her mouth like a cat.

Ian, still tipped back, looked like a cat himself. How he loves to sit back and watch life unfold, I thought. But I couldn't be annoyed with him. He looked from me to Jenny, then back to me again, and nodded almost imperceptibly, as if to say, everything will be all right.

When Cliff arrived, I let him take charge. I was like Ian then, watching.

"Let's have a look at this young lady who's come all the way from America on her own. So—" Cliff stood before Jenny, grinning, and she grinned back. "You just made up your mind to come to London and took the first plane without a word to anyone. Is that true?"

"My friend, Cara—she knew. She took me to the airport. I told my parents I was spending a few nights at her house because her mom was out of town."

"Plucky one, eh?" Ian said.

"Indeed she is," said Cliff. He looked at Jenny for quite some time, then at her worn backpack with the colorful buttons on it: "No Nukes." "Save the Whales." "I Brake for Elvis." He turned to me. "You've got buckets of work to do here. And that little flat of yours would be insufferable with two people in it. How about we trade for the time Jenny's here? She'd be comfortable in Monica's room, I think. And I've got some field sites to visit in the next fortnight; I wouldn't mind a bit having her tag along. She can be my assistant. That'll keep her busy in the day. That is," he said to Jenny, "if you want to have a go at it."

"Field sites? Wow. Yeah, I'd love that." She paused and looked at me. "If it's not too much trouble?"

I was staggered by Cliff's generosity, more than a little anxious about being so indebted to him. Yet he seemed so pleased at the prospect of solving my problem, and Jenny so clearly smitten by his idea that there was no way I could have sent her back to Indiana on the next plane, which every instinct was telling me to do. "If Cliff says it's okay for us to use his flat, it's okay," I told Jenny. "And if he says it's okay for you to go out to the sites with him, that's okay, too. As long as your parents agree."

"They'll let me, Aunt Evie. I know they will, if you say so."

Ian dialed the phone number Jenny had given him, and after a few moments, he handed her the receiver.

"Mom? Mom, it's me. Jenny? I'm sorry to wake you up. No, nothing's wrong. I'm fine. Yes, fine. Honest. No, it's not a bad connection. Mom, I'm not at Cara's. I'm in London." Jenny looked at me. "London. Yeah, I came to London. Last night. Cara took me to the airport. What? I don't *have* my job any more. I mean, I quit on Friday. Yeah, I know. I'm sorry. *I'm sorry.* Mom? Don't freak out, okay? Listen, I bought the ticket with my own money. From working. I have all that other money from Aunt Lily, you know. Since I don't need my own money for school any more, I took it out of the bank Friday when I quit work. No, no. I got travelers checks, like I did last year, for France. Mom, I'm okay. Really. I'm with Aunt Evie. You're not mad, are you? Mom. Here. Ask her. She'll tell you it's all right."

I couldn't remember the last time I'd talked to my sister. A year, maybe? Not at Christmas. I'd sent everyone postcards from China, where I'd gone to avoid the holidays. In May, I'd gotten Jenny's graduation announcement and sent a gift. A note that said, "Good luck. So sorry I can't be there."

Now when I took the phone from Jenny, Angel said, "Evie, I don't know what to say. I can't believe Jenny would do such a thing, barging in on you that way. I don't know what's gotten into her. You must think—

"Oh, Evie. Did you—" She stopped short.

"It came yesterday," I said. "Your letter."

"Well, thank God for that," she said. "I'm so sorry, Evie. Your finding out that way. But—"

"It wasn't your fault," I said. "You did exactly what Aunt Lily asked you to do."

"But I didn't want it to be that way. And the last thing you need right now is worrying about Jenny." She started to cry. "My God, what in the world is the matter with her? Here Matt and I thought she was at Cara's house. We didn't even miss her. We just went off to bed as if everything were normal."

I glanced at Jenny, who was back at the table, picking up the crumbs of scones, looking anxious.

"Angel, she's fine," I said. "I can't say it wasn't a shock to find her here this morning; the truth is, I'm still in shock. But she's okay. We're both okay. And a friend of mine has offered to trade flats with me while she's here; the one the museum rented for me is so small. He's an archaeologist; he'll take Jenny around to some of the sites with him, he says. While I work. Listen, why not let her stay a few weeks? There's no sense in sending her right back, unless you and Matt really want me to."

"You're sure?"

"Yes," I said, though I wasn't. "It's all right. Really."

"Evie, talk to her," Angel said. "Please. I don't know what's wrong with her, but all summer, especially since Aunt Lily got sick, something's been wrong. She's so unhappy. She's just not herself—" She began to cry this time, harder than before. "I'll talk to you later. When I've had a chance to talk to Matt. To get what she's done solid in my brain. Okay?"

"Of course," I said, and assured her once again that everything was going to be fine. As if I were such an expert at happiness that I was perfectly qualified to take on the task of fixing Jenny's life.

Chapter Eleven

*T*he taxi roared down Whitehall, approached Westminster Abbey and the Houses of Parliament. "Oh look, Big Ben!" Jenny said. "Grandma used to pass it on the bus every day on her way to work, she told me. It looks just the way she described it. Did you know it was the last time she saw her brother, Aunt Evie? Right there, by Big Ben. Just before he died."

"No," I said.

Her eyes filled with tears, as if she had known Peg's brother herself. She glanced back for a last glimpse of the clock as the taxi passed the government buildings. "Right there," she said again. "Wow. It's so weird to actually see it, you know? All this stuff she's told me about. Anyway, they'd been to the movies and to tea on the day it happened, Grandma and her brother. Grandma was meeting one of her girlfriends to go dancing, so she took him to the bus stop to make sure he got on all right. He wanted to stay. He kept teasing her, dancing around, saying, 'Take me with you. Why can't I go with you?' You know, like kids do? He was only fourteen, they wouldn't even have let him in. But he kept bugging her anyway.

"She made him get on the bus. Then, just as it started over the bridge, the air raid warning went off. She didn't know what to do. All the people around her started running. They'd go down in the subways—the tube, I mean—during the bombings, Grandma told me. It was safer there, underground. But she felt so terrible about making her brother go on the bus, she was so scared about what might happen to him that she just stood there, watching the bombers go over. Actually watching them. Can you believe that? She saw the corner of the hospital just across the bridge get hit and catch on fire. That's when she started running.

117

"A policeman tried to stop her, but she wouldn't stop. She ran all the way across the bridge, that one we just saw. She told me she saw bits of beds that had been blown out the side of the hospital. Bits of bodies, too. A dog's head in the gutter. Is that gross, or what? She saw a baby buggy all twisted and bent, and, Aunt Evie, a little baby's hand, still in the sleeve of its sweater."

"And her brother?"

"Dead," Jenny said. "In the bus. It fell into a big bomb crater and caught on fire. She was the one who had to tell her mother."

"I never knew that," I said. "She never told us that."

"I know. She only told me because I was doing this report for school. On World War II? I had this weird history teacher last year. Mr. Edwards. He made everyone talk to some person who'd been through it. He kept saying, 'Details, people! Details! History is made of details.' I wanted to get an 'A', so I kept bugging Grandma to think of the weirdest details she could. When I turned my paper in, he asked me if she'd come in and talk to our class.

"She was so great," Jenny said. "The kids thought she was really cool. They asked so many questions that we were late to our next period classes. Mr. Edwards taped all of it. He said she was better than any book. You can listen to the tape if you want to. I have a copy." Jenny patted her backpack. "I brought it with me. I thought I'd listen to it again, after I saw all the places she talked about."

Just then, the cab pulled up at Cliff's flat; I asked the driver to wait. I took Jenny's suitcase and she hefted her pack on her shoulder and followed me. Using the key Cliff had given me, I opened the door. I had never entered his apartment alone until that moment, and I felt strange as I stood inside, his whole life surrounding me. The presence of his books, all he knew. The photographs of his children. I had only glanced into his daughter's room before, on my way down the corridor. Now I led Jenny there.

Monica's room was wallpapered in a pretty Laura Ashley print— bouquets of violets tied with yellow ribbons, on a white background. The draperies were made of the same fabric, and so were the throw pillows on the lavender duvet. Real African violets in clay pots were lined up on the marble sills. There was a white wicker armchair upholstered in the violet print, a little wicker dressing table dotted with photos

and knick-knacks and more violets. Poor bedraggled Jenny looked out
of place in the antique mirror above it. Ian wouldn't call her plucky
now, I thought. She'd grown very quiet. She looked almost scared, as if
she'd suddenly realized the enormity of what she'd done.

But I turned down the bed as if I hadn't noticed. More Laura
Ashley violets on the sheets. "A good, long nap and you'll feel like new
again," I said. "I'll go on back to the museum and work for a while.
Later, we'll have some supper with Cliff and go out exploring a bit, if
you feel like it." When she stood, as if frozen, I teased her. "We'll get
you a nightgown made of this fabric. I've seen them. You'll be like one
of those exotic African insects, camouflaged. Nobody will be able to
find you."

She smiled then, dropped her backpack, kicked off her shoes and
fell onto the bed. Before I could show her where the bathroom and
kitchen were, or tell her to make herself at home until I got back, she
was fast asleep. I covered her, stood a moment watching her, thinking
again how like Angel she was. Then I pulled the shades to darken the
room. I left her a note with the phone number where she could reach
me.

I had thought the distraction of Jenny's appearing might make it
hard to concentrate, but I worked well that afternoon, finishing the
repair on the most serious of the three cuts at last. I bridged it on the
back of the canvas with small linen fibers, shaving the surplus away so
that the patched area was as thin and unobtrusive as possible. Now it
was time to move the canvas from the structural lab up to the vast,
warehouse-like area on the top floor of the museum where I would clean
it.

It was much more pleasant there than in the lab downstairs. It
brought to mind the perfect painting studio that Da Vinci had imagined in his writings: ". . . black and a slanting roof with openings to
let in shafts of light." And Caravaggio, who was known to have placed
his models in dark rooms, exposing them to light that was placed high
above them. The high walls of the National Gallery's paint lab were
painted blue-black, and natural light fell in through the slanted glass
roof, providing conservators an atmosphere that, on good days, cre-

ated gradations of light and dark that must have been similar to the scale known to the early painters. But London sunshine being, at best, unreliable, the lab was fully fitted with fluorescent lighting as well.

Countless jars of paints and solvents cluttered the dark wood cabinets and counter-tops; fat hoses vented the fumes to the outside. There were X-rays of paintings everywhere—on desk-tops and tables, propped against the walls. Books, art journals, and written notes dotted the work surfaces. Huge metal easels that looked like scaffolding held wall-size panels or canvases. The easels were equipped with wheels so that conservators could follow the sunlight as they worked, and with ancient hydraulic chairs that allowed them to move up and down, across, to gain access to the farthest corners of the painting. Richly stained oak easels held the smaller works. Their ornate frames propped, empty, against the blue walls seemed at first glance like pictures of the night.

With a keen sense of anticipation, I cleared the quiet corner that had been assigned to me and organized my notes and the equipment I'd need for the cleaning. I set the canvas, which I'd mounted on a work stretcher, face-up, on my table. Until today, I had worked on the back of it. Whenever I had needed to look at the picture to center myself, it was the print tacked above my work table or the one I kept in my flat that I looked at. Now there she was, the real woman, before me.

I was struck, as I always was in the presence of a Vermeer, by the smooth perfection of the surface. His paintings seemed like jewels to me, polished until they glowed. What patience it must have taken to apply layer after layer of color, each one so thin that, still wet, it must have been transparent.

That afternoon, when I looked at the woman, she seemed to be smiling. But I couldn't put my finger on what kind of smile it was. Indulgent? Had it given her pleasure to stand hours at a time, watching the painter work? Was it a patient smile, the practiced smile of a woman used to doing things for others? A secret smile, the kind that hides the real person inside?

If she was his wife, the mother of his children—as many art historians believe she must have been—how had she had time to pose for him? And why this pose? Had he watched her playing the virginal in a stolen moment, caught her look up from it to tell the children, "Wait," and wanted to capture the expression on her face forever? It is always tempting to make a story of Vermeer's life. But there is no story. Not enough facts are known to weave one. We know this woman, who appears again and again in the pictures, but we cannot be certain that she was his wife. We know he had fifteen children—most of them daughters—but we're not certain how many of them survived; we know virtually nothing about their lives. We know his serene corner: the leaded window, the checkerboard pattern of black and white marble on the floor, the gray-white wall. But the inventory of his possessions made at his death records no musical instruments. No woven rugs, no Delftware, no tapestries.

"The Sphinx of Delft," Thoré-Burger called Vermeer. He painted these perfect golden moments and vanished. Yes, sphinx-like. That described the woman's smile, too. I turned to my work, thinking that if there were a heaven, Vermeer would certainly be there; and I imagined him looking down, watching me try to puzzle all this out, with an expression on his face much like the one that he had given this woman.

One look at the painting showed me that where I'd adhered the strips of mulberry paper to the cuts on the paint surface that first week, the varnish had turned whitish. I cleaned those areas first, using cotton swabs soaked in a solution of alcohol. I stopped when I realized that the light had changed. The lab had grown shadowy. It was nearly five. I stepped back. Now, with the varnish gone and the color brought up, lightened, around them, the re-woven slashes looked like thin wounds that were healing.

Jenny was sitting on the edge of a chair, absently leafing through a *National Geographic* when Cliff and I arrived at his flat. She had showered and changed into a clean pair of jeans and a red INDIANA T-shirt. Her hair was still wet, slicked back and braided. Drying tendrils escaped and framed her face, which wore an anxious expression.

"I was really dumb," she said. "My mom would kill me. I didn't bring anything but jeans and stuff like that?"

"You're the perfect mate for me then," Cliff said. "I go to the Savoy in jeans. With a coat and tie, of course."

Jenny laughed, visibly relaxed.

"So," he said. "That bit of high trauma behind us, there's a pub down the street where we can have a bite. Then if you've the energy for it, we'll take the tube to the Tower and start off your stay in London right. I've done some work down there and gotten to know a fair number of the Yeoman Warders—the Beefeaters, those fellows in fancy red suits you've probably seen photographs of. Now and again, if I've someone very special to show around, they'll sneak me into the Ceremony of the Keys without a pass. Are you up to that tonight, do you think?"

"Oh, yes, please. That's the place I want to see more than anything. My grandma told me all the stories about it, when I was little. She's English, you know?"

Cliff smiled. "So your Aunt Evie's told me."

I smiled, too. I was touched by Jenny's pride in Peg, as if having an English grandmother made her special, set her apart. I remembered myself at that age, how I had wanted so desperately to believe I might be special in some way myself.

I began to relax about having agreed to let her stay. She was a smart girl; she'd become caught up in her experiences here and stop talking about Peg all the time. And after a few days, she'd be just Jenny to me, not only a disconcerting reminder of the sister I had lost. Cliff would help. It was a lesson to me right now, the way he was talking with her. At supper and on the tube, the two of them chatted comfortably. He spoke to Jenny as he would have spoken to any other person he'd just met, a person with interesting opinions, with a life worth knowing about. He spoke as if he assumed she'd feel the same way about him. And clearly she did, listening intently as he talked to her about his obsession with the past.

"History is no more than a story that never ends," he said. "Take the Tower. There's the story of the land itself, before men even knew about walls. The story of the need to build walls, then the story of building them. The stories of all who ever lived inside, the kings and queens and scullery maids. The poor blokes whose heads rolled. Now the history of the place and the people who come to experience a bit of the past are the story. You see what I mean? The Beefeaters, who exist solely to perpetuate the rituals and legends. You, the girl from America with a history of your own, who's come to see for yourself this place you've heard about all your life. Me bringing you here. Your Aunt Evie."

He glanced at me. "Perfect example of another idea I have—the

Tower is," he said, and I laughed as he knew I would. "History gains weight, you know. Wars and plagues. Laws and charters. Kings and queens, all with their own idea of what a country should be. Artists and inventors making it up as they go along. Then add to that people like us, the weight of ordinary lives—

"History piles up on itself until there's so much of it that a country can very nearly grind to a halt under the weight of it. Like England." He puffed out his cheeks, curved his arms out and staggered off the train like the fat lady in the circus to show what he meant. Even laughing, Jenny hung on to his every word.

It was near dusk when we came up from the tube and saw the Tower, vast and shadowy, before us. Cliff walked to the guardhouse and said something to the man inside. Within a few minutes, he returned carrying three passes, and we joined the little group waiting at the outer gate. When the Beefeater opened it, we walked across the drawbridge and through the arched main gate onto the grounds. It was eerie. When I'd visited the Tower before, it was in the daytime, along with droves of tourists. Now there were just forty or so people there to follow the Chief Warder through the nightly ritual of securing the Tower, to witness a tradition of nearly a thousand years.

We gathered at Traitors' Gate, and I saw Jenny look a long time at the cement stairs leading down to the dock where the prisoners had been brought in, saw her look up and back again, then scribble something in her notebook. I wondered if she was imagining, as I was, what it must have been like to walk up those stairs and glimpse the barred windows of the prison for the first time. The Warder stood at attention on the cobbled walkway and waited for the group to quiet. His body, the spikes and turrets along the walls made long, attenuated shadows in the unnatural light from the lamp posts.

Suddenly, the man bellowed. It was an animal-like cry, raw and piercing. It was answered by another bellowing that traveled with the wind along the walkway where we stood, echoing off the high stone walls. The Warder moved from gate to gate then, his great gold ring of keys jangling. We passed the executioner's block, which seemed more real without the daytime crowd of tourists snapping photos; the White Tower, where legend said the little princes had been buried; the Jewel House. At each gate, the terrible bellow and its answer. The beating of wings as pigeons flew up and settled again in their places on the lawn, the walls. It grew dark. Returning to the Traitors' Gate, the fortress secured, we heard the slap-slap of heels on the cobblestone, and the sentry appeared. When he spoke the password, the Warder relinquished the keys to be taken to the Resident Governor. By the yellow light of the old lamp posts, I saw that Jenny's eyes were shining.

None of us had said a word during the ceremony. Even on the tube, returning to Cliff's flat, we were subdued. But, later, when Cliff had stuffed a few days' clothes in a duffel and prepared to leave us alone, Jenny threw her arms around him and said, bumbling, blushing beet-red, "I'll never forget this. It was the best night of my whole life. Thank you."

He hugged her back, winked at me. Then he was gone.

Neither of us was sleepy. "Tea?" I asked, and Jenny nodded eagerly. She helped me in the kitchen. "Now, tell me again how you managed to have a passport?" I said. "This trip to France you mentioned earlier—"

"France? Oh, it was this special thing. You had to apply to get in. Have an interview, take a test. My French teacher said I should try. No way I ever thought I'd get accepted. Plus, it really cost a lot, and I didn't want my mom and dad to spend that kind of money. But then I got this scholarship—

"Actually, it turned out to be kind of weird. I mean, most of the time we stayed in this little village in Breton? We had to live with these families, which I didn't like all that much. I wasn't exactly homesick. I was just, I don't know, I felt sort of like I'd disappeared. Like, who *was* I? But I liked going to school, doing only French. That was neat. And speaking French all the time. I started thinking in French, even dreaming. And I really liked it when we got to go to Paris. I liked seeing all the stuff I'd read about, or seen pictures of. Seeing what it was really like. Did you ever live there, Aunt Evie?"

"No. Florence for a while, and Rome. Amsterdam. I've been to Paris many times, but I've never lived there."

"Well, I think I might like to live there. I might like to study languages. I'm pretty good at French now. I've taken Spanish. I like knowing how other people live. But even if I don't do that, I'm glad I got to be in the program. Boy, was it was weird going back to Indiana, though.

And high school."

"But you're finished with all that now."

"All of it, that's for sure," she said in an odd voice.

She didn't want to talk about it anymore, I could see that, and I guess it was to avoid an uncomfortable silence that I asked about Aunt Lily. I felt awful when she started to cry.

I'd never seen anyone cry so suddenly, so quietly. She sat there on the sofa, her mug of tea balanced on her lap, cupped with both hands. She looked so sad, tears pouring down her face, that I began to feel a tickly feeling at the back of my own throat; my eyes burned.

Aunt Lily, dead.

"I didn't go see her," Jenny said finally. "I didn't go see her one time when she was sick."

"Oh, Jenny." I went and sat beside her, took the mug, and set it on a table. She wouldn't look at me. "You didn't know," I said. "Your mother told me that no one thought Aunt Lily was going to die yet."

"I did. I mean, I knew she might. And I wouldn't have gone to see her anyway. I hadn't been to see her for a long time, and I wasn't going."

"You were scared to go. To see her so sick. Jenny, you're eighteen years old. No one expects you to be perfect. You know Aunt Lily didn't. What matters is all the times you did go see her. How much she loved you. I know she did. She used to write to me about you all the time. How pretty and smart you were. How proud you made her." Lightly, with the tip of my finger, I turned my niece's face toward me. "Jenny, I hadn't been to see her for a long time, either. When I got your mother's letter, I felt terrible about that. More than once since then, I've had to say to myself, 'Aunt Lily knew how you felt about her.'"

"That made you feel better?" Jenny's voice was small.

"No," I had to say. "Not much anyway. I still feel awful. I still can't believe I'll never see her again." I felt that tickling in my throat again, and willed it away. "I just found out yesterday, you know. I got your mother's letter—"

Yesterday. It seemed like a lifetime ago that I had slept with Cliff here, in his apartment, dreaming of Aunt Lily. Just yesterday morning, I woke, smiling, drank the coffee Cliff brought to me in bed, and set out for the museum so full of happiness that I felt as if I might have flown there on my own power.

"You know something?" I said. "I'm suddenly exhausted. You must be, too. It's been a long day." I stood and took her hands to pull her upright beside me. "We'll talk more tomorrow."

She stood very still for a moment, then hugged me fiercely, as she'd hugged Cliff earlier. "Thanks for everything you've done for me, Aunt Evie. Really, thanks a lot," she whispered, then disappeared.

I was tired, I hadn't lied about that. But I was restless. I put my nightgown on and stood at the open window in Cliff's bedroom, look-ing out on the street. The laughter of a group of young people hurry-ing toward King's Road drifted up. Cars whooshed by, even at this late hour. I'll read awhile, I thought, and rummaged around in my brief-case for some professional journals I'd been carrying around, meaning to catch up on. Just as I'd put my glasses on and piled the pillows just so behind my back, the phone rang.

"You're settled in, then?" Cliff asked when I answered it.

"Yes," I said. "Jenny's gone off to bed. I'm feeling overwhelmed, I guess. I thought I'd try to read myself to sleep. It's strange being here, you know."

"In my bed," he said. "I was getting rather used to your being there with me."

"And now, suddenly, I'm somebody's mother."

"You're not angry at me—are you, Evie? For saying I'd take charge of Jenny."

"No," I said. "I couldn't really have sent her back, could I? I am her aunt, after all—even though I hardly know her. And she must be terribly upset about something to have done what she's done; it's Aunt Lily, I suppose. Oh, Cliff, she cried as if her heart would break this evening. She's got it in her mind that because she didn't go see Aunt Lily those few weeks before she died, Aunt Lily thought she didn't love her—

"As if I could help her with that," I said.

"I don't know," Cliff said. "Maybe it's a good thing for both of you. She's a lovely girl, so curious and full of life. I look forward to taking her off exploring; she'll be excellent company, I think." He laughed. "You know, Evie, it occurs to me you might have been right about one thing all along. Why *shouldn't* we be allowed to choose a parent who suits us? You'd have had a right life with your Aunt Lily. I might be so lucky as to have a child like Jenny come to me. It would be much more fun that way, wouldn't it? Perhaps we should propose it to Parliament: give unhappy children the option to go off in search of of the perfect parent. Someone who thinks they're brilliant and charming just the way they are. No guilt, no looking back."

"She's so like my sister," I said. "Jenny is."

"Like you, too, at that age, I imagine."

"She is," I said. "Angel looked like me as a teenager."

"It could be a good thing," he said again. "We'll see. But I'm not at all sure about this interruption in *our* lives. I do miss you, Evie."

"Yes," I said. Just the sound of his voice set off the racing in my heart that I'd felt since we'd begun this new phase of our time together. I wanted to be with him. It was a feeling both exotic and somehow comfortable, like coming home. But I still had no idea what it meant, or would mean, and I wasn't really sorry for the bit of breathing space that Jenny's arrival had allowed.

When we'd hung up, there was a knock at my door.

"Aunt Evie?"

There she was again: Angel. She wore a long white nightgown. She had unbraided her hair, and it fell in waves around her shoulders. In her hand, she carried her Walkman and a cassette tape, which she held out to me. "It's Grandma," said my sister's voice. "You know, the tape I was telling you about? From school?"

I took it from her, thanked her, speaking her name. Jenny. She had no way of knowing how I felt about Peg. The tape was meant as a kind of gift, I knew. I felt I had to listen.

Chapter Twelve

*M*y family lived in the East End of London. Cockneys, they were. Working people. Very strict. When I was your age, before the war, I used to love to go dancing. But I had to go secretly. If my dad had known where I was setting off to, he'd have kept me in. No matter where I went, I was never allowed to stay out past ten. Once my partner and I won a contest, and we had the chance to go into London proper, to dance in the finals of the London ballroom dancing competition at the Savoy. My father forbade it.

I begged him to let me go. My partner was a boy I'd known since I was a little girl, my parents knew his parents well; but that made no difference to my father. For the first time in my life, I right-out defied him. My auntie helped me: Auntie Viv, his youngest sister. She was closer to my age than to my father's. She had a handsome young husband, a clever fellow well up in the union already. He spoiled her with pretty clothes. And jewelry—my father was scandalized by Auntie Viv's jewelry. She lent me a lovely dress the night of the competition, a flowered silk. And glass beads. She made up my face and dabbed me with her perfume.

I was a bundle of nerves when we set out. Even at the last minute, I thought, "I can't go against him." I adored my father in spite of his strictness. I wanted to please him more than anything. But I wanted to dance, too. I'd made up my mind about the contest, I was determined. Go for it, you'd say.

The class laughed.

It was one of the most wonderful nights of my life. I'll never forget it. The Savoy, so elegant. Just as I'd imagined it. And the band, all

128

done up in their tuxedos. Me in Auntie Viv's best. Bill, handsome in a rented suit. We came in second! Our pictures were taken for the newspaper. We won five pounds each—a fortune in those days. I was so happy I'd half-convinced myself that my father would be proud of me when he found out—right until the moment I saw him through the window, waiting up in the parlor in his dressing gown. It was midnight, mind you. Not exactly the wee hours. But the look on his face made me say goodnight to Bill very quickly and go to face whatever punishment he intended for me. It was simple enough. I would go nowhere but to work—in England, at sixteen, you were out of school and working at a job—and to church with the family until further notice. Months and months!

The war changed everything. Suddenly, no one could expect to live the way they'd lived before. The air raid sirens would start up and everyone would hurry off to the shelters. All cramped together—men and women, boys and girls—propriety went by the wayside. There were worse things to worry about than that. The people you loved might die. You might die yourself. You might very likely come up the next morning and find everything you owned blown to bits.

Were you scared?

Oh, yes. We were terribly frightened when the war began. They rolled in the big anti-aircraft guns. They piled sandbags in front of shop windows so that when the bombing started, the broken glass wouldn't go flying everywhere. There was an immediate black-out. No street lights at night, and all the windows covered with heavy dark curtains. You'd creep along the street, feeling for the edges of the pavement with your feet, tripping over the mountains of sandbags. We just didn't know what to expect. That was the worst part.

But it was a long time—from September to the spring, when France fell—before we had anything real to be frightened of. You've read about Dunkirk in your history book, maybe even seen pictures of it, but you really can't imagine what it was like to see hundreds of boats setting out to cross the channel and rescue the troops that had been stranded off the coast of Normandy. It was our fathers and brothers and boyfriends they were going after. Yachts, tugs, trawlers, merchant vessels. Some of the boats were pitifully small, just fishing dories. There were so many of them you could hardly see the river itself. People crying, waving as they watched them heading out to sea.

It was a terrible shock to us, Dunkirk. We'd been prepared for air raids and shortages, but we never believed the Germans would set foot on English soil. Now they were just the English Channel away. We began to fear an invasion. Practically overnight, the Home Guard took down street signs and railways signs, hoping to confuse the Nazis if they came. They erected vast metal hoops over any roads that might be used as airfields. They hammered rows of wooden stakes across open fields. Rumors spread that German parachutists were infiltrating the country. We were warned to be suspicious of everyone and everything.

To this day, I don't understand why the invasion never happened. There was the Battle of Britain that summer, of course. After France fell, the Germans naturally wanted to try to gain control of the air over Britain, and the Luftwaffe began its attack. You could see them fighting in the skies over London. We'd stand and cheer for our boys as if what we were watching was a cricket match. But then, for no good reason, the attacks on the RAF Fighter Command stopped. Some say Hitler couldn't bring himself to invade England, after all. His respect for the English was so great that he didn't believe he could defeat us. He did have great respect for the English, you know—or do you? It was a pure race, worthy in his eyes. He'd always hoped the English would come round to his side.

But you want to know about the bombing, I suppose. The Blitz. That began almost a year to the day after the war began. "Black Saturday," it came to be called. English people remember it the way your American grandparents remember Pearl Harbor—

I can see it as plainly as if it happened yesterday: my whole family gathered round my grandmother's table for our weekly Saturday supper. My grandad saying, "Another false alarm," when the sirens went off. Then the look on his face when he saw the planes. Like a flock of terrible black birds.

Funny, what comes to mind is the first Fourth of July holiday I spent in this country. It's mentioning the bombs, you know, that makes me think of it. It was just a year after the war was over, 1946. I'd just been in America a month. I had my first try at baseball that day. And my last, I might add.

Laughter.

I'm afraid I wasn't very good, even though my husband was determined to make an American of me. We'd gone to the Fourth of July parade that morning. We spent the rest of the day at the park. I had my first corn on the cob. And fried chicken. Imagine! Eating food with your fingers. I thought, if my mum and dad could see me right now.

Laughter.

I laugh now, but I really was terribly, terribly homesick. Nothing in America seemed at all right to me. I'd begun to fear I'd never fit, and that holiday celebration didn't make me feel any better. By sunset, I was done in. Hot and sticky and grimy after a long day in the sun. The children in the park had grown quite wild. Boys tossed firecrackers into the rubbish cans and ran off laughing as they exploded and made the picnickers start with fright. I began to feel uneasy. When I saw heat lightning flickering on the horizon, I remembered the way you could see the fires for miles those first days of the Blitz. All of London burning. I wanted to leave the park before the fireworks display, to go back to our little house that was finally starting to feel familiar to me. But Tom, my husband, had been so looking forward to his first Fourth of July back in the States. I knew he'd be disappointed if I asked him to leave.

Just calm down, I told myself as darkness fell. Don't think about it. But I couldn't help remembering. The whistle of the fireworks as they were shot up into the sky, the explosions they made took me back to the long nights of the Blitz. The bombs screaming down, incendiaries crackling. I remembered the anti-aircraft guns—the way each one had its own different sound, how together they made a kind of awful music. And smoke like acid and everything around you black and burning. Night after night, the explosions shook me to my bones and I'd wonder if they would ever stop, ever in my whole life. Then when they did stop, it was little comfort. In the terrible emptiness the quiet made, I'd listen for the sirens to start in wailing again.

Anyway, as I stood there that Fourth of July, watching the fireworks, I began to tremble. I remember clenching my jaw to keep my teeth from chattering, saying to myself, 'The war's over. You're here. In America. Safe.' But I grew so weak I couldn't continue to stand. It was when I knelt to the blanket where my baby lay, as if to check on her, that my husband turned and spoke my name.

Immediately, I was brought back, of course. But I couldn't stop crying. I felt foolish trying to explain to him why the fireworks had frightened me so and even more foolish hearing him try to explain it to the people we were with. I knew that none of them really understood, not even Tom. He'd lived through only part of what the war had been.

Although, I must say that maybe the strangest thing about the Blitz, after all, was the way people did get used to it. You'd hear the sirens. Then the whomp-whomp of the anti-aircraft batteries in the Thames Estuary. Then the bombers coming. If you got caught above ground, you could look up and see the silver barrage balloons in the sky, like Goodyear blimps—hundreds of them. They kept the bombers from strafing too low. You could see smoke in the distance from the first bombs. Then the smoke got closer and closer and you could see the planes above you, the bombs raining down.

Like I said, after the war had gone on a while, most people were quite calm about it. The shelters proved not so safe. Sometimes, if there was a direct hit, people were trapped inside and died there. So toward the end of the war, lots of us just stayed above ground and took our chances. We went about our business as best we could.

Was your house ever bombed?
Peg laughed.

Details. Your teacher likes details, does he?

Laughter and groaning.

Well, here. I'll give you some details about a bombing. My grandad kept a portrait of his father—my great-grandfather, a grumpy old crank he was—above the mantel in the parlor. "My Father's Likeness," he called it. It was his pride. My poor grandmum secretly despised it. "That man," she'd say when Grandad wasn't around. "Even death can't keep him from casting a pall."

The picture survived the bombing of their house, only that one wall stood. When we came up from the shelter, there was Great-Grandad looking out over the rubble most disapprovingly. Grandad carried the picture to my Auntie Alice's, and it survived the bombing of her house as well. By the end of the war, everyone was living in my mum and dad's house and, for want of space, "My Father's Likeness" was stored in the attic. Near the end of the war, a bomb fell through our roof, straight to the cellar, where it lay, undetonated. After the bomb squad defused it, you could stand in my mum's kitchen and look right up to the sky through the perfect circles the bomb had made falling through each story. That's where everyone was when my Uncle Bert appeared, carrying "My Father's Likeness". He was grinning like a cat, his own face stuck through the hole where the old man's face had been.

"Well then," my grandmum said, her face deadpan. "Seems Mr. Hitler's not such a bad egg after all."

Laughter.

It may seem strange to you, telling such funny stories. It's another thing people often don't understand. But people laughed a lot during the war. What else could you do? You had no control over the things that were happening all around you. My younger brother died when the bus he was riding on was bombed. My poor little sister, Rita, was tagged like a parcel and sent away to the country after that, out of danger. When I saw her again she was all grown up. I hardly knew her. My fiancé—Bill, my dance partner, was my fiancé by then—went off to North Africa. He was killed there. You just carried on. But people were kind to each other in a way I've never seen again, since the war. Everyone was in the same boat. People say, Oh, it must've been so terrible. And it was. But there was this kindness, too. And a kind of recklessness. If you were young, like I was, it was very exciting—

Remember, I was coming from that strict household. Though I loved both my parents dearly, I felt as if I'd been set free. Young people were expected to serve, and I left home as soon as I could, to join the Women's Air Force.

Did you fight?

No, no. This was well before women's liberation, you know. We were part of the support staff. We manned the switchboards, packed parachutes. That sort of thing. We worked long hours. There never seemed to be enough of us. But we were young and full of life. We always managed the strength to cycle into town for the dances they held to entertain the servicemen.

Is that how you met your husband?

Actually, I met him on a train. I'd been in London on leave. I'd been delayed, I had to run I don't know how many blocks, lugging my kit bag, to get to the station on time. I must have looked a wreck because he offered me his seat. Which was no small gesture those days. It was miserable trying to get anywhere on the trains. People jammed in the aisles, in the spaces between the cars. And, as if being packed like sardines weren't bad enough, the trains were hot in the summer, freezing cold in the winter. And the windows were painted with black paint. You couldn't even see out.

Normally, I shied away from American boys. It wasn't that I disliked them. They were a friendly lot. But wild. And the English boys on our base made us feel guilty if we went out with them. The Yanks had lots of money to spend and cigarettes and gum and candy. Our boys accused us of liking them for that.

But I let that American soldier give me his seat that day, and I was grateful to get it. And since he stood in the aisle beside me all the way to Cambridge, it seemed the least I could do was talk to him. It was near Christmas, and he was feeling awfully lonely. He told me all about the place he lived: Indiana. He made it sound like a paradise!

Laughter.

By the time we reached Cambridge, we'd struck up a friendship. It turned out that we were both going on to Newmarket; he was stationed near there, as I was. I let him buy me supper in a pub near the station while we waited to make our connection. That's how it was then. Men and women met and became friends, almost by accident, and their whole lives changed because of it. Of course, that day on the train, I never dreamed things would turn out the way they did.

One more question before the bell rings. Yes?
The day the war ended, do you remember it?

Oh, the streets full of soldiers! Just full of them. You can't imagine. All mixed up with butlers and grannies and wild little children. There were vast conga lines in Piccadilly Circus, people laughing and crying at the same time. And all the lights on at last! There I stood in the midst of it, still a girl really, tears streaming down my face—part for happiness and part for fear, thinking how I didn't have the faintest idea what my life was going to be like from that day forward.

Chapter Thirteen

I slept like a dead person. I didn't dream. When I woke up, I believed for an instant that I was in my own bed, in my apartment, in New York. Then I opened my eyes, and there were Cliff's things all around me. Jenny's headphones and her Walkman on the bedside table. I heard Peg's voice in my head, as clear as if it had been on the tape the moment before I had switched it off. "That's how it was then. Men and women met, almost by accident, and their whole lives were changed by it."

So matter-of-fact: *Their whole lives were changed by it.* And no mention whatsoever of anyone else caught in the wake of those changes. A small child, for instance. Myself. But I resolved not to let what Peg said upset me. If Jenny asked me what I thought of her grandmother's stories, I'd say, interesting. Wasn't it nice of her to come and talk to your class.

I needn't have worried, at least not that morning. After a good night's sleep, Jenny was so full of energy, so excited about Cliff's plans for her that she seemed to have completely forgotten about the tape. She asked me a dozen questions about his work, which I answered as well as I could, describing the sites I'd been to with him. When I showed her the row of detective books on the shelf in the study, the ones he'd written, she said, "He's a writer, too?" She took the book I handed her and held it as if it were made of glass. I left her in the study, absorbed in it, waiting for Cliff, who was due to come for her in an hour.

It was a pleasant walk to the museum from my little flat in Pimlico; but it was too far to walk from Chelsea, so I headed for the tube station at Sloane Square, mingling with the neighborhood yuppies, who were off for the Temple and Fleet Street, their *Timeses* stuck in the side pockets of their briefcases. As I walked the tunnel to the platform, I remembered the stories Peg used to tell us about taking shelter in the

136

tube stations during the war, despite my resolution to put her out of my mind. Some people who'd been bombed out had practically lived in them, she said. They salvaged ragged pillows and blankets from the wreckage of their homes and lined up every afternoon, waiting to be let in. Old men passed the time playing cribbage, women knitted. It was terribly crowded inside, she told us. If you wanted to use the trains, you had to step carefully around whole families sleeping head to head along the platforms. Sometimes late at night, after the trains stopped running, people even climbed down into the deep wells where the train tracks were, and slept there. I peered down into the filth and could not even imagine it.

I thought of the story Jenny had told me about Peg's brother, too. He'd died in the war, that's all she'd ever told us about him. All these years, and I hadn't known until yesterday that he had died in a bombing, that she had run across Westminster Bridge, bombs falling all around her, toward the burning bus that, moments before, had carried him away from her. She'd polished away the sharp edges of her memories just as Mrs. Murray had.

I felt like crying. Why, I don't know, when Peg's life no longer had anything to do with my own. Nothing she said or did could really affect me. But no matter what I told myself—that Aunt Lily's dying was the real reason I was in such a state, not to mention the shock of Jenny's appearance—I could not get the sound of Peg's voice out of my head. Everywhere I looked, I saw the ghost of the girl she had been in this city long ago, hurrying with her heavy kit bag to the train, where she would meet my father.

I hurried myself, to the upstairs lab, where the bottles and beakers shone in the sunlight pouring in through the glass ceiling. Where I knew Peg's voice could not follow me. I sat a long time in the silence I found there, letting my eye travel Vermeer's painting from the Cupid—the rosy, blond tempter pressing his playing card to the very edge of the picture plane—to the gray wall, to the harpsichord, to the face of the woman. Always the face of the woman. Turning from the Cupid toward some person, some vision we can never know, she seemed to say, "Be calm. Listen." I could almost hear the first resonant notes struck on the instrument before her, the beginning of some elegant complexity of sound, and I was blessedly myself again, calm as she was, capable and ready for my task.

Today I would begin to clean the surface of the canvas. Oh, cleaning, people say, if they're unfamiliar with what I do. As if cleaning is the easy part of restoring a priceless painting, comparable to cleaning their kitchens or their cars. But it is, in fact, the most delicate of tasks, the truly dangerous part of the restoration process. If it is done poorly, details of the work may be obscured, others wrongly highlighted; contours may be hardened. The delicate modeling of forms may be flattened, lost. And all these effects are irreversible.

I worked all morning on one small corner of the Vermeer, using Q-tips and cotton balls to remove the old discolored varnish. When Ian came for me at lunchtime, I was glad to take a break. My shoulders ached, my neck felt stiff. The blast of sunlight that hit me as we walked outside rendered me momentarily blind.

We walked into St. Martin's Lane, peering into the windows of bookshops along the way. We passed the Freed dance shop, where we could see little ballerinas preening in the mirrors as they waited to be fitted for pointe shoes. The pub where we often ate lunch was cool and dim. We went to our usual table in the far corner.

"So Cliff and Jenny have gone off on their first field excursion, have they?" Ian said, sipping his ale.

"St. Albans, I think. He promised her lunch at the Crypt Cafe."

He smiled. "And last night? The Tower?"

"Oh, she loved that," I said. "It *was* wonderful. Spooky. That weird call the Beefeaters make back and forth, the sound of their boots on the path. Close your eyes and it could as easily be the sixteen-hundreds as now. Which made being there with Jenny all the stranger."

Ian raised an eyebrow.

"She looks so much like my sister," I said. "I look at her and see Angel, and for one crazy moment I think, it's not too late for her to have the life she could have had. If I grab her and hold tight—

"And as if that weren't disconcerting enough, she presents me with this tape of Peg, my stepmother, talking to her history class; and I either have to tell her right then how I feel about Peg, how I've felt about Peg all my life, or I have to listen to it."

"So you listened," Ian said.

"Yes. I listened to Peg telling a whole classroom of kids the romantic story about how she met my father on a train, never dreaming he was the man she'd marry."

"Did you expect her to tell them everything, then? The whole truth?"

"It *was* a history class," I said.

"Yes, history. But what happened was more than forty years ago now; what difference does it make how she remembers it? Why is it that you're still so angry at her, Evie? You've never really said. Was she so cruel to you? Did she conspire to set your father against you?"

"No. Nothing like that. Good God, she fell all over herself, pushing my dad at me. When he wouldn't have needed pushing if his life had turned out right. If she hadn't taken him from the family he already had—

"I know, you're going to say it was his fault, too. It takes two people to have an affair."

Ian shrugged.

"You don't know her," I said.

"And she's not here now, is she? So why is it that you've decided she's to blame for Jenny appearing at your doorstep on top of everything else?"

"I never said that, Ian. I said, I don't want to talk about her. Or think about her. I don't want to hear how wonderful Jenny thinks she is. I sure as hell don't want to hear her voice."

Several heads turned at the tables surrounding us, and I realized my own voice had risen. The waitress came with our meals, and stood nervously before us.

"I'm sorry, Evie," Ian said, after she'd served us and left. "I've upset you when I know you must still be feeling terrible about your aunt."

I shook my head, pressed my fingers hard against my eyelids. Yes, I did feel terrible about Aunt Lily. But it wasn't just her death, as Ian thought. It was the diary she'd left me, all she'd said there about Peg and Dad and my mother. It was knowing that I'd be thinking about Peg right now even if Jenny hadn't appeared so unexpectedly, even if she hadn't brought me Peg's voice. But I couldn't tell Ian all that now. Where would I begin?

"Evie—" he said.

I opened my eyes, reached across and squeezed his hand reassuringly. "I'm okay," I said. "Really, I am. You're right, I still haven't quite taken in the news about Aunt Lily. When I do, maybe Jenny's surprise appearance won't seem so large."

"You *could* tell her how you feel." He smiled wryly. "Perhaps a bit more mildly than you told me. But why not tell her, Evie?"

"I could never do that," I said. "There's no point in it. I'm sorry I even tried to explain it to you. I mean, look at you. You've known me forever and it's obvious you think I'm being totally absurd."

"Not absurd," he said.

"It is absurd," I said. "Even I know that. It's just, God, I don't want to go backwards and it seems to me like that's all I've done since I've been here. I'll tell you something, being overworked in New York is beginning to sound good to me. Who cares if it's ninety degrees, noisy, filthy, and full of crazy people who'd just as soon shoot you as look at you."

He laughed.

"It's not funny," I said.

"It is, actually. You might just as well face it. And not the least amusing is the fact that your biggest problem last week is this week's saving grace."

"Cliff, you mean."

"He's in his glory with Jenny, isn't he? A willing victim."

"He's wonderful with her. Watching him with her made me think, surely, his relationship with his own children can't be as bad as he believes—"

"Oh, it's every bit as bad as he believes," Ian assured me. "Despite the way Jenny's rather exploded into your life, she's first-rate, Evie. You must see that. Believe me, Robin and Monica are nothing like her. First off, neither one of them would go tromping off to St. Albans with him on a bet. Robin demands a motor car museum or a fun park. Monica wants to go shopping."

"But maybe they're not like that all the time," I said. "Maybe they're only that way when they're with him. He feels he's failed them, you know—the divorce, all that. He's still trying to figure out how to make things right. You're exaggerating, aren't you? Come on. They can't possibly be as bad as you say."

"You'll see," he said.

"Not me. I have no intention of seeing them. Why would I?"

Ian took one of his long thin cigarettes from the pack and tapped it on the table before lighting it. All the while looking at me, as if waiting for me to admit the stupidity of what I'd just said.

I tried to change the subject. "I went over to the Wallace Collection last week and looked at the Watteaus," I said. "I'd heard they'd made a mess, cleaning them. God, they look terrible. Flat. It was good for me to see them right before starting cleaning the Vermeer—"

"Evie, you'd never make a mistake like that. That's why you're here." Ian blew three perfect smoke rings, tipped back on his chair. "Unless you believe in kismet," he said. "Karma, planets colliding." He spoke in his usual wry voice. He was probably just trying to get a rise out of me again. But I couldn't be sure.

Cliff had work to do at his office that evening, so Jenny and I went out to get a bite to eat. I took her to a place I liked in Covent Garden, an outdoor cafeteria with good Italian food and strawberry tarts made with Devon cream. I had thought it might be easier for us there than in a quiet restaurant, and I was right. Just beyond where we sat, a mime worked a growing crowd of tourists. More tourists threaded in and out of the brightly lit shops. Jenny laughed when a bird hopped onto the table next to ours and ate what had been left behind as if it had been set out for him.

"Tell about your day with Cliff," I said.

Jenny took her battered spiral notebook from her backpack and leafed through until she found the page she wanted. "Verulamium." She pronounced the Roman word clumsily. "That's the city underneath everything else. It's so weird, Aunt Evie. There's this big area? It looks maybe like a football field, except it's neater. You know, like mown. And real green. Perfect. But there's all this stuff underneath it, Cliff said. Parts of the Roman town—

"I love how history was all piled up there. All hooked together." She looked at her notebook again. "Like, did you know that Alban was England's first Christian martyr? The Romans killed him. The church— cathedral—is built over the spot where he died. They built it with bricks they took from something Roman. And part of the Magna Carta was written there, in the cathedral. That's a whole *different* time—

"At home, it's so boring. I mean, what's in Indianapolis?

"The Speedway," I said. "In a thousand years, they'll excavate the Indianapolis Motor Speedway. Maybe your grandparents' house, it's so close. But do you think they'd ever guess that the Speedway High School marching band marched from the football field to the track on race day at seven in the morning, playing 'America the Beautiful,' waking up the whole neighborhood?"

Jenny laughed. "Or the way race fans come right up in the yard and pee on Grandma's begonias? Can't you see them digging up STP baseball caps and going, 'huh?'"

"People will be getting PhD's trying to puzzle it all out. Like Cliff and his Romans."

"He's so cool," Jenny said. "He's really smart, but he doesn't act smart the way some teachers do. You know what I mean? He tells you things in a regular way, not like it's some big deal. God, Mr. Edwards— you know, the history teacher I told you about—he'd just love Cliff. He has such great ideas. Like today he told me about the Wild Card Theory of History—

"How, now and then, something nobody could've predicted is bound to happen and throw everything into chaos. Like maybe I'm the wild card in your history, Aunt Evie," she said. "That's what Cliff said."

I laughed.

"And, isn't it neat how he knows about such bizarre places?" she went on. "Like, today, we had lunch in this crypt. At first, I thought it was going to be *too* bizarre—you know, gross kind of. Eating lunch where all those dead people are. But we go in and there are all these little round tables with pink tablecloths on them, and these church ladies fussing over you. They were hilarious. They thought I was Cliff's daughter."

"Did they?" I said. "And what did he think of that?"

"He looked sad. When I asked him why, he told me his daughter was mad at him. Because of the divorce." Jenny closed her notebook and slipped it into the outside pocket of her backpack. "I told him about my friend, Cara. Her parents got divorced, and she hated her dad for a really long time. At least she said she did. But then, after a while, she got used to his being gone and things got better. Almost everybody's parents are divorced, you know. Except mine. Can we start back now?" she asked abruptly.

"Walk awhile?"

She nodded. We passed the Covent Garden tube station and wandered along side streets and through the narrow lanes behind the theatres, where crowds of people stood outside pubs drinking huge mugs of beer. We lingered in Leicester Square a while, where a girl with hair as green and crinkly as Easter basket grass was playing the flute like an angel.

"Sometimes I think I'd like to do something really crazy like that," Jenny said. "Dye my hair green. Or purple. Maybe just a big streak."

"But your hair's so pretty."

"Exactly what my mother would say. Then I'd say, 'Mom, pretty is boring.' It is boring, you know."

"Well, that's certainly true in paintings," I said. "It's tension that makes you want to look at a painting. The painting I'm working on, for instance: the woman in it isn't pretty at all. But the expression on her face makes you wonder, what does she see?

"That's what makes a painting come alive: tension. Not only in the faces, but in the way a painting is put together. The balance of shapes in space. The tonal balance in the color—" I stopped. Don't get carried away here, I told myself. You're talking to a teenage girl.

But Jenny was looking at me curiously. "You like tension?" she asked. "I mean, I always thought tension was bad. People are constantly saying to me, don't get so tense. Calm down, settle down. It drives me insane."

"That's not exactly the same thing," I said. "Although I guess most people would have to admit that a certain amount of tension in their lives makes things more interesting."

She grinned. "Like you meeting Cliff? He told me that the first time he met you he really wanted to be friends with you, but you weren't so sure."

Oh, wonderful, I thought. The two of them were wandering around St. Albans all afternoon, talking about me. "Jenny," I began.

But she'd already segued into another topic. Her mind, I decided, was a lot like a big cauldron of soup into which she dipped the spoon of her consciousness and brought up a perfectly random blending of ideas.

"Like, my mom and dad have a lot of room to talk about tension lately," she said. "They spent my whole life being the calmest people in the universe. Then last fall, they started acting like maniacs. Where are you going, who are you going with? You're late. It's five minutes after twelve! Grandma said all parents get strange when their oldest kid is a senior in high school. Like suddenly they realize you're really going to be grown up and gone, and they think of all the things they wish they would've done better, but now it's too late. She said that's how she and Grandpa felt when you were that age."

"Peg said that?" I asked. "About me?"

"Oh, yeah," Jenny said. "Plus, she wasn't your real mother, so that made her feel even worse. Anyhow," she continued. "When I told Cliff what Grandma said, he said she was probably right. And I'm the only kid. So that makes it even harder. He said, sometimes when he gets mad at his kids, he doesn't really know why. It's like he's scared for them, but he can't say that. So he yells at them about something stupid."

She seemed to be waiting for some response from me, so I said, "Is that the reason you left, then? The tension between you and your parents?"

"No." She stopped, as if to study something in the shop window we were passing. But when I looked more closely, I saw that she was furiously blinking back tears. "I just wish they didn't think things were so simple, you know? I go to college in the fall, then law school. I marry Justin when I get finished and we have our kids and live happily ever after."

"Justin?" I said. "Who's Justin?"

"My boyfriend. My ex-boyfriend, that is. He was on the football team. Probably the best quarterback my dad ever had."

"But you don't want to marry him."

"Actually, Aunt Evie, I did. I mean, I thought I did. But then we broke up, and I'll tell you something, I'm glad. I'm glad I found out what he was really like before—"

"Jenny, you're too young to be thinking about marrying *anyone*," I said. "Your parents can't have been encouraging such a thing, at your age." I felt myself flush when I remembered that Angel and Matt were already married at the age Jenny was now.

But it was as if she hadn't even heard me. She began walking again, and I followed, the two of us chatting about things we saw along the way. We passed the Switzerland House with its wonderful mechanical clock, the street vendors with their plastic Bobbies' helmets and toy double-decker buses and tacky T-shirts. We crossed Wardour Street and saw the bright neon characters above the shops and restaurants, marking London's Chinatown. Merging with the jostling crowd in Piccadilly Circus, I said, "Your Aunt Vicky thought Piccadilly Circus was a real circus, when she was little."

Jenny smiled, but it was a wistful smile. "You want to know what really drives me nuts about my parents?" she asked, as we made our way to the tube stop. "How much they love me. How, no matter what I do, no matter how mad they get at me, they always end up saying, 'But we only want you to be happy.' It makes me feel bad," she said. "I'm all they have, I know that. But I'll never be the person they want me to be."

"What kind of person is that, Jenny?" I asked. "What do you think they want for you?"

"You know, a pleasant life." She thought a moment, perplexed by her own words. "Not that I don't want a pleasant life," she said. "I mean, who wants to be unhappy?

"So, what *do* you want?" I asked.

"Oh, I only know what I *don't* want." Her voice was light, mocking.

"Which is?

"Not to be like them. I can't."

Chapter Fourteen

*B*e happy: Jenny's words took me back to the small, cramped house we lived in: long evenings with the television blaring in the living room, Dad snoring on the sofa. The Queens shrieking with laughter, Peg yakking on the telephone to one of her girlfriends, the next-door neighbors arguing.

That brought back walking home from school on cold, gloomy winter afternoons: My toes numb with cold in my cheap shoes, my bare legs freezing, my arms aching with the weight of the books I carried. Sometimes, walking, I grew so tired that I wanted more than anything to stop and lie down right there on the sidewalk. But I kept walking; I had no choice but to keep walking toward that place that was even more hateful to me than the walking itself. Home.

It was impossible to think of being happy in such a place. Couldn't Peg see that? By then, Dad saw very little from the treadmill his life had become. He worked, drank enough to make him dull and sleepy, ate when he had to, worked again. He's tired, he works so hard, Peg would say. She wouldn't wake him up. She ignored the pint bottles of whiskey when she came upon them hidden in the crevices of the couch, in the water tank of the toilet, in the toes of his shoes. When Uncle Paul called and said, "Tom, I need you," Peg wouldn't say, "Don't go."

Uncle Paul drank, too—everyone knew that. Even Aunt Lily admitted it. But it was because of what had happened to him in the war. I used to try to imagine the Uncle Paul that Aunt Lily told me about, young and full of life, but I could never make what I saw in my mind's eye match up with the Uncle Paul I knew: thin and shaky, his eyes cast downward, except when he looked toward Aunt Lily for some direction. She said my father was the only one who could bring out a glimmer of the Paul she'd fallen in love with. Which was probably why, as mad as she was at him about what she believed he had let happen to my mother, as much as she disapproved of Peg, she never tried to keep the two brothers apart. And why Peg, who knew how much it mattered to my father to be redeemed in Lily's eyes, did not interfere. In those days, it was probably the only thing the two of them agreed on.

Looking back, I see that it must have been at least partly the slow build-up of pressure he felt as we children grew up, grew into ourselves, that caused my father to shift from his role as rescuer to one who needed to be rescued himself. There were too many of us, we were so needy. There were shoes and coats to be bought; school books to be paid for; toothaches, broken collar bones, and strep throats to be attended to; sacrifices made to provide our small occasional pleasures. But all I saw then was that, finally, he'd been caught and twisted in the loop made of the unexpected happiness he'd found claiming Peg and the guilt he felt about my mother's death, which had made claiming Peg possible. It seemed to me that he'd gotten just what he deserved—and Peg, too. The very fact that she ignored what he'd become and wouldn't try to save him from himself seemed proof of it.

Be happy. The best I could imagine was calmness, beautiful things in their right places. But as Uncle Paul got worse, I couldn't find that calmness with Aunt Lily. If he was there when I went to visit, Aunt Lily was distracted, one ear always tuned to the living room, where he sat in his stained easy chair for hours at a time, drowsing, waking abruptly to rant about the way people treated him at work, about how the whole world conspired against him, and then winding down like an old Victrola until he was drowsing again. If he wasn't there, she was distracted, too, worrying that he might come home any minute, in who knew what shape. Even the beautiful things in their right places were gone. He had broken some of them; others she had put away for safe-keeping.

She worked. Day and night, you could hear the drone of the sewing machine, see the beautiful fabrics transform beneath her fingers. She loved me, I knew. But I saw that my presence in her life caused her more pain than pleasure, and I tried not to depend on her. I would go away, I told myself. I'd find my own calm place as soon as I could. I'd take Angel with me.

Now I longed for the calm place I'd made, the feel of my own beautiful things in their right places. The bland unfamiliarity of my little flat in Dolphin Square had given me an odd comfort. In it, I might have been anyone; emerging from it, anything was possible. But in Cliff's flat, the presence of his whole life pressed against me. The time we'd spent together seemed so small in the balance.

Then there was the presence of Jenny—the way the sight of her, the sound of her voice brought back Angel in a rush, what Angel might have been. Worse, this mind trick brought back my own young self, too, and at unexpected moments gave me the illusion that my real life was still before me, waiting to unfold. During that first week Jenny was with me, I dreamed myself in achingly beautiful places, exotic places. I was with Cliff in the dreams, sometimes with Angel. Surrounding us in odd, surreal juxtapositions were common household objects: plates, glasses, baskets, bowls, each one rendered in vivid color, shimmering with light. Each of these dream images was balanced, complete, and perfectly still. Each was framed in gold as resonant and surprising as the gold frame Vermeer had painted on the wall behind the woman at the virginal. The image hung like a still life in my mind's eye while I slept, suspended there, until the first crack of happiness split it, and it fell away, leaving nothing but an expanse of dull, blank mirror.

In the morning, I'd stare at my face in the real mirror, shocked by the lines I saw there, by the slack skin already beginning to pull away from the bone. I would feel the crack of the dream again, and I remembered why it was calmness I had decided upon so long ago: It was what I could afford.

Still, I was capable of being drawn into the force field made of Cliff and Jenny's pleasure. He was true to his promise; he took complete charge of her. Then, having deemed her curiosity sincere, he went one step farther and set out to show her parts of England most tourists never discover. He chose roundabout routes to drive to the official sites they visited, stopping in at obscure museums that held little-known treasures, sometimes stopping the car at the side of the road and hiking a mile or so to some Celtic tomb or crumbled medieval turret he knew of, hidden in an oat field. In the evenings, all three of us took long walks in the city, and Cliff delighted in showing us traces of Rome in the most unlikely places: a tile drain in the wall at All Hallows, a stretch of wall preserved in an underground parking lot, the Temple of

Mithras on Queen Victoria Street.

"There's so much to learn," Jenny would say. "I feel so stupid sometimes. It just kills me what I don't know."

Late one afternoon, she and Cliff arrived at the lab unexpectedly. "We're off to Avebury," Cliff said. "And we mean to take you along. No excuses, Evie. Let's go! It's a bit of a drive. We can't be dawdling."

It was nearly evening by the time we drew close. The sun had retreated, and the light but steady rain that had begun to fall made the thick hedgerows lining the country road we drove on seem waxed, not quite real. Misshapen boulders lined the narrower road that Cliff turned onto. Perfectly spaced along the whole distance of the road that led into the little village, they resembled pulled teeth, broken, rotting.

The car park was nearly empty. We got out and followed the directional signs toward the village center, nodding at the few tourists hurrying past in the opposite direction, their rain coats turned up for better protection against the weather. Rain collected and fell in big splats from the leaves of the tall old trees lining the path. We walked past the National Trust Shop, a tearoom, a low stone farmhouse until we reached a place where, when you looked out, you could see no evidence of anything man had built except for the occasional roof of a car moving along a distant road that, itself, was hidden from view.

And the alien curve of stones. These ancient gray stones were massive, magnificently shaped by the elements. The one nearest to us loomed above us, taller and wider than we were. Those farther away were no less imposing. Perfectly spaced, like the smaller boulders along the road, the stones looked like sentinels circling the green space. There was nothing else in the lush green landscape like them. You would not have had to know a thing about history to be absolutely certain that they hadn't gotten there by any force of Nature.

Cliff told us that all archaeologists really knew was that the stones—the heaviest of which is nearly forty tons—were hauled from the Marlborough Downs in the late Stone Age, and set up at least two hundred years before Stonehenge.

"Whole lifetimes have been spent puzzling the meaning of Avebury," he said. "We've been to the moon, but we haven't been able to find a single, solid clue about what men and women did here, on this little patch of land in England. We probably never will."

I shifted and saw a light go on in the farmhouse we'd passed. I heard an engine start up. I noticed that, standing in the tall grass, my feet had gotten soaking wet.

"Move away from the stone a moment, will you, Evie?" Cliff stepped back, aimed, and focused Jenny's camera on her. "There." The shutter clicked, and clicked again. "There's another one for good measure."

The sky was slate gray, heavy with rain. It seemed to press against the earth, against the stones that had been carried here in a time so long ago we could not even imagine it. Jenny's yellow anorak, her white Reeboks looked inordinately bright. Her face, turned toward us, open, waiting, looked so young.

"You'll take this photo out when you're berating yourself sometime, Jenny. For not knowing something you feel you ought to have known." Cliff smiled that smile of his and paused a long moment, concocting one of his educational effects. I thought of Silchester—the way, at harvest time, the streets and walls of the ruined city struggled up through layers of time, presenting themselves to the sky. I waited, as I had done on that day, for the lesson he would teach.

"You'll remember this place then, won't you?" he said to Jenny now. "And remember that, really, none of us knows very much at all."

Jenny never seemed to tire. We'd get back to the flat after a full day, and she'd say, "Tea, Aunt Evie?"

"Oh, sure," I'd say.

She'd fix it, and we'd sit up talking till all hours like two girls at a slumber party. Unwittingly, she told me the story of my own life, a version obviously concocted from listening to Peg, Aunt Lily, and Angel. What they remembered from my childhood had been tempered by time. What they knew of the person I'd become was limited by the narrowness of their own lives and by my reluctance to be with them. In the ingenuous manner of the very young, Jenny told me that I'd been considered an odd, intense child. That I was admired now for what my family perceived as glamorous, if obscure work. For my adventures in the wide world. For my intelligence. I was pitied because no husband or child loved me.

Jenny herself loved the idea of what my life had been, and she was full of questions about it. What had it been like in Florence, during the flood? she wanted to know. Were the houses in Amsterdam as pretty as they looked in pictures, did the houseboats along the canals really have windowboxes full of flowers? Was all Delft blue and white, like the pretty pottery I'd sent her mom?

I showed her a print of Vermeer's townscape, and told her about the time I had gone to Delft in search of the very spot it had been painted from. As I spoke, I could see my young self leaning just-so to frame the leaning tower of the Oude Kerk in my hotel window. It was so close. It seemed to me that I could almost reach out and touch the black-faced clock with its gold numerals, the red lions, the gilded town crest. Four turrets, sturdy as soldiers, lifted the gothic spire toward the sky. It was early morning. The church bell tolled six times as I entered the street and began to walk through the town.

It had been raining for days, and the patches of blue sky seemed brilliant, surprising as they pressed away the clouds. The wet tree trunks were black, the wet brick pavement looked smudgy, as if it had been rouged. Ahead of me, the arched bridges and their reflections in the still water of the Oude Delft Canal made circles as lovely and elusive as a string of painted pearls.

I passed the Prinsenhof Museum, the white house with the plaque informing passersby that the painter Pieter de Hoogh once lived here, once an orphanage with two stone children above its door. The leaves on the ancient trees that lined the canal were as big as hands, here and there translucent in the light that poured through the narrow brick passageways.

It was then that I had the odd sensation that one of Vermeer's daughters was with me, that I had tumbled backwards with her to this same street, on an early morning more than three hundred years ago.

"I've never told this to a soul," I told Jenny. "It was so strange, I thought no one would believe it. Or they'd think I was crazy. I didn't see her like you'd see a ghost. It wasn't like that. I sensed her, then I saw her in my mind's eye. This girl—" I showed Jenny a print of the painting that hangs in the Met: a homely girl, small thin-lipped, with wide-set eyes.

Talking to her, the magic of the morning came back to me. The girl had seemed as real to me as anyone I'd ever known. I knew she'd awakened, thrown her clothes on, and followed her father into the day. She kept a distance from him, but still she saw what he saw—the pattern a certain group of houses made, unremittingly vertical, except for the elegant curve of their lace curtains; the points of light that gathered on the ripples a gull made skimming the surface of the canal. She squinted straight into the sun to make the gables and roofs and towers that rose into the sky go fuzzy at the edges, to dissolve all detail so that whatever she was looking at became simply the essence of itself.

I could almost see Vermeer striding ahead of her, through light and shadow, to the place where the Oude Delft Canal emptied into the small harbor at Kapelsbrug. Stopping there, his mind's eye already refining the geometry of the landscape, his fingers aching for the brush. I could see him turning by chance, smiling, at the sight of his daughter.

I had stood that morning on what was the yellow quay in the painting, a roadway now. Vermeer's villagers were gone, replaced by commuters hurrying to work in cars, on bicycles. The town wall, the turreted Scheidam gate had disappeared. The beautiful blue boat was gone. But the teal water rippled in the light breeze and made the houses reflected in it hazy, dream-like. Red roofs glowed. The spire of the Nieuwe Kerk still rose in the distance, bathed in light.

It was possible that Vermeer had stood here with one of his daughters, I'd thought. Possible, too, that something in the way she looked at the scene before them had made him decide to teach her to paint. Why not? The women painters history had recorded were more often than not daughters or sisters or wives of artists. And there was no evidence of Vermeer ever having taken on apprentices. Someone must have helped him make brushes, mix pigments, prepare canvases. Why not a beloved daughter?

Then and now, this thought moved me nearly to tears.

Turning from Kapelsbrug that morning to walk the streets Vermeer and his daughter might have walked together, I felt as if I were floating in time. First, Acterom, a narrow passage, cool and dark, where the canal was murky, with lily pads crowded along its slick mossy walls. Then beyond, to where it turned and was struck by sunlight, so that the tangled strands of grasses floating just below the surface looked unnaturally green. Achterom became Turfmarkt, then widened into Brabantse, where the shopkeepers were beginning to stir. A slice of Great Markt Square came into view, but Vermeer and his daughter would have turned before entering it. North, toward home and family: the room with the lovely mullioned window.

"Wouldn't it be wonderful if it were true—" Jenny said, her eyes shining, "her father teaching her. It could be."

"Yes," I said. "It could."

We talked about Cliff then, how much Jenny was learning from him, the strange and wonderful way he saw the world. Being with him was like living in one of those optical illusion pages in the game books that she'd loved as a child, she said. Like "Find the Elephants in the Trees." At first glance, the picture seems perfectly normal: a house, a swing set, trees and flowers. Then, suddenly, the outline of the first elephant appears in a configuration of leaves. Then another in the pattern of bark on a tree-trunk. Then another, and another. And once you've seen them, you can't un-see them. What you thought was a tidy little world has been completely transformed.

I laughed at her analogy, but it was true that, since I'd known Cliff, the world had changed for me in just that way. No matter how many times I told myself that this relationship was temporary, that I would go back to New York when my work on the Vermeer was finished and resume my life, no matter how many times I looked at myself in the mirror and saw the limitations of that life in my own face, the world continued to open up when I was with him, continued to surprise me. I still could not imagine how my real life might change to accommodate him. But late at night in Cliff's flat, talking to Angel's daughter, I knew I was no longer the person I had been.

Chapter Fifteen

Six months ago, in New York, I'd never have agreed to spend a Saturday on what smacked of a family outing. But that first Saturday of Jenny's visit, Cliff collected us early and we set out—Cliff and I in the front seat of the Rover, Jenny in the back. As we drove, she pored over the worn map of England that Cliff kept in the glove compartment. Now and then, she leaned over the seat to show us something she'd discovered.

We were headed for Newmarket, the town where Peg and my father used to meet during the war. Yesterday, the end of the work week, Cliff had said to Jenny, "Tomorrow, you choose." And that's what she had chosen.

"Is it all right, Evie?" Cliff asked in a private moment.

It wasn't, quite, but I didn't say so. By then I'd grown fond enough of Jenny to go along with almost any plan.

I wouldn't have remembered the name of the town where Peg and Dad had courted, it was just one of any number of things about them that I'd put out of my mind years ago. But that morning, as Jenny talked about the place, I began to remember things that Peg had told us. The little train that ran between Cambridge and Newmarket, trees growing so close to the track in places that the train brushed against them; the flat farmland sectioned by hedges. Just outside the town, we came upon the emerald heath dotted with stables and paddocks, just as she'd described it. War or no war, she said, the sleek racehorses were exercised every single day.

"Imagine this spot in wartime," Cliff said. "The deafening roar of planes in and out at all hours. All night, search lights like long cold fingers raking the sky."

He pulled off the road at a gap in the thick hedgerow, and we tramped onto the heath, where a crumbling cement block sat amidst the swaying grasses. "It's a machine gun emplacement," he said. "Pill-boxes, they called them. For shooting down parachutists, or low-flying planes. You'll find them all over England, actually. And old airstrips, too, moldering back into the earth for archaeologists like me to discover chunks of two or three hundred years from now."

I turned and started back to the car, cold suddenly, as if someone had walked across my grave. The poppies that grew along the roadside reminded me of blood. I thought of the story Peg told about a lone German plane that appeared out of the clouds one winter afternoon and strafed Newmarket's long main thoroughfare, killing dozens of people in seconds, leaving splintered wood and shattered glass along the whole length of the town. It might very easily have first appeared just above where I stood now, waiting for Jenny and Cliff. I looked up at the gray, rain-heavy clouds, half-expecting to see a glint of silver.

The odd feeling stayed with me as we parked the car and walked along High Street toward the Golden Lion Pub. Beside me, Jenny chattered, telling Cliff about how Peg kept running into that GI she'd met on the train, every time she cycled into Newmarket. Eventually, they'd become friends. "Isn't it weird?" she marveled, handing him her camera. "If they hadn't, I'd never have been born. And here I am now."

She stood beneath the growling yellow lion on the pub sign and smiled when Cliff took her picture. "Now Aunt Evie, too." She gestured toward me and I joined her, posed.

Inside, the gloom of the day was repeated in the cool dampness of the place. The thick curved panes of bottle glass in the bow windows allowed a minimum of light. The framed pastels of horse-racing scenes on the salmon-colored walls were predictable enough, but the furnishings seemed quite surreal: pale green leather banquettes, bamboo tables with Tiffany lamps hung above them, bamboo stools. Mirrored pillars stood between the bar and the eating area.

"You're quiet, Evie," Cliff said.

I agreed, but I didn't elaborate. How could I explain that from the moment I'd stood on the heath, imagining the fighter plane emerging from the clouds, I'd felt surrounded by ghosts? It was just midmorning, the pub was deserted; but I could almost hear the big band music spilling out of the dance hall in the back, smell the cigarette smoke, hear the laughter of the soldiers and their girls. I was thinking about Aunt Lily's diary, too. All during the war, Aunt Lily had cared for me. It wasn't her fault she'd come to love me too much. My own mother was who-knows-where; she didn't want me. My father was here in this very place with Peg.

The wavy glass rendered the world outside hazy, impressionistic. The old brick Rutland Arms across the street probably looked the same now as it had looked more than forty years ago to the soldiers who had sat here, gazing out, dreaming of home.

Or not dreaming of home at all.

Cliff went to the bar to get our coffees, and came back with the barmaid in tow, a matronly woman in her late fifties, who was delighted by Jenny's story about her grandparents, eager to tell us all she remembered about the pub in wartime.

"They'd bring the GIs in on liberty trucks. Ooh, crammed full, they were. The boys would fall out in a pile and there we kids would be. 'Got any gum, chum?' we'd say. And they'd laugh at us and give us gum—and sweets, if they had them. I had a very pretty older sister, Miriam, and if she was with me, they'd whistle and cat-call and give me more than my share to try to get into her good graces. Oh, they were handsome!

"Miriam used to crank up our dad's old Victrola and make me practice dancing with her evenings, before she came up here with her girlfriends." She laughed, took a funny little dance step and sang in a flat voice, "'Horsey, horsey don't you stop, just let your feet go clippety-clop.' 'The Palais Glide,'" she said. "Ask your granny if she remembers it."

I glanced at Jenny, who was scribbling madly in her notebook. Ask your granny if she remembers how she justified her affair with my father, too, I wanted to say to her. Ask Peg if she ever thought about me.

I couldn't stay. If I did, I'd say something I'd regret. I excused myself and went to the ladies' room. "What are you doing here?" I whispered to my reflection in the mirror. I'd come to England to work, for God's sake. How had I let myself get so far off track? The longer I looked at myself, the more disoriented I became.

When I came out, It was clear that Cliff and Jenny hadn't missed me. The barmaid had sat down at the table, and the three of them were laughing uproariously. They didn't even look up when I walked past them and out the front door.

It had begun to drizzle. I pulled the collar of my raincoat up high, walked quickly, with my head down, dodging young mothers pushing prams, housewives with plastic carrier bags brimming with the fresh vegetables they'd bought at market. I passed through the business district of the town, passed brick houses with lush gardens blooming in their tiny yards. The wet roses looked like velvet. I passed a cemetery surrounded by a low stone wall, then paddocks that smelled of weathered wood and horse manure and leather.

The town ended abruptly. The heath rolled out, even greener in the rain. A sign read, "Cambridge 12." My world, I thought. I longed to lose myself for the rest of the day in the Fitzwilliam. Or in a bookshop. But the distance between where I stood and what could save me seemed as great to me at that moment, as impossible to breach, as it had seemed all through my childhood.

I thought of Joris, the impossibility of what we had felt for each other—the catch-22 of it that never ceased to cause a twisting inside me. Sometimes I believed I had loved Joris most of all because he had said no to me. Because he had done what my own father had not had the courage to do with Peg.

I turned into the cemetery. Partly because I thought that the huge trees would shelter me from the rain that had begun to come down hard. Partly because the way I felt made the cemetery seem inviting. I walked the path that had been worn along the inside of the wall. Beyond the wall, I saw horses grazing. On my side of it, a brown rabbit hopped in the tall unkempt grass. Shining dark ivy grew up the trees and wound around the occasional weathered benches. It covered whole sections of the stone wall and whole grave stones. It seemed to be erupting from the lidded tombs.

To keep myself from thinking, I read names and tried to imagine who the people had been. Beatrice Gibson, Colin Butcher, Annie Moody. "In fond memory of Mrs. Elizabeth Pudney from friends at the Black Horse Hotel." John Hindle, John Hawtry Capes.

I thought I had calmed down considerably until I looked up and saw Cliff. Years of working outdoors had rendered him oblivious to the weather, and he strode toward me, with no more than his heavy Irish sweater to protect him from the rain. His hair was wet and curling. The overwhelming desire I felt at the sight of him made me turn away.

His hand on my shoulder made me shudder.

"So you dragged yourself away from Jenny and that waitress?" I said.

He turned me toward him, and the look on his face showed me that he was as shocked as I was by what I'd said. But it didn't stop me.

"Don't ever try to talk me into any more of these family expeditions, Cliff," I said. "Jenny doesn't know the half of what went on between Peg and my father and all the pain it caused. What they did was wrong, you know. Wrong. Where is she, anyway?" I asked. "Jenny."

"She was going to buy postcards for—" He paused. "To send to her family. Then she wanted to see the Horse Racing Museum. We'd meet up in an hour, we decided. Evie, she's just a girl. She's got these romantic notions about your parents, that's all."

"It's a lie, what she believes," I said. "You know it."

"It was years ago. She loves them. What's the harm? But if it means so much to you, maybe you should tell her the way you see it."

Oh," I said. "Not tell her the truth. Tell her the way I see it. So you think I'm lying?"

"Evie, don't be absurd. Nobody's lying. Surely you can see that at least some of what happened is a matter of point-of-view."

"It was wrong what they did," I said. "That's not point-of-view. That's fact. I just wish for once someone would admit it. And I'll tell you something else. I've had it up to my ears with these people, and the last thing I need is you taking their side. If I'd known you were going to take everything I've told you about my family and twist it around—"

"Evie," he said.

"Evie what?"

"I'm not taking anybody's side. There *is* no side, that's what I'm trying to say to you. You know as well as I do that no two people see the world in the same way, so why can't you accept what that means in the case of your parents? They lived their lives. They had the courage to do that."

"Meaning?" I asked.

"Just that they loved one another enough to take a chance, to try to make a go of it together. So they made a mess of things. Who doesn't? That's what life is, you know," he said bitterly. "A bloody mess. Or maybe you don't know, Evie. Maybe you never will trump up the courage to jump in and make a mess of it yourself. Maybe that's the real problem between us."

I felt myself go as cold as the granite angels surrounding me. I felt like lying down, stretching out along the length of someone's grave. I said in the coldest voice I could muster, "I never wanted to start up this—this *relationship*, or whatever the hell it is we have—in the first place, you know. Now I wonder why I've let it go as far as it's gone. I don't need this, Cliff—you interfering in my life, acting as if it's one of your made-up mysteries, some puzzle to be solved. And as for dragging Jenny all over England, if I'd wanted to go around playing Happy Families, I'd have had one of my own."

Cliff looked stricken, completely confused. I was crying. By then, even I didn't know what in the world I was talking about. The truth was, until this morning, I'd loved the time the three of us had spent together."

"Oh, just forget it," I said. "Forget everything. This whole day is stupid."

I started to walk away, figuring he'd follow. I'd collect myself and we'd go find Jenny.

I'd just get through whatever else the two of them were bound and determined to do. If they cooked up any more Peg-and-Dad trips, I would politely refuse.

"Evie, wait. Please," he said, catching up with me.

I kept walking.

"I do this, you know. I get obsessed. Here you are, thrown for a loop, what with your Aunt Lily's death and Jenny appearing all in a week's time, and I'm dragging you on some field excursion you don't want to go on. Evie, will you stop? "

I stopped. "You're not responsible for me, Cliff. I could have said no."

"I didn't say I was responsible for you, Evie. I said I haven't been paying attention to what you need. I know I've gone off half-cocked since Jenny's been here. Ah, Christ," he said, "I feel so bad about my own kids: the bloody divorce and all that's happened because of it. It's as if, with Jenny, I can somehow make up for it. It's foolish, I know. It's not right. But Evie, being with Jenny is just the way I always hoped it would be with Robin and Monica."

I let him pull me against him. His sweater was damp and scratchy against my face. My eyelids, my limbs felt heavy as I leaned into him. I could have slept standing there, I was sure of it. He fingered my hair, combing it lightly with his fingers, letting it fall back against my neck.

"I haven't even asked you about your Aunt Lily," he said. "Tell me about her, Evie. Tell me how you feel."

"Like my heart has cracked," I said. "That's all. I think of the way her life turned out, so sad and small. I think of how much it would have meant to her if I'd gone home one last time, if I'd seen her. I think, Angel should have told me. But I know it wasn't Angel's fault. If I'd stayed in touch with Aunt Lily the way I should have—"

I cried for her then, as I had needed to cry since I'd learned the news, my tears soaking into Cliff's sweater. I don't know how much time passed before I spoke again, before I pulled away from him and we began to walk slowly toward the town.

"It doesn't seem real, Aunt Lily being gone," I said. "I mean, the idea of her death makes me sad. And that diary she left me, all those things she'd kept from me. What am I supposed to make of that? But, I feel—I don't know, like it's ridiculous to be so out of balance. I hardly saw my Aunt Lily in the last ten or fifteen years, I rarely even talked to her—

"But that doesn't erase the fact of her death."

"No, no. I know that. In fact, it only makes me feel worse. I can't quit thinking about that postcard I sent her from Housesteads getting there too late. Other things, little things, remind me that she's gone, and suddenly I feel like I'm four years old again, taken away from her. I guess there'll come a time when I finally understand what losing her means. Both times."

"Perhaps." Cliff looked thoughtful. "But then perhaps we aren't meant to fully understand. My Robin said the most amazing thing after Metta's mum died. He was just three at the time. Old enough to have been terribly attached to his granny, but too little to understand what her dying meant. I sat him down and said, 'Robin, a very sad thing has happened. Granny was very, very ill. So ill that her poor body quit working, and she died. We shall never see her again, but we shall always remember how much we loved her and how much she loved us.'

He cried as if his little heart would break. It was good for him to grieve, I thought. Get it out of his system.

"Not six months later, Metta and I decided to take a trip down to Cornwall to visit her father. The children had been there many times and loved to go. When we told them of our plans, Robin, especially, was pleased. 'We're going to see our grandad!' I heard him boasting to his playmates. 'Our granny, too.'

"I was beside myself. He hadn't understood at all what I'd told him. So I sat him down and explained it all over again. Evie, he looked at me with the most bereft expression on his little face, and said, 'Oh, Daddy, *again?*'

"Isn't that what death is, after all?" Cliff said. "That *again?* Sometimes, when I was a boy, I'd stop short in the middle of whatever I was doing as if I'd been hit on the head with a hammer, and I'd think, I still don't have a father. He's still dead in France. He will never come and fetch me. Every time, the grief felt absolutely new. I still feel it sometimes. And I never even knew him."

"I'd take grief," I said. "What I hate is this awful confusion. I turn Aunt Lily's diary over and over in my mind, trying to figure out what it means. Wondering what more she'd have written if she'd had the time. What else is there that I don't know?"

"Couldn't you talk to your father about that time?" Cliff said. "Wouldn't he tell you what he remembers?"

"I'd never ask my father," I said.

"Why?" Cliff asked. "Evie, why do you hate him so much?"

"I don't hate him, I just never wanted to be with him—not after he married Peg. Why couldn't they have just let me stay with my Aunt Lily, where I belonged?"

"Because they loved you? Because they wanted you with them? Parents are like that."

I heard in his voice the sorrow he felt for his own children. I kept quiet, though. I knew if I spoke, I'd say what I'd said all my life: "Peg isn't my real mother."

What would be the point?

So in silence, bent against the rain, we walked along the High Street of the little English town, where Peg and my father had walked together years ago and, in spite of themselves, fallen in love.

Chapter Sixteen

*L*ater that evening, when Jenny asked if she could please, please, please call Peg and tell her about Newmarket, how could I say no? I could hear her from where we sat in the dining room, finishing our meal. She was talking fast, as she always did when she was excited.

"Grandma? Guess who? It's me, yeah. Jenny! You won't believe where I went today with Aunt Evie!"

She talked for a long time, pausing only if Peg asked her a question. "It *is* still there," she said. "I took pictures for you. Yes. The dance hall in back. We met this lady who told us all about how it was then. Yes, I'm taking tons of pictures. Okay, I promise—

"Aunt Evie," she sang out, "Grandma wants to talk to you." She held the receiver toward me, beaming.

I glanced at Cliff, who raised a sympathetic eyebrow.

"Evie," said the voice on the other end of the line. "Jenny's having such a lovely time with you. It's so good of you to have taken her in the way you have." Was it the overseas connection, that slight time delay, that made Peg's voice sound so unfamiliar? So American.

"Imagine, the two of you in the Golden Lion Pub! It means a lot to me, Jenny's interest in all this. She's talked my ear off, and your dad's, too. Not that either one of us would've encouraged her to jump on a plane the way she did and—

"Oh, there I go, blathering on," she said, more like the Peg I remembered.

"She's a wonderful girl," I said. "So much like Angel was."

"She is," Peg said. "But I see a lot of you in her, too. I've always told her that. She's always been so good in school, you know. And so— determined."

Willful, I thought. You mean I was willful.

"But, Evie, what I really wanted to say was how sorry I am about

Lily. I know you must be heartbroken. I've written, of course. But now that Jenny's phoned, I can tell you myself how much I've thought of you these past days. You were so close, Lily was so good to you. You do understand, though, don't you? About the letter? Angel was frantic trying to find you when Lily took a turn for the worse. None of us realized—"

"I understand," I said. "It's all right. I should have thought to let someone know where I'd be."

"Oh, honey," Peg's voice broke. "Who'd have thought? But Lily went peacefully, bless her heart. I'm sure Angel told you that. And you do know how much she loved you."

There was an awkward silence, which I broke, asking about my father.

"Fine, he's just fine," Peg said. "He's run out to the grocery. He'll be sick when he gets back and finds he's missed talking to you—

"Oh, I just can't *believe* you're there, "she went on. "London. Dad and I always thought we'd go back someday—"

She went on in the cheerful voice that used to drive me absolutely mad. "Oh, but Jenny said she's been taking lots of pictures for me. And she said you'd to try to go see my sister if there's time. Wouldn't that be something, after all these years? My goodness. Rita."

When I hung up, I thought, over my dead body am I going to visit Peg's relatives. But even as I thought it, I knew I'd go. I'd been so careful not to say anything about Peg that might upset Jenny; now, if I refused to go see Peg's sister, I'd have to tell her why.

"I wish Grandma could come here," Jenny was saying to Cliff, when I returned to the dining room. "It isn't fair, you know? How she never got to come back? She told me that at first she used to get so homesick for England she thought she'd die. People in America weren't all that nice to her, either."

Who? I thought. Me? Aunt Lily? Maybe if Peg had told Jenny the truth about my mother, Jenny would have understood perfectly well why she hadn't been met with open arms.

"Well, not really mean," Jenny continued. "It's just that they thought she was strange. Her accent, mainly. They'd ask her to say things just so they could hear how different she said them. They didn't do it to hurt her feelings. Actually, Grandma said most people thought it sounded neat the way she talked. But they made her feel like a pet, or something. Like she was doing tricks for them. She wasn't a shy person before, she said. But after she came to America, she was. And she felt dumb a lot of the time, too. Like nothing she did was right.

"People don't always understand—" Cliff began.

"They don't understand *anything*," Jenny interrupted. "I hate people sometimes. The way they act like everybody has to be just like them. The way they don't want to know anything that matters—"

She stopped short, near tears, then she made a face, as if to make fun of herself. "When I was little and I'd get all bent out of shape about something? My mom and I worked out this thing where she'd give me a signal and I'd just go to my room until I calmed down. Boy, she'd be giving it to me right now." She stood up. "I'm really tired," she said. "Is it all right if I just go on to bed?" She didn't wait for an answer, but bent over and kissed my cheek, then Cliff's, and thanked us again for the day.

"You don't have to go visit Peg's sister," Cliff said when he heard her turn the shower on. "I'll take her."

"I'll go, I'll go." I got up and went into the living room. I stared at the wall of Cliff's tapes, alphabetized, labeled in his meticulous hand. I chose Mozart, a piano concerto. Relaxing. "It's just another week, right? She'll be gone, back to Indiana, and I can get to work seriously again. Maybe even concentrate."

The expression on Cliff's face when I turned to face him, that half-smile, made me say, "Okay, I admit it. I adore her. There's no way I'm going to hurt her feelings if I can possibly avoid it."

He laughed then, but it didn't make me angry. "God, just don't tell Ian," I said, going to stand beside him at the big bowed window that looked down on the street, slipping my arm through his. "He'll never let me live it down."

"Promise," he said.

Outside, it was still light. It had stopped raining, and the sky was dove gray, luminous. A silvery light shone on the people who had begun to emerge into the streets. It glinted off parked cars, bled into the Victorian buildings, turning the red brick pink.

Still restless, I wanted to go out into the evening. Cliff listened at Jenny's door and pronounced her fast asleep. He could tell, he said. If you had children, the first thing you learned was how to tell when they were sleeping.

We disengaged the telephone, left a note, and crept out, closing the front door soundlessly behind us. We walked off quickly, like thieves, away from the lights of Kings Road, toward the river. Though neither of us spoke, we both knew exactly where we were going.

Cars sped past on Grosvenor Road, their headlights like cats' eyes in the last light. Lamps went on in the riverside flats one by one, revealing living rooms with sofas and televisions, dining tables groaning with food and wine, bright cheery kitchens. There were silhouettes of bicycles and prams chained to the wrought iron railings of balconies and gardens; silhouettes of flowers, nodding, heavy with moisture— and the smell of them. There was a damp smell, too, coming off the river. And the sound of barges whispering past, tatters of music from the occasional pleasure boat, the mournful hooting of fog horns in the distance, all floating up from the silver mist that was all we could see of the Thames. In time, the lights of Dolphin Square came into view. The dark windows of my little flat.

Cliff opened the door. There were his books and papers spread out on the table where my books and papers had been spread out a week before. His jeans, his shirts hung in my closet. All these things I saw just the shadows of, because it had grown dark and we had not turned on the lamp. Cliff bent to remove the sofa cushions, flipped out the hide-a-bed, then twisted easily out of his heavy sweater. The white T-shirt he wore underneath it gleamed.

When he turned to me with a slow smile, he was like a boy. Like James Dean just off his Harley, the kind of boy you used to look at with longing and some measure of dread, and who made you feel reckless, as if, given the chance, you might do anything at all with him. I had never in my life felt the hunger I felt now; I knew that if I took that first small step toward it, toward Cliff, I'd be lost. And I took that step. The parked car, the motel at the outskirts of town: I understood this now. Lost was what I hungered for.

Afterwards, lying drowsily in Cliff's arms, I tried to explain to myself what had happened between us that night. Was it the idea of Jenny, abandoned, with no knowledge of where we were? In fact, no one knew where we were. There was something reckless about that, something younger than I had ever been. And daring. Or was it the presence of the stuffy academics in the flats surrounding us: historians, linguists, students of literature bent over their books at midnight while we were making love?

Or the night itself, that luminous silver? But I could not explain it, and the thing that surprised me was that I didn't care.

"Something's wrong with Jenny," Cliff said, his first words since we'd left his flat. "You saw it, didn't you? Tonight she was near tears."

"She was all wound up, thinking about Peg and my father. She gets so—involved. Things are so real to her."

"It's more than that, Evie. Yesterday, driving back from Reading, she started to cry. At first, I thought it was about your Aunt Lily dying. She's awfully sad about that, I know—"

"She didn't go see Aunt Lily when she was sick, she told me. She feels guilty."

"Ah," said Cliff. "Well, that's something. But I think there's more. I've sensed her about to tell me something several times, but then she stops. And this evening. That wasn't about your Aunt Lily."

I shifted position, suddenly uncomfortable with Cliff's arm wound so tightly around me. "Is this what married people do? Make love, then lie in bed and talk about their children?"

"Actually, yes." Cliff laughed and pulled me back against him. "Awful, isn't it? Let's don't be anything like them."

Late the next morning, I woke in Cliff's bed, alone and disoriented, piecing together bits of the night before as if piecing together bits of a dream. As the world began to focus, I heard voices, and got up and followed them to the kitchen: Cliff and Jenny. The two of them were deep in conversation, a dozen or so scribbled index cards scattered before them on the table.

"Aunt Evie!" Jenny said when she looked up. "Guess what? We're making a mystery."

"A priceless cache of Roman jewelry found beneath the bombed-out ruins of houses near the Barbican disappears," Cliff said in a stage announcer's voice. "The president of the petroleum company sponsoring the dig accuses the workers of a conspiracy, and feels no obligation to continue the promised six month's funding. But the workers suspect the president himself, whose frequent visits and endless questions had heretofore seemed only annoying, but now seem extremely suspicious to them—"

"Even Giles Bardon is stumped," Jenny said.

"Until—" Cliff grinned.

"An American woman shows up at the site—"

"Not exactly American," Cliff said.

"Right. American now. But she's English, really. She married an American soldier and is coming back now, for the first time, to see the neighborhood she grew up in."

"She's brought flowers," Cliff said. "Roses, we think. She means to leave them as close to the doorstep of her old home as she can."

"Which just happens to be exactly where the dig is," I said.

"Good, Aunt Evie!" Jenny said. "But the important thing is: see, she's wearing this necklace. Well, a chain, really. With this thingamabob on it that turns out to be exactly like one of the Roman things that was stolen. You know, an earring, maybe. A piece of a set—"

"And?" I asked.

Jenny looked to Cliff, who shrugged and laughed. "We haven't the faintest idea," he said. "Except that time is of the essence, since at any moment the bulldozers may move in to ready the site for the skyscraper that's to be built there, and bury the evidence. And, of course, we know the necklace she's wearing is the clue to everything—"

"But then, that's the fun of it. Puzzling over everything that seems to matter, everything that floats up until, suddenly, you see it all adds up to one thing. The story, you know? At some point, there it is—inevitable."

"Life should be so simple," I said.

But neither seemed to hear me. They were back at it, head-to-head, jotting notes on index cards and adding them to the growing pile. I drifted through the apartment, tidying the study, making the bed in Robin's room, where Cliff had slept. I made a cup of tea and crawled back into Cliff's bed with it, propping myself up with pillows. Rain pelted against the windows, making a comforting sound, and my thoughts turned to my own mystery: the lady at the virginal, the painter who had made her.

There was no solution to this mystery, I knew. There was no detective in the world who could add up what was known about Vermeer and make a complete picture of his life. Town records show that he was born in 1632, baptized in the Nieuwe Kerk in Delft. His father was Reynier Janszoon, an innkeeper and dealer in fine arts, who had been trained in the trade of silk weaving as a young man. His mother was Digna Balthens. He had one sister, Gertruy, twelve years older. It is not known when or how the young Vermeer's artistic talent was recognized, nor is it known with whom he studied; but the fact that he was accepted into the St. Luke's Guild in 1654 implies that he served a traditional apprenticeship with a master, for this was a requirement of membership. His master might have been the Delft painter, Evert Van Aelst, known to have owed Vermeer's father money in 1639, when Vermeer was nine. Or, maybe it was Carel Fabritius, one of Rembrandt's last students, whose name was linked with Vermeer's in a poem written on the occasion of Fabritius's untimely death. Or Leonard Bramer, a highly commissioned artist of the time, who vouched for Vermeer's good character in 1653, when Maria Thins protested the young painter's betrothal to her daughter, Catharina Bolnes. Catharina was Catholic. Vermeer was not. Her family was richer than his. It is not known whether either or both of these factors caused Maria Thins's misgivings, nor is it known why she changed her mind. We know simply that Vermeer and Catharina appeared at the town hall for betrothal on April fourth of that year, and were married April twentieth at the Catholic Church at Schipluy. We know that they lived with Maria Thins, in her house, most of their married lives.

Receipts and inventories show that Vermeer was a dealer in fine arts, as his father had been. The records of the St. Luke's Guild reveal that he served several terms as president, and at least once traveled from Delft to the Hague on guild business. But nothing is known of his life as an artist. Little is known of his life as a man, just a smattering of entries in record books: the births and deaths of children noted, deeds filed, witness made, bills owed.

He died at forty-three. This, the only explanation of his death, was given to the town council by his widow when she applied for financial assistance.

During the long and ruinous war with France not only
had he been unable to sell any of his art, but also, to his detri-
ment, he was left sitting with the paintings of other masters he
was dealing in. As a result and owing to the very great burden
of his children, having no means of his own, he had lapsed into
such decay and decadence, which he had so taken to heart that,
as if he had fallen into a frenzy, in a day or day and a half he
had gone from being healthy to being dead. He was buried in
the family plot in the Oude Kerk, the small coffin of his most
recently deceased child resting upon his own.

Feeling melancholy, I sipped my tea and looked at "A Lady Standing at the Virginal", which was thought by many to be Vermeer's last
painting. Was the woman his wife? Was the mystery beyond the picture plane her knowledge of this growing burden that her husband felt?
And, if so, had she posed for the chance to observe him, hoping to find
a way to help him out of the morass of debt and trouble? Or, only to
give him a moment's ease? I could look at the painting for the rest of
my life. I could add up all I knew a million times. Still, there would be
no answer.

My own life, documented, would add up to little more. My birth
certificate, my father's army discharge papers showing he had served
in England, my mother's obituary, certificates recording Peg and Dad's
London marriage and my sisters' births: these things would define my
childhood. There would be nothing to connect me to my Aunt Lily,
except maybe the fact that my father's army checks had been sent to
her address during the war. And certain photographs. But those weren't
really reliable. One could only guess at why the people in them were
grouped the way they were. Why only some of them were smiling.

Peg's letter, which arrived at the museum the next morning, would
have added little to the true picture. It was just Peg being Peg: ram-
bling on about how glad she was that she and Lily had finally become
friends these last years, how much we would all miss her, how sorry
she was that they had not reached me in time. And to think of me in
London! It made her homesick to think of it, even though it had been
so long now that she could hardly remember what home was like. And,
of course, the city must have changed drastically since the war—

I sat and stared at the Vermeer a long time, trying to lose myself in it. Yes. Its pure color was coming up beautifully: the Madonna blue of the shawl, the pale gold of the skirt. Under the raking light, I could see the evidence of Vermeer's brush. The thread-thin drag of dull white that he had used on the edges of the folds to make the fabrics shine. The quick stipples creating lace and pearl.

The cleaning had been going extremely well, not so much due to my efforts as to the nearly perfect condition the painting had been in before the damage was done to it. Seventeenth century Dutch paintings almost always aged well; it was one of the joys of working on them. Idly, I thought of the painters of that time: so stereotypically Dutch in the care they took with their materials, in the meticulousness with which they went about their work. It had always intrigued me, the way their rigid lives opened out so marvelously the moment the careful preparations were completed and the brush connected with the canvas.

Their workmanlike curiosity about science intrigued me, too, and I thought again about all that was not known about Vermeer's life, all that could be possible. The scientist Van Leeuwenhoek, for instance, was born the same year as Vermeer, their names recorded on the same page of the baptismal records of the Nieuwe Kerk. When Vermeer died, Van Leeuwenhoek was named executor of the estate. Were the two men friends? Was Van Leeuwenhoek Vermeer's model for "The Geographer" and "The Astronomer," as some art historians believe? Did his knowledge of optics appeal to Vermeer, an artist who left not a single drawing, who we are almost certain used the camera obscura in the first stages of a number of his paintings? Looking at Vermeer's work— recognizing the paradox of such deep serenity existing with the unmistakable insistent pulse of real life, feeling the exquisite tension that such a paradox creates—it is hard to imagine the artist tinkering with lenses and mirrors until the shadow outline of his model was cast on the canvas to his satisfaction. There's something cold in such an image, calculated. Some evidence that the beauty he made did not come only from his heart—

Which brought me right back in a loop to where I had been: feeling out of balance, wrestling with the matters of my own heart. I would just leave, I decided. Take the day off. I could afford the time. I'd have a leisurely lunch, then go back to the flat, take a long bath, and try to get myself in the right frame of mind for the visit with Peg's sister that Jenny had arranged for that evening. I had just turned to gather my things when Jenny appeared in the doorway.

"Aunt Evie?" she said. "If you're not real busy, would you want to come shopping with us? Cliff says I should wear a dress to the supper tonight."

I glanced again at Vermeer's woman before answering. Was it a daughter's voice the woman turned toward? At that moment, the expression on her face seemed weary.

"Cliff's up talking to Ian," Jenny went on. "He said if you can go, good. We should go up and get him. If not, don't worry, he'll take me and we'll just meet you later, like we planned."

I turned toward her then. I saw how tentatively she stood there, how pretty she looked in the sunlight slanting down through the skylights, and I couldn't help smiling at her. "Of course I'll go with you," I said.

In the Laura Ashley store off Sloane Street, that same bright sunlight slanted in through the big front windows. The polished wood floor shone. Cliff passed the husbands and fathers who sat patiently on the chintz couches, and the three of us joined the shoppers riffling the sale racks of dresses in a frenzy of indecision.

An American girl about Jenny's age grabbed a blue-flowered sailor dress. "Oh, my gosh, can you believe this? Eighteen pounds." She fished in her mother's big leather shoulder bag for a smaller purse that held a calculator, which she removed. She punched in the numbers. "Mom, it's only, like, thirty dollars! I'm going to try it on."

We picked out floral prints in several different styles, and Jenny disappeared into the dressing room. "This one?" she said, emerging. It was a fitted dress, with a square neck and puffed sleeves that fell just short of her elbow. The bright reds and pinks of the print deepened her suntan and made her dark hair seem even darker.

When the American woman said, "That dress is absolutely darling on your daughter," Cliff grinned and said, "Yes, it certainly is."

Chapter Seventeen

We set out on the tube just past the rush hour, Jenny in her new dress, Cliff in clean jeans, a starched shirt, and a tie for the occasion. Jenny laughed when he told her the stop we were looking for was Elephant and Castle.

"*L'enfant de Castille,*" he said. "Originally. That's what the English have done to it."

Outside the station, traffic thundered in the roundabout. Trash skidded along the sidewalk in the breeze. There was graffiti on the sides of buildings, on the walkways. It was nothing like I imagined it would be. Peg used to talk about the terraced houses with their flower gardens—like embroidered handkerchiefs, she said. Each house had a brass door knocker, and you'd see the ladies out every morning, shining them. According to Peg, everything in England shone.

But following the directions Rita had given us to her house, we saw no flower gardens. Just long rows of brick townhouses, all the same except for an occasional squatty frame house wedged into an empty spot—where the original house had been bombed out, Cliff explained. There were whole blocks where no houses stood, vacant lots glutted with weeds and garbage. Cliff said those whole blocks had been bombed away.

Jenny looked confused. "But the war's been over more than forty years," she said.

"Think how many years it took to build London. In forty years, with limited funds—" Cliff shrugged.

"But where did all the people go who lived here?"

"Out to the suburbs, some of them, others into council estates—like your subsidized housing in America. They built them in the new towns that sprung up around London, as well. Families that had lived here in the East End for generations split up and went off to wherever they could find a place. They had no choice. Think of it," he said. "People going along, certain that their lives would be more or less the same as their parents' and grandparents' before them had been, and then the war comes along and changes everything. Now there's the reality of history, isn't it? Not the facts and figures on the page, but the course of any one person's life changed irrevocably by forces completely beyond his control. Like my mum ending up in the north of England the way she did. And my whole life, my career shaped by that coincidence. Here," he said. "Twenty-seven. Here's the house we're looking for."

Rita flung open the front door when she saw us coming up the walk. It was like seeing Peg before me: she was thin and blue-eyed, her wiry red hair threaded with gray.

"Oh my, look at you," she said, embracing me and planting a kiss on my cheek before I could even say hello. "Peg's girl. Oh, and this must be Jenny! Come now, Harry," she called to her husband. "They're here."

He met us in the corridor, a florid man, who pumped our hands and declared, "Blimey, I thought the old girl would have a heart attack before you arrived!"

"Harry," Rita said. But she was laughing. "Here, love," she said to Jenny, patting the seat beside her on the sofa. "I still can't believe it. Peg's family, after all this time. You must tell me everything."

"Grandma's fine—" Jenny began.

"Grandma," Rita said. "Oh, dear me. You know, the last time I saw my sister, she wasn't too much older than you are now. Just a girl. But go on, love. I'll pour us some tea and we'll sit back and have a good chat before supper. I do want you to tell me everything."

Jenny pulled out a snapshot that had been taken earlier that summer at her graduation party, and named everyone for Rita: Peg and Tom, her parents, her aunts and uncles and cousins. Her aunts were hilarious, she said, always bossing everyone around—her grandpa said it was because they'd been named after the Queens of England and thought they had the right.

"Still the joker, is he?" Rita asked. "Tom used to have us in stitches with his funny stories. I was quite smitten with him, you know. I'd been evacuated early in the war, so I never knew him till he came back for Peg, when I was twelve. I'd had been to the market for Mum, and when I came back there was this man in the kitchen. Peg looked a fright— big as a house she was, with Vicky. Laughing and crying at once while he spun her round and round. Lord, when I realized who he was, I dropped the whole blooming bag of groceries!

"Wasn't I swooning?" She laughed. "Just like in the movies, I thought. All the while he was here, I followed him around like a puppy. You look like Tom," she said. "And your mum, Angel, isn't it, dear? She looks like Tom, too, doesn't she? And you, Evie. The others look like us. Like Peg."

"Peg isn't actually my mother, remember."

Rita cast me a blank look.

"You were evacuated," Cliff said. "Were your parents living here in this part of London during the war then, Rita?

"Oh, yes. Right in the thick of it. Our brother was killed, you know, and Peg went into the WAF soon after that. My mum and dad wouldn't have it any other way than I be sent off to a safe place. I was seven. I remember howling when my mum left me with all the other little ones at the station, tagged like a parcel. A tiny village near Chipping Camden was where I was billeted. With kind folks," she said. "I was lucky that way. They treated me like their own, and I came to love them. Indeed, coming home after all that time was just about as hard as leaving had been. Maybe harder. I was at that age, you know. Beginning to feel grown up. Both Mum and Dad remembered me as a little girl, though, and that's what they wanted me to be. As if they could turn back the clock. But Peg always stood up for me. I adored her. I thought she was so glamorous. All she'd done! I was thrilled when Tom came for her, of course, but I felt cheated, too, when I realized he'd be taking her away. I'd grown so attached to her, you know. And I was so looking forward to the baby—"

She stood and took a small square silver frame from the mantel; it opened like a book, with a photograph two girls on the right side of it. "It's Peg's compact," she said, handing it to Jenny. "The one she carried all during the war."

"Oh!" Jenny said. "It's you, isn't it? The little girl in the photograph. With my grandma."

"It is," Rita said. "Taken just before the war, on my eighth birthday. Odd, isn't it? Peg must have been about the age you are now. She gave the compact to me when she left for the States. I'd need it, she said. I'd be the one going out dancing from now on. But it was so beautiful, so special to her that I could never bear to use it. So I had it made into a little frame to remember her by. And, look. On the empty side, it's engraved."

Jenny peered at it, then read, "Peg From Bill, January 29, 1939."

"Perhaps she's told you about Bill," Rita said. "The young man she was engaged to before she met your granddad."

"He was a pilot," Jenny said. "Killed in the war."

"Yes," Rita said. "This was his engagement gift to her. I never could have felt that it was truly mine." Her eyes filled with tears, and she fluttered her hands as if to wave them away. "There, now. Enough of days gone by. Dear me, Harry's right, I've been a basket case since you rang yesterday." She leaned toward Jenny and took her two hands. "I'm so happy you've come. You too, Evie. You must tell me everything about Peg. All these years, I haven't let myself think about how much I miss her."

I sat back while Jenny and Rita talked, the open compact with the photograph of Peg and Rita clearly in my view. The two of them at the seaside, Peg's arm encircling Rita's shoulder, Rita smiling up at her, a smaller version of her sister. I wondered if Peg had looked at Angel and me together sometimes and remembered this photograph. Whether watching us together made her lonely for the sister she'd left behind.

I answered the occasional question Rita asked me, adding something now and then that I remembered. Cliff chatted with Harry on the other side of the room—about Harry's work as a lorry driver, his upcoming retirement, his boyhood during the war. I could see him taking in the details of Rita's parlor as he talked, cataloging them in his mind: the bright orange curtains and throw pillows, the brown flowered carpet, the doll dressed in orange net that was displayed on the bottom shelf of the television stand. Would they end up in one of his detective novels? Imagining the wry Giles Bardon, a character not unlike Ian, in that room made me smile, and I relaxed a little.

Now Rita was chronicling the lives of her children: her daughter, Janet, who lived in Surrey, and her son, Simon, who'd gone to find work up in the north. They grew from babies to adults in the clutter of photographs on the wide mantel. There were photographs of her five grandchildren, too. A photo of Peg in her WAF uniform, one of their brother, ancient sepia photographs of their parents and grandparents. There was a photo of Rita and Harry on their wedding day. And the photograph taken on Peg and Dad's wedding day, one I'd seen before in their album at home: Peg's head tilted up toward my father's face, the two of them oblivious to Peg's whole family lined up on the church steps on either side of them. Then I saw a long narrow frame that had four faded school photos in it: myself at about age ten, dressed in a Girl Scout uniform, and Vicky, Bets, and Anne.

Rita saw me looking at it. "I found that, and the photo of Peg's wedding in my mum's things when she died. She kept all the photographs Peg ever sent of you girls. She'd show them round. 'Evie's the smart one,' she'd say, and tell about the prizes you won at school. She was so proud of you. She kept all Peg's letters, too. Here," she said, nodding toward a fat packet of airmail letters on the table beside her. "I dug them out when you phoned. I thought you might like to take them back to her. I thought she might get a kick out of reading them after all this time."

"But don't you want to keep them?" Jenny asked.

"They're not mine, love," Rita said. "They were my mum's. I never read them. I just couldn't bear to part with them when I came upon them in her things."

"Okay," Jenny said. "If you're sure. Wow, I bet it will be strange for her, reading them. She was really homesick when she first came to Indianapolis, you know."

"That I remember," Rita said. "Mum getting those letters. She'd say, 'Oh, poor Peg,' and Dad would say, 'She's made her bed, Margaret. Leave her rest in it.' I used to get so angry at him."

"She cried the whole way over on the boat," Jenny said. "She looked like a wreck when she got to America, she said. Then every time she tried to do something, it turned out wrong. Like, my dad made popcorn for them sometimes and once, when he was gone, she decided to make some herself. But she forgot to put the top on the pan and, when the popcorn started to pop, it went everywhere. She got used to things after a while, though. She got more American, then she felt better.

She still says 'tom-*ah*-to,' though."

Rita laughed. "And still drinks her tea, I'll wager."

"Oh, yeah," Jenny said. "Tea, with milk and sugar. No way she'll never get over that."

She zipped Peg's letters into her pack, out of sight, but the presence of my own name, which was surely written in many of them, made me feel distracted. When Rita turned from Jenny to me and asked about my life, I felt myself floundering as I tried to explain why I was in England. The idea that I'd been brought here to repair a torn picture seemed quite beyond her, as it had to Cliff's mother. "No children?" she asked.

"No. I've never been married."

"Oh. Well, then," she said.

Cliff went with Harry to collect Auntie Viv, who was to join us for supper, the two of them still chatting animatedly as they walked down the front walk. Harry stopped and pointed at something in the vacant lot across the street. Cliff nodded, and they walked on. I admired the ease with which he met all kinds of people, the way he put them at ease. Jenny had that same quality. She hadn't known Rita an hour, yet trailed her into the kitchen, talking a mile a minute. Rita handed me a family album, and while she and Jenny put supper on the table, I leafed through it, still feeling that I did not belong here.

It was Auntie Viv who finally calmed me down. She appeared, beaming, with Cliff on one arm and Harry on the other. She was slim, her long nails perfectly manicured, painted red. Her jet black hair was pulled back in a chignon. She was dressed in an amazing embroidered silk dress. From Hong Kong, she said. Brought by one of her nephews who'd gone there on business. She wore spike heels.

"Eighty-three is no reason to turn stodgy, now is it?"

"Absolutely not," Cliff said, settling her at the table.

It was clear to me right off that Auntie Viv was not a person to be corrected, so when she said to me, "So you're Peg's oldest girl," I said, "Yes." Nor did I insist that Cliff was just my friend, after I'd said it once and she arched her eyebrows and gave me a knowing glance. She was so full of life it was impossible to be annoyed.

Jenny was charmed, too. She took out her book and wrote as Viv talked, explaining that she didn't want to forget anything that Peg might want to know. While the rest of us ate Rita's roast chicken, Viv told about her granddaughter, who was a weather girl for the BBC, about one of Peg's cousins who'd bought up land near Ascot after the war and had ended up sitting pretty on it in the middle of a posh country club, about the neighbor boy who'd become a film actor and still came back from time to time to visit. "Peg's sure to remember him," she said. "Donnie Morton. Poor thing. His own mum didn't have the time of day for him. Everybody on the block used to look after him and his sister, and he never forgot it."

"Donnie Morton," Jenny wrote. Then she asked Viv to tell her about Peg's parents.

"My brother, John. He was Peg's father, your great-grandfather. Just have a look at him." Auntie Viv gestured toward the mantel at the photograph of him and she pursed her lips, mimicking his dour expression. "Not much fun, was our John. I used to drive him mad, living the way I did. Me and my husband, Bert—we used to go off to the pub on Friday nights for dancing right up until the time Bert passed on, bless his soul. Ten years ago now that was. John thought we were scandalous.

"It was a pity, though. Poor John never did get used to all the changes the war brought. He broke his own wife's heart in the end. Never forgave her for letting Derek go off with Peg that day. Never forgave Peg for going to America, even though he made her life a misery all the while she was with them."

"He didn't like Grandpa?" Jenny asked.

"John didn't like Yanks," Viv said. "Any Yanks. When Margaret, your great-grandmother, put her foot down that one time and insisted they go over to visit Peg, you'd have thought she'd dragged him to darkest Africa. It wasn't long after that trip to America that your mum began to fail, isn't that right, Rita?"

"It was," Rita said sadly. "It never crossed my mind that Dad wouldn't have written Peg to let her know Mum was sick until it was too late for her to come. And I'd so grown busy with my own family by then that I'm afraid I didn't give it a lot of thought afterwards. I'd quit writing to Peg long ago, in any case."

"As I had," said Viv. "You set out with the best intentions, you know, meaning to keep up writing. Then suddenly you realize it's been

months or years since the last time you heard from one another, and it
isn't as if you wouldn't still like to keep up the connection, but you don't
even know where to start."

"You'll write now, though, won't you?" Jenny asked. "I'll write
down Grandma's address before I leave, okay? I know she wants to hear
from you. I'll tell her to write, too. Maybe she could even visit you."

"Wouldn't that be something, Rita?" Auntie Viv said, and for the
first time she looked truly old. "I can't imagine our Peg anything but a
pretty young girl. I still remember the last time I saw her, the day before she sailed for the States. She brought the baby by to see me and we
took a walk, down to the shops. It was warm, I remember. Summer.
Roses straggling up through the rubble. Like ghosts they were, marking the places where gardens had been.

"The two of us stopped and watched a crew of workmen tearing
down the last of the Camberwell factory. Plasters had been manufac-
tured there, bandages. The children used to call it the butterfly factory
because of the huge Camberwell moth that was painted on one wall.
That butterfly wall stood when the rest of the building was bombed
during the Blitz. It seemed a bit of a miracle—that butterfly, floating
over the rubble. A good luck charm, if you will. That day, the wrecking ball was battering it away, brick by brick, leaving nothing but terrible choking dust.

"I saw Peg getting teary at the sight of it, and I said to her, 'You're
better off going, you and the baby. You'll make a new life there.'

"Ah, now here *I* am, teary," Viv said. "All these years later. A teary
old fool." She turned to Jenny. "Write this in your book, love. You tell
Peg her Auntie Viv remembers everything. You tell her I may get over
and see her yet, the way I promised her I would that day we watched
the wrecking ball together. Eighty-three's no time to sit down, I say.
You tell Peg her Auntie Viv still goes out dancing Friday nights when
she can find a man who's able!"

Chapter Eighteen

*T*he morning after our visit with Rita, Vermeer's woman regarded me with an expression I used to see on Aunt Lily's face when something I said or did at a family gathering caused a tense, quiet moment among us. My behavior could not be commented on for fear that we might suddenly find ourselves talking about verboten subjects, but it could not be ignored. So my Aunt Lily just looked at me. *I expected you to be a better person than that,* she said with her eyes.

All those years, consumed by my own misery, I had never once considered what Peg had left behind to marry my father, what she'd lost. Now I could not stop thinking about the pretty silver compact, lovingly polished to keep its high shine. The photograph of Peg and Rita in it, the engraved date of her engagement opposite them. I wondered if, in the most difficult times, Peg had imagined what her life would have been like lived amidst her family, married to Bill. In the kitchen, up to her elbows in soapsuds, crying, what was she crying about? She had mentioned Rita, Auntie Viv, and others in the stories she told over the years; but while she described England in vivid detail, the people were drawn in broad, usually comic strokes. They didn't seem a bit real to me.

Or maybe I just wasn't listening.

Jenny and I had stayed up late again last night, talking. Rather, Jenny talked. About Rita and Auntie Viv, trying as she spoke to patch together what she knew of Peg's life in England with things she had observed or learned during our visit.

"The butterfly factory," she said. "Grandma never said a word about that. And isn't it so sad about her fiancé being killed in the war? It must have been awful for her when she found out. Every time she opened up that compact he gave her, she must have thought of him.

Even in the Golden Lion Pub, when she was with Grandpa. It just kills me to think about that." Her eyes filled with tears. "But, Aunt Evie, it's so strange, isn't it? If he hadn't died, I wouldn't be here. I never would have been born."

Now, putting my work away for the evening, I, too, found myself pondering two truths that seemed to contradict each other. I could not imagine a life that was not in some way defined by hating Peg; I could not imagine a life bereft of the joy Jenny that had brought into it.

She greeted me cheerfully when I arrived at Cliff's flat and found her setting out the ingredients to make a cake. "I'm warning you, this could be one big disaster," she said. "The first time I ever baked a cake— I was about eight—I thought the recipe said thirteen cups of water instead of one and a third. Made perfect sense to me. It was going to be a surprise for my mom. I'm in the kitchen, pouring away, and she comes in—and she's surprised, all right. She about had a heart attack. She's always telling people I'd better marry a chef or I'm going to starve to death. I'm great at decorations, though." She picked up a plastic bag with "Museum of London" printed on the front. Inside, there was a package of miniature Roman legions made of plastic. "I got sugar cubes, too. I figure I can dip them in tea to make them brown, then stick them together with icing. Hadrian's Wall, right?" She grinned.

How she'd found out the date of Cliff's birthday, I don't know. But she had, and she had insisted there must be a party. She'd be in charge of the cake and decorations, she informed me. I could be in charge of dinner. There wasn't really much for me to do, though. Once I'd assembled the chicken casserole and put it in the refrigerator, I just sat in the kitchen and watched Jenny work.

"Gosh, I love birthdays," she said, organizing the bowls and pans and utensils she'd need. "When I was little, my mom would make me a crown. It was so cool. I even like birthdays that aren't mine. Probably because of the way Grandma used to give all us kids a present, an unbirthday present, every time it was anybody's birthday. Like in *Alice in Wonderland*." Mom told me she did that when you guys were little, too."

"Yes," I said.

She bit her lower lip as she bent over her task, concentrated on measuring the ingredients into the bowl. "Do you have a present for Cliff yet?"

I nodded. I told her I'd framed a postcard of the Vermeer painting, just the right size for his desk.

"Cool," she said. "Aunt Evie, do you think it would be okay if I gave him my INDIANA tee-shirt, that red one? I went shopping, but I couldn't find anything, you know—special. That tee-shirt's almost new. I got it just before I came here. Do you think it's too tacky, though? I mean, giving something used?"

"Absolutely not. Cliff would love that tee-shirt."

She turned the electric mixer on, then turned it off again. "Now, Ian's coming for sure, isn't he?"

"Honestly, you're sounding as fussy as Aunt Lily," I teased. "Worrying over the guest list. Everything having to be just right." I immediately regretted my words when I thought, *she's gone,* opening that empty space that had been Aunt Lily. I saw on Jenny's face that she felt it, too.

"It's going to be wonderful," I said. "You know how pleased Cliff was when we told him about it. No matter what you give him or who shows up, he'll love it. And, yes, Ian's definitely coming. He said he wouldn't miss it for the world."

Cliff was not allowed into the flat the next morning, for fear that he would see the cake Jenny had made or the crepe paper decorations she had strung up in the dining area. I sent her out with a smile of complicity, and a twinge of guilt for keeping the other secret I knew. Cliff had made plans to put her to work with one of his assistants so that he could double back and spend the day with me.

I put on Vivaldi and got into the bath, thinking that not once in my entire life had I ever missed work in the interest of something so completely self indulgent. I was still in the tub when I heard the key turn in the lock, heard Cliff's footsteps. I turned toward the doorway, where he appeared smiling, carrying a wrapped present. He held it out to me.

"It's *your* birthday," I said. I climbed out of the tub, wrapped myself in a big towel.

"Open it."

It was a long white silk nightgown, perfectly simple. When I put it on, it felt cool against my skin.

"Yes, it's lovely on you," he said. "I thought it would be. Look."

But in the steamy bathroom mirror, I was all blurred at the edges, exactly the way I felt.

We took our time. We ate the buttery croissants that he'd bought in the shop down the street. We listened to more music. Talked. When we moved, we moved slowly, deliberately, the space between us shifting almost physically. When we did touch, at last, I felt like I was burning.

Later, at the party, we still felt connected. It was something that had never happened to me before, almost frightening: the sense that each move I made, each thought I had, each feeling racing through me had its counterpart in Cliff's body. And feeling his rhythms, his very consciousness inside my own.

Ian noticed, I could tell by his even more bemused than usual expression. But Jenny, bent on making it a perfect evening for Cliff, seemed oblivious. The cake was a grand success, and the presents. Ian's was a book of photographs of New York. He said, "You'll be going to see Evie, of course. You'll want to read up. That, and sharpen your switch blade."

Then the phone rang. "Hello?" Cliff said, still laughing.

And I saw his face change, felt the connection between us snap.

"Oh. Yes, Metta. Well, thank you. Lovely day, yes. Yes." He glanced at us. "Some friends in for dinner. The children, you say? Yes, put them on." I got up to clear the table.

"They spoiled everything, didn't they?" Jenny said when Cliff and Ian had left. "His kids. After he talked to them, I could tell he wasn't having fun any more. You know, Aunt Evie, I feel so bad for Cliff sometimes. I don't think his kids are all that nice to him. He says they think he's weird."

"I don't know them," I said, suddenly feeling in very rocky territory. "Maybe it's just that they're still upset with him. About the divorce—"

"Well, I told him what Grandma told me one time," Jenny said. "You know, about how you were when she first married Grandpa. How you were still really upset about your own mom dying. How you were used to living with Aunt Lily and wanted to go back and have things be the same as they used to be. She said kids don't always mean what they say. They don't always purposely hurt you. It's just when they're hurt themselves, they can't help it sometimes—they just act bad. All you can do is love them. You don't think Cliff could have really awful kids, do you Aunt Evie? I mean, don't you think they're really, really okay? You know, like down deep?"

She looked at me. I had to say something, but my throat felt tight and all I could manage was, "I don't know. I hope so."

That night, I couldn't sleep. I saw Peg and my father dancing in the living room. All those dimes on the coffee table. My father offering to give me all I could carry. Then I saw myself years later, near Jenny's age, offering money to him. I had wanted something desperately. I couldn't even remember now what it was, but my father had sold his own father's pocketwatch to get it for me. I knew how much he valued the watch, but that had not made me grateful for the gesture. Rather, it made me speechless with rage. I did not want to owe him, he should not have put me in the position to owe him. If he hadn't spent our money drinking, he would have been able to give me what I needed without having had to sell the precious watch. I vowed that I would earn the money to pay him back, every single cent—and I did earn the money, and what I saw now was the hurt look on his face when I insisted that he accept it.

I saw that narrow picture frame on Rita's mantel: myself in my Girl Scout uniform and my sisters, each one of us exactly the same size.

"Girl *Scouts,* not Girl *Guides,*" I remembered myself saying when Peg told me how nice I looked in my uniform.

I couldn't shake the bad feeling all the next day. I kept thinking of Cliff, remembering the look on his face when he picked up the phone the night before, the way the happiness of the evening had visibly drained away at the sound of Metta's voice.

And then the letter from Angel came. We'd talked several times since the morning Jenny arrived, mainly about her travel plans for home. Each time I reassured Angel that things were fine, really they were.

"You're sure," she'd say.

Yes. I was glad Jenny had come, glad for the chance to know her. Each time I said it, I meant it more, and I think she finally believed it. We had not talked about ourselves, our lives. Now I sat there, her thick letter in my hands.

"Dear Evie," It began. "I've wanted to write this for a long time.

"But for a long time I thought you wouldn't want to hear what I had to say. I'm not real sure you want to hear it now. Evie, I know how disappointed you were when I got married. I know how stupid it seemed. I was so young, I could have done a million things—anything, you taught me that. But you never knew Matt, how good and smart he was—and still is. How much he loved me. You couldn't see that being with him was the right thing for me. You wanted me to be like you. But I wasn't. I never was.

"I always knew you weren't happy. I knew I was the only one in our family that you loved. I could see that before I understood what it meant, before I could name the thing about myself that made me different from you. I swear, Evie, sometimes I think I was born loving everyone in the whole world in exactly the same measure. You, Mom and Dad, Vic and Bets and Anne, Matt and Jenny, every little child that ends up in my classroom. I feel like a big tuning fork sometimes, love running through me like a kind of sound that never stops. Life hasn't been very hard for me. For the most part, I'm ridiculously happy. But that love. God, sometimes it makes me so tired, wanting all those people I love to love me back—and to love each other.

"I don't blame you for being mad about what I did. All the time you invested in me, the way you believed in me. I know it's such a small thing I've done with my life—just roomful after roomful of little kids down through the years. But, you know, I figured out once that what I do for them is not so different from what you did for me. You made my world big and small at the same time. I mean, the way you taught me everything you knew, the way you listened to me, and asked me questions, as if what I thought mattered. The way you chose me. I felt special, knowing you really, really wanted to be with me. You gave me the happy childhood I want those little ones to have.

"You gave me a way of being in the world that made me feel safe inside. It was why I could live with the tension in our household all those years and not feel like I was dying. I guess it's also why I failed you. Why I never needed to leave. I remember how I used to think, if I could only make Evie love Mom and Dad, she'd be happy, then we'd all be happy—but of course I couldn't make you love anyone. Maybe it wasn't even my place to try. But even in that way, long after you were gone, you kept on teaching me, because Jenny was like you. I think I knew it the very first time I held her. Like the way I can look at a child in my classroom sometimes now and know right off whether she's a child the world is going to be kind to or whether she's a child who's bound to wrestle with the world all her life.

"It means so much to me that Jenny's with you. When she was growing up, sometimes I'd think, what would Evie do? What would she want? I couldn't make Jenny happy, I knew that. But it still took millions of mistakes for me to face up to the fact that all I could do was try and try to see who she was, and then when the time came, let her go and hope she'd find her own happiness, like you did when you left Mom and Dad. Does that make any sense at all? Honestly, it seems to me more and more that things just go in a circle, eventually lapping themselves, like cars on a race track, until there's no way to figure out what's what. Mostly I don't even try. I mean, how could I ever explain the way I can still be so sad about Aunt Lily dying, and at the same time know that if she hadn't died I never would have gotten up the courage to finally write you this letter and say, even after all these years, Evie, I still miss you.

It seemed these days I was always crying. Angel's letter, the sudden sense of her absence in my life that it brought. Years lost because of my own stubbornness, another thing that could never be fixed. "Maybe I'm the wild card in your history," Jenny had said. Maybe she was. But it shouldn't have been that way.

I tried to work, but Vermeer's woman mocked me. You should have let yourself be interrupted, she seemed to say. You should have looked up, you should have seen.

I'll go out into the galleries, I thought. I'll look at the paintings, just look at them. I was always reminding myself that I didn't do that enough—just enjoy them.

It was midday. As I walked through the door that separated the working part of the museum from the galleries, I was confronted by crowds of people milling on the wide staircase. I made my way through them to the galleries, which were also crowded. In some places, people stood three and four deep straining to view the paintings. I stood awhile and looked at the blank spot where my Vermeer belonged. When the crowd thinned a bit, I looked at the Dutch paintings that surrounded it. Women scrubbing, sweeping, cooking, bending over children. Men drinking, throwing dice, peddling wares. Doors revealing rooms full of the accoutrements of living, windows thrown wide, gates opening into the street. For the first time, it was the mess of it I saw—the real world the painting had been made of—not the stillness of the caught moment. Voices speaking, dogs barking, children crying. And I saw that the light I so loved, the light illuminating the simple, lovely objects would shift any second and move on across the morning, the day, the lives of the people within the frame.

Cliff was right. I had been so careful to avoid the mess of real life. For what? When there was nothing that could save me from the light: the shift of it bound to leave a coldness, its inevitable path toward the dark.

I wanted him now. I wanted to call him up and say, okay, I'm in the mess now, but I feel worse than ever. You were the one who dragged me into it, so tell me what to do. But he had taken Jenny up to see Hadrian's Wall and they wouldn't be back until the following day. When he decided on the outing, earlier that week, I'd been pleased at the prospect of a whole, quiet evening to myself. Now, my enthusiasm for an evening of solitude waned considerably. I imagined Cliff and Jenny, cozy, in Mrs. Murray's kitchen, and it made me feel lonely. In Cliff's flat, alone, I figured all I'd do was sit around and think.

"Oh, horrors," Ian said, when I phoned his office and invited him to dinner. "Think. God forbid you should do that." Later, over drinks, he asked, as I knew he would, "So, Evie. What are these terrible thoughts you're trying to avoid?"

"You name it," I said. "These days, I'm like a radar screen gone bad. Everything gets through, everything has equal weight. For years, my life's been in perfect order. Now—as if finding myself in so deep with Cliff weren't enough—it seems that every member of my family suddenly has something to say to me, some speaking directly from the grave. Do I need this? Aunt Lily informs me that everything she told me about my mother was a lie. But if Aunt Lily was so unreliable, how do I know whether this set of facts is any truer than the set I had before? Or the set in the other diary she says she burned? And if the new facts are true, so what? Am I supposed to go home, become a child again and start all over?

"No, wait," I said when Ian clucked sympathetically. "You haven't heard the rest. Yesterday I got a letter from Peg, telling me how happy she was that she and Aunt Lily eventually became friends. Plus, I actually received a joint sympathy card, a religious sympathy card, I might add, from my three sisters. Each one wrote a little note and sent pictures of her children—

"Ian, my sister Vicky dots the "i" of her name with a little heart. Don't laugh," I said. "If you don't see what a disaster this is by now, you can throw in our weird visit to Peg's sister the other night for good measure."

"How was that?" Ian asked. "I didn't get a chance to ask you at the party."

"Nice," I said. "I mean really, really nice. Which only made me more confused. Peg's sister tried so hard, and there was this aunt, Aunty Viv—oh, you'd have loved her. Eighty-three and dressed in a Suzy Wong dress. I'm surprised Cliff hasn't told you about her already. He thought she was wonderful.

"But listen, will you? Today I got this letter from my sister, Angel."

"Angel," he said, looking really interested for the first time.

But having gotten his attention, I realized I'd have to go all the way back to the beginning of time to be able explain what the letter had meant to me. And anyway, Cliff was the only one in the whole world who would understand.

"Oh, just pour me another glass of wine," I said. "I am sick to death of all this. I just want one small thing, okay? I want my boring old life back. Do you think you could arrange that?"

"Alas, not possible." He went on in an affectedly ponderous voice. "Things change. That's Buddha's Fourth Noble Truth—condensed a bit, mind you."

"Please," I said. "You sound like an undergraduate."

He laughed. "Fine. Let's look at things on a less cosmic level then, shall we? The family dilemma is quite a simple one, after all. At most, you re-think some things. You left all those people behind you long ago, Evie. You're just browned off because they've reared their heads. You either decide to try to sort it all out, or simply take care of what needs to be done and leave them all behind you once again. Except Jenny, maybe. You've grown fond of her in spite of yourself, haven't you?"

I acknowledged that I had. "But it's Cliff," I said miserably. "That's the real problem. Ian, I think I'm in love with him. No, no, I *am* in love with him. And I don't know which frightens me more: the thought that in a few weeks it will be all over between us, or the thought that— it won't. And don't look so shocked at what I'm saying. You're the one—"

"But I never thought—" he began. "Oh dear, I have made a muddle of your life, dragging you over here, haven't I? What will you do?"

"Do?" I asked. "You think there's something I can do?"

He didn't answer. Clearly, there was nothing more that either of us could say about Cliff and me, at least at the moment. Ian, who could always be counted on to know the right thing to do, poured the rest of wine, ordered another bottle, and launched into the latest museum gossip, which kept me in peals of laughter all through the meal.

Later, after we'd parted, I had the taxi drop me at the flat in Dolphin Square. I remembered how I had been so content in my drab little flat those first few weeks, so focused, and I hoped that, just for tonight, I might be the person I had been there again. I'll just put Cliff's things in the closet and close the door, I thought. His books and papers were always so neatly stacked and labeled that I knew I could move them without worrying whether I'd disturbed the order. But as soon as I entered the room, I knew it had been a mistake to come. Cliff might as well have been present, the flat had become so much his own.

There was no sense in putting his things away and getting them all back out again in the morning. I opened the hide-a-bed and lay down. The pillow smelled of him, so I got up and went to sit at the desk. I leafed through the book of Roman jewelry I found there, smiled at the index card I saw on top of the rubber-banded pile next to it—a list of jewelry in the Giles Bardon mystery that he and Jenny had been cooking up the other morning. I couldn't resist taking the rubber band off the index cards and looking through them. There were details of setting: the particular location of the dig, near the Moorgate tube stop; facts about the corporation president's childhood during the war; a sketch of the Roman charm the returning war bride wore on her chain. The card with her description on it stopped me cold. "Peg's history— married to a GI after the war. But she looks like Evie. Small, dark, smartly dressed. Elegant, like E says her Aunt Lily looked. Like Evie herself will look at that age."

I stared at Cliff's crabbed handwriting, not reading the words, just staring at the shape of them on the card, and for a moment it seemed to me that the loops and lines he had made there were all that was left of me. How dare he appropriate my life? And, God! That he would merge me in any way with Peg! That it would be my face as an old, finished woman that compelled him. Not some fantasy of what my young face had been, not my face as he knew it now.

I understood then that no matter how I felt about it, a part of me was irrevocably his. Anger, panic, a terrible curiosity, perhaps fear all mingled inside me. And an odd relief. What was his, he would be determined to understand. What was his, he would never, ever let go.

Still, I did not see how this could translate to real life at all. Especially when I turned from Cliff's mystery to leaf through the mystery he'd left on the table by the bed: the latest P.D. James, his place marked with a postcard. The picture showed a curve of blue ocean. When I turned it over, I saw that I had guessed right: the Mediterranean, the South of France. The message read: "Dear Cliff, the children and I are having a lovely holiday. The weather has been superb. I just wanted to remind you that we'll be returning 15 August and that Robin and Monica look forward to seeing you at that next weekend. I'll ring you on our arrival to make plans. Metta."

I thought of how I'd felt the night before while Cliff was talking on the phone to his children. I felt again the pain of the snapped connection. The sense of my life flowing through him into the words I'd just read. And I remembered Ian's last words tonight. Having said goodnight, we were just about to part and go our separate ways. But, impulsively, I touched his arm to hold him back. We hadn't mentioned Cliff for well over an hour, but Ian knew exactly what I meant when I said, "I'll go back to New York when I'm finished with the Vermeer, you know. I have to. Do you think that'll be the end of it?"

"Maybe," he said. "I don't know. Certainly the end of the beginning."

Chapter Nineteen

"**S**ay you have a dog," Jenny said. "Okay. You've had it ever since you were a little kid. You're nuts about it. Every day when you come home, the dog comes running up to meet you, wagging its tail and licking you all over. Like, no matter what kind of crummy day you've had, or how big of a jerk you've been, this dog is glad to see you."

She paused. "Now suppose it's time to come home one day and you know your dog will be there waiting for you, like always—but you know something else, too. Later, when your mom or dad or husband or wife—or whoever—gets home from work, they're going to take the dog to the vet and have it put to sleep. They're not doing it to be mean. The dog is real sick and it's going to die anyway and if it isn't put to sleep, it'll suffer. What do you do?"

"Do?" I asked her.

"Yeah," she said, in an encouraging, teacherish tone. "What do you do? Give me some possibilities."

We were sitting in a café in Bloomsbury, waiting for Cliff to join us for the evening. We'd been talking about all the things we wanted to cram into the next few days before she left, and suddenly Jenny had launched into this explanation of an idea she'd learned in her world lit class. What dogs had to do with world literature—or with our sightseeing plans—I could not fathom. But her earnestness was so endearing that I followed her train of thought as best I could.

"You could avoid going home," I said. "Go somewhere else and stay there till you know the dog will be gone. Or I guess you could be extra nice to the dog. Spoil it: you know, maybe let it eat whatever it wants. I have a friend whose dog loves olives, for example. If she doesn't watch it like a hawk, it'll climb up on a chair and eat a whole tray of them from a buffet table, then proceed to throw up all over the Persian carpet in the living room."

Jenny disregarded my attempt at humor. "You could ignore the dog," she prodded. "Or be mean to it and pretend you didn't like it all that much anyhow. You could get mad at your parents or the veterinarian and blame them."

"Yes," I said.

"Or you could take that dog to the place it loves more than any other place. The woods maybe, or the park. And you could have the best time you ever had with it in its whole life that day because it's going to die. Because," she repeated. "That's the important part—

"See, when you know you're going to lose something you love, it should make you enjoy it more. Those things don't seem to fit together, but they do. *Duende,* the idea is called. The Spanish made it up. Bullfighting has it. It's in the dance the bullfighter does with the bull, the audience all the while knowing that any minute one of them is going to die. It's life and death, happiness and sadness becoming the same thing.

"So—" she concluded. "I guess that since I love being in England so much and love being with you and Cliff—and I know it's about to be over, I should be really, really happy right now, shouldn't I?"

She leaned toward me. "But I can't get past the fact that I don't want to go home, Aunt Evie. I hate it how ideas sound so cool that you absolutely *have* to believe them, but then they don't work. I mean, I loved that idea when I learned it. I thought it would change my whole life. But it doesn't work. I mean, I believe it in my head—I *do.* But I can't make it change how I feel." She laughed, but did not smile. "My mom says I have only one problem: I want everything. All the time."

"There's nothing wrong with wanting, Jenny. It's good to want. When you go after what you want, you grow."

"But it doesn't make me grow," Jenny said. "It just makes me upset. It makes me feel guilty. My mom would be mortified if she heard me complaining about having to go home. I mean, after all I've gotten to see and all you and Cliff have done for me. You're supposed to feel grateful when something good happens to you, right? Not greedy, always wanting more."

"You want what you want," I said. "Wanting isn't a moral issue, it's a feeling—and you can't control how you feel. So how can you be judged for it?"

I left it at that, and turned the conversation back to our plans. If I'd gone one step farther, I knew I'd have been making judgments myself, telling Jenny that what life had taught her so far was ignorant and wrong and that she'd better make up her mind to be what she wanted to be, and be it right now, while she still had the chance.

Worse, I might have told her what I was feeling as the date of her departure grew nearer. I didn't want her to leave. It seemed to me that the three of us might go on indefinitely as we had these past weeks. "If she could just stay with us, I know she could be the person she needs to be," I'd said to Cliff. Then I stopped short, embarrassed.

"Oh?" He smiled at me. *"You're* staying then?"

"You know what I mean," I said. "Jenny might make it if she could stay away from Angel and Matt for a while. She might finally believe that what she's living is her own life. God, there are things she could do that she hasn't even yet imagined—"

"And if Jenny stayed, you'd stay too?"

"Cliff," I said.

"What about all the things *you* hadn't imagined?" he persisted. "That I hadn't imagined before I met you?"

"Like the American woman in your new book?" I asked.

I was astonished by my own words and by the anger bubbling up around them. I hadn't said a word about discovering the index card with my description that night I stayed at Dolphin Square. I certainly didn't want to confront whatever I felt about it right now. I wanted, instead, to erase Cliff's shocked expression and go backwards, to our conversation about Jenny.

Still, I continued. "Who knows what your Giles Bardon would've done next if you hadn't had my life to appropriate for his next adventure," I said. "How handy that I showed up when I did. So convenient that all the things I've never told anyone else in the world about my life, you can *use*."

"Evie—" Cliff began

But neither of us knew how to go on.

"I'm sorry," I said, finally. "Really, I am. The last thing I want to do right now is get into an argument about *us*. I shouldn't have been reading what was on your desk, I know that—"

I tried to turn away, but gently he took my face in his hands so that I could not help but look at him. "You can read anything of mine," he said. "You can have anything. Evie, if I write you down, I can keep you. Can't you see that? Those books, foolish as they are, are the only way I've ever found of hanging on to what I love. And whether we talk about it or not, I do love you."

"I know, I know," I whispered. "But I'm so afraid."

He put his arms around me then, and held me a long while. "I know your impulse is to go away from me," he said. "Maybe you will go away, in the end, maybe you should. But where does the love go, then? What's to be done with what I remember? All I know to do with it is to write it down. Things never change in a book. You open it and there's a person, a world you once knew. Or worlds you might have known, lives you might have lived. Evie, you *do* understand that—"

I said yes, though I didn't—not really. Later, I agreed when Cliff said that it was important to enjoy the time left we had with Jenny, not to spoil it. What he told me about the books made sense, of course. A good idea. But I was like Jenny: I couldn't make it work. I couldn't stop being sad.

We decided to spend her last full day with us at Bath. We set out a bit subdued, each of us lost in our own thoughts as we traveled out of London, into the green hills beyond. If I glanced into the rear view mirror, I could see Jenny's pensive face. I wanted to turn and comfort her, but what would I say, Everything will be all right? I wasn't at all sure that I believed it. Each time I glanced back, I was filled with a kind of yearning I had never known. That morning, on the way to Bath, I think I understood something about what having a nearly grown child must be like: love and helplessness and gratitude mingling. A certain disbelief that the complete person before you could have grown out of you into herself. Would my own mother have felt this ache if she had lived to watch me secretly, as I watched Jenny now? Could Peg have felt it? Before Jenny entered my life, I would have said, impossible.

It was cool when we arrived in Bath, the sky was cloudless—the same light color of the stone that the elegant Georgian houses were made of. In fact, everything in the city seemed to be that same milky gray: the pavements, the shops along Great Pulteney Street, the bridge across the Avon, the gracefully arched colonnades. When I glanced up at the hills beyond the city, the green seemed extraordinarily brilliant to me.

The green of the baths amazed me, too. The museum was darkened for effect. The artifacts gleamed in their lit cases, but they could not compete with the effect of the still, jade water in the baths, the steam rising from it, shrouding the carved nymphs and goddesses so that they seemed like ghosts.

Cliff read from the guidebook, "'One of the ways the Romans put the Sacred Spring to use was with curse tablets, a means of bringing retribution on an enemy. If someone had done you wrong, for example stolen your cloak, and you were not quite sure who it was, you would go to the temple scribe and ask him to help compose a message to the goddess. It would normally be inscribed on pewter, in a standard form written in a kind of legal language." For example—Cliff laughed. "'May he who stole my cloak, whether he be man or woman, boy or girl, freedman or slave, become impotent and die.'" That's right to the point, isn't it? You'd add the list of suspects, throw the piece of pewter in the springs and the goddess would dispense with them.

"Curses, ladies?" He grinned and flung his arm toward the steaming water.

An expression I hadn't seen before flickered across Jenny's face, but she remained silent. I remained silent as well. A while ago, I might have half-seriously cursed Peg or my father, but with the recent turn of events I didn't know who to be mad at anymore.

We walked on. Out of the museum, past yet another house in which Charles Dickens had written a novel, toward the Royal Crescent, where, looking at the long curve of perfectly uniform Palladian houses, I felt, for a moment, that it might as easily have been 1787 as 1987, the year it was. I wondered who I might have been in that other time and whether my life would have been equally painful and confusing and full of joy. And then the moment passed.

After lunch, we explored the cathedral. It was smaller than many we'd seen, and big windows flooded it with an unusual brightness. I admired the kneeling cushions the women's guild had designed and stitched in needlepoint. I'd admired them in every church I visited in England—even the tiniest country churches had them. But what kept us in the church much longer than we'd planned to stay were the memorial plaques that covered the walls. There were hundreds of them, all sizes. Some were simple, with just a name and the dates of the person's life. Others were intricately carved, with lovely epitaphs that made you remember that it was a real person you were reading about, someone deeply loved. We moved slowly around the sanctuary, sometimes reading the plaques aloud.

"Look," Jenny said. "'Robert Walsh. By the death of this gentleman an ancient and respectable family in Ireland became extinct.'"

I hadn't noticed the curate until that moment, when he joined us and explained to Jenny that the broken pillar carved on the memorial stone symbolized the end of a bloodline. He smiled when she jotted the piece of information in her notebook.

"One doesn't often see young people take an interest these days," he said to me, peering over his glasses. "Lovely girl, your daughter." Before I could correct him, he continued, "Here, let me show you a great favorite of mine." We followed him across the church, threading through the tourists, and read the memorial he pointed out to us.

"Sacred to the memory of Anne, the only daughter of George Finch, of Valentines in Essex. AN EXCELLENT PERSON. Her life being the more desirable in that the first real occasion of grief she gave her sorrowful mother was her death. LUGE ET IMITARE."

"Grieve and copy," the curate said. "The Latin."

I expected Jenny to write down what he'd said. Instead, she turned and regarded us with an expression so desolate that I reached instinctively to comfort her. But she bolted, making her way in a straight line through the crowd of people, startling them as she headed toward the door. Cliff hurried after her.

"Oh, dear me," the curate said. "I *am* sorry. I—"

"Please, no. It wasn't your fault. She's been troubled, lately—" I didn't know what more to say, so I touched his arm hoping to reassure him, thanked him for his kindness, and left him standing there, perplexed, polishing his eyeglasses on his black vestments.

I was shaking when I got outside. The sun had come out suddenly, full force, and I had to shield my eyes with my hand. I studied the scene before me, trying to find Cliff and Jenny among the hundreds of people milling in the square. Finally I spotted them not far away, on a bench. Jenny was pale, her head bowed. Cliff's hand was on her hand; he spoke in a low voice, urgently, leaning toward her. Then she looked up and saw me, and began to cry.

"I'm sorry, Aunt Evie," she said. "That man was so nice to us, and I was rude to him. I'm so sorry."

"Oh, Jenny, I don't care about that," I said.

"Come, now." Cliff offered her a handkerchief. "Come, let's take a walk, shall we?"

In silence, we made our way to the gardens along the river, where children played and lovers picnicked. Old men dozed in striped deck chairs, their newspapers folded over their faces.

We found a quiet spot beneath a big chestnut tree on the riverbank, and settled there.

"I'm sorry," Jenny said again, almost a whisper. She stared a long time at the peaceful water. "It's just—that thing the man showed us, about the daughter. It made me feel so ashamed."

"Why?" Cliff asked. "Jenny, you're an excellent person yourself. I can't believe you've done anything shameful."

"You think so," Jenny said bitterly. She looked him square in the eye. "What if I told you I had an abortion?"

Both Cliff and I regarded her, dumbfounded.

"I did, you know. Have one. Because I'm stupid. Stupid to have gotten myself in such a mess in the first place. Stupid—really, really stupid—to have believed the person whose baby it was loved me. What did I expect, that he'd be thrilled to give up his football scholarship and get married? Even I didn't want that. But I wanted him to act like he'd have married me if it *had* been what I wanted—or at least considered it. But no, he couldn't get away fast enough. He gave me all the money he'd gotten for graduation, big deal. He mailed it to me from the summer camp where he was working. Where my dad got him a job.

"It's why I couldn't go see Aunt Lily," she said. "All her life she wanted a baby, everybody knew that, just one little baby, and I just couldn't go to see her knowing what I'd done. God, I didn't even have the nerve to tell my parents. I let Cara's mom lie and sign for me, like she was my own mother. She took me. Oh, it was so awful, Aunt Evie. That room with everything so clean and shiny and the nurses being so nice. And it hurt. It hurt a lot. And all that blood. It makes me sick now just to think about it. "

"Jenny," Cliff said.

"Wait, just wait," she said. "You haven't heard the worst part yet— I'm not sorry. I mean, I'm real sorry I was so stupid to let it happen in the first place, and I'm sorry the baby had to die because I didn't want it. It *was* a baby, you know. I believe that. At least, it would have been a baby if I'd left it alone—like my parents left me alone and let me be, even though having me made their lives a whole lot harder than they would have been. God, I'm just turning out to be nothing but a big disappointment to them. They probably wonder why they wrecked their lives having me, since I don't even want to be the person they want me to be—

"It's them I feel worst about, my mom and dad. Not telling them. And I can't ever tell them," she said, crying now. "Because I can't tell them I'm sorry for what I did. I had to do it, I'd do it again, too. And I'm not sorry. That's what they could never accept."

I drew her to me, felt her hot tears soaking through my cotton dress. As on that very first evening she was with me, she cried absolutely silently. "Oh, Jenny," I said, "Jenny. You were right to do what you did. And it's all right to keep it to yourself for a while, until you know better what it means. Who knows? When you go home, you may find that you want to tell them, after all. Or you may decide it's right not to—at least not now."

"But I don't want to go home," she said in a small voice. "Not ever. No, it's stupider than that. I want to go home the way it was before, to go all the way back to the day I said yes to Justin and say no instead. I want for everything not to be spoiled, to not have to think about college, or what I want to be. I want to stop awhile and just do something I love, the way I've done with you guys. But I know I can't. I have to go home, don't I?"

No, I wanted to say. You don't ever have to go back there. You don't have to be with them. Stay here with me, with us. It seemed a long time before I could say, "I think you need to go home. I think you need to see your parents before you can decide what you really want to do."

"I know," she said. She sat up, took a deep hiccuppy breath.

"You could surprise yourself, you know. You may take one look at them and know exactly what's right. But, Jenny, whether or not you decide to tell your parents about the abortion, be careful not to make the same mistake with them that you accuse them of making with you. You get upset because you think they have this idea of what your life should be," I said. "But aren't you doing that yourself when you assume that your mom and dad really wanted the life you have before you, now? You feel guilty because they had you when they were so young. You think their lives could have turned out a million other ways, better ways. But the truth is, all the two of them ever wanted was each other."

Speaking those words, I believed them for the first time myself. I felt Cliff watching me. "They love each other," I went on. "Do you know how rare that is? Real love? If your mother had her life to live all over, she'd do exactly the same thing again. Having you, making her life around you and your father—that was the right choice for her.

"It's just, whatever you choose you have to live with. You have to have the courage to look straight at the things that happen as a result of it, and live with them. In the end, that may be the hardest part of all about taking charge of your life, making up your mind that it *is* yours, that it's not going to be like any other life ever lived.

"I know about this," I said. "But I've done everything with my family the *wrong* way, Jenny. That's why I know how important it is for you to see clearly now."

Cliff watched me as intently as Jenny did. I was unaccustomed to this kind of honesty, a little frightened by the effects of it, which I saw in their eyes, in the way that their attention was riveted upon me. My own heart was pounding when I said, "Almost no one knows this, Jenny. But a long, long time ago, I almost got married. It was the spring I finished college. Everyone was thrilled. His family liked me, my family liked him. Rob was his name, we'd been friends since our freshman year. Your mother especially liked him. She was still a little girl when I met him, and he always went out of his way to be kind to her. The wedding date was set for June, Aunt Lily had made my dress.

"But it didn't work out. A few weeks before the wedding, he came to me and confessed that he was gay. Queer, he said. That was the word people used then, and always in such an ugly way. It was much different for gays at that time: most people—including me—considered homosexuality to be a terrible, embarrassing disease. It would have been a scandal if anyone had even suspected such a thing of someone like Rob: a boy from a nice family, a fraternity boy. And although I was devastated by what he told me, I did still love him. I knew he loved me, too, in his own way. I had no desire to make him suffer any more than he already had. And I was so humiliated myself that I couldn't bear to tell anyone the truth about why there was no way we could ever marry.

"So I lied. I told Dad and Peg and Aunt Lily that I had changed my mind. It seemed to me the only possible thing to do under the circumstances. I made the choice not to tell the truth to my family. Just as you may choose not to tell the truth about the abortion to yours. It may turn out to be right for you not to tell them. At least for now—

"But Jenny, whatever you decide, you've got to do a better job of living with it than I did. I ran away with my secret. Worse, I wasn't honest with myself. I convinced myself that if I never saw Rob again and stayed away from everyone who'd ever seen the two of us together, it would be as if I had never known him at all. Never loving anyone again, never letting anyone love me, I could keep my heart from breaking. I thought that was being strong."

"But what *is* strong?" Jenny asked. "What am I supposed to *do?*"

I shook my head. "*Something.* That's all I know, you have to do something. You have to make a decision, then face up to what you've decided the best way you know how. And go on."

"But how?" she said. "How can I ever be really strong if I can't stop thinking about the little baby that would have been? Just gone. Lost. I don't know how I can ever make up for that."

"You can't," Cliff said. "Jenny, there's always something lost. Always. No matter what you do. No matter what choice you make. Thankfully, it's not very often something so dear as a baby—but every time you turn down one street instead of another, every time you board a bus in this direction instead of that, a thousand things are lost. Someone you might have met, something you might have seen to make your whole life change."

"But how do you stop thinking about all that?" she asked. "How do you stop being sad?"

"Maybe you can't stop thinking about it, maybe you never stop being sad. And if that's the case, you learn to accept loss and sadness as part of who you are. What's to be learned here, after all, is that you can only move forward, and when a choice presents itself, do the thing you feel is right."

Cliff tipped Jenny's chin up so that she was looking at him. "So you will go forward, won't you?" he said. "Starting now. You'll go home tomorrow, then in a few weeks go off to university and have a lovely time studying whatever pleases you. After all, who's to know exactly what you're doing while you're there? That's the great charm of being at university, isn't it, Evie?"

"It is," I said. "College is a whole different world, you'll see. And once you've made the break from your parents, once they see you're happy there, they'll quit worrying so much. They're just scared to death now, letting you go. They love you and they don't want to have to think anything they did or didn't do spoiled some chance you had to be happy. They're doing the best they can—"

I had to stop and collect myself before I could go on. Even so, my voice shook when I said, "Peg and my dad and Aunt Lily did their best for me—though, God knows, it's taken Cliff browbeating me with my own memories, you appearing on my doorstep to make me finally see what a fool I was for so long. Your mother was right a long time ago when she told me that if I'd ever had children of my own I'd know that our parents' best effort was all it was fair for any of us to expect. I should have listened to her. And Cliff." I smiled. "Who I believe may have said something similar. Just like you should listen to me now."

"I love you, Aunt Evie," Jenny said.

And I took Angel's child into my arms, held her to me, and felt the hard shell of my old life crack away.

"How come you never had kids?" Jenny had asked me during one of our late-night talks.

"My work," I told her. "I was selfish, I guess. I wanted my life to myself."

"Sometimes do you wish you would've had them?"

"No," I said, and that was true. I loved my work, I loved to travel. I loved being alone.

Children didn't fit into the picture. They were so messy, noisy. They were always hungry. You had to spend half your life ferrying them from here to there. Years dissolved while you wiped their noses, smoothed Band-Aids on scraped knees. Every day, at least once, you'd think, God, if I could just get them grown! And then it turned out that grown was harder than anything that came before. Grown meant things couldn't be fixed anymore. Grown meant letting go.

All this, I had heard people talk about. But that night, as I helped Jenny pack to leave, I understood what it meant. "Are you sure you have everything?" I asked her stupidly, like someone's mother. "Passport, ticket? The things you bought, they're in a safe place?"

I thought, if I could come to love a child in two weeks as much as I'd come to love Jenny, how could I have borne a real daughter's departure? How could anyone?

I slept fitfully that night, waking and worrying in circles—thinking of Jenny all alone in the clinic, how frightened she must have been; thinking, what if she hadn't gone to the clinic at all, what if she'd married the boy, had the baby? I wouldn't have gone to the wedding, of course. Maybe I wouldn't even have learned about the baby until later, when the announcement came and I counted back the months from the birth date. I knew, though, the bitterness I would have felt. Again. A waste. Lost. But I wouldn't have known her, so I wouldn't have thought of her as someone lost to *me*.

This last incomprehensible thought drove me out of bed, into the dark kitchen. There, I found Jenny sitting at the table, her hands cupped around a mug of tea, her eyes closed, washed in moonlight. I started to turn away, to leave her there alone, but she blinked and saw me.

"You can't sleep either?" I sat down beside her.

She shrugged, smiled. "I thought maybe if I stayed up all night it would seem like I was here longer. Really," she said, "I got up to think—

"You know, my friend, Cara?"

I nodded.

"Like I told you before, she's real screwed up—because of her parents' divorce and all.

"So she reads all these weird books. Psychology stuff. Eight hundred and twenty-two roads to inner peace and happiness. Stuff like that. Anyhow, she told me about this thing to do: You take some problem that's bugging you and you try to really see it in your mind's eye. Then you try to see a place to *put* it, and you put it there and that makes it go away. The problem, I mean. So I thought, okay, maybe instead of trying to stop thinking about what the baby would've been like, I should think about it on purpose, make myself see it. Does that sound dumb?"

"Not dumb," I said. "Maybe, I don't know, a little dangerous—"

"Maybe." She smiled again. "Anything Cara thinks is a good idea usually is. I did it anyhow, though. I mean that's what I've been doing. Sitting here, looking at the baby in my head. It was a little girl baby," she said. "I was glad of that."

Be careful, I thought. This is real to her. I asked "Was she pretty?"

"Oh, Aunt Evie, she was. She had this funny black hair sticking out all over the place. And this little pointed chin and blue eyes. She was smiling. She had on a ruffly pink sweater with pink ribbons that I just know Grandma made for her. And little pink shoes. I looked and looked at her, it seemed like forever. Cara said that's what you're supposed to do, just keep looking at the thing until all of a sudden you know what to do."

"Did that happen?" I asked.

"Yeah," she said. "That's the weirdest part. It was like she was just floating there in my mind—real still, like the lady in your painting, and then she *was* a painting, with a beautiful gold frame all around her. And, Aunt Evie, that's when I saw that the thing to do was give her to you." She looked at me, her eyes shining with tears. "And you took her from me—

"Oh, I know it's not really real," she said. "One of Cara's wacky things, right? But it seemed so real, like it really happened."

"Well—" I smoothed her hair and drew her to me. "I don't know, maybe it's not so wacky, after all. Think about it. She *is* the perfect baby for me, the only baby I'd ever have wanted to have. No bottles, no crying. No messy diapers. Pretty as a picture—"

We laughed and cried at the same time. And in the shadowy

kitchen, the moon in the window, the real world of cars and trees and houses no more than outlines against the sky, I felt the weight of Jenny's lost child settle inside me.

Chapter Twenty

When Jenny left, Vermeer's woman looked sad to me, as if she were glancing one last time toward an empty place where someone she loved had stood, the terrible absence pressing her fingers to the keys. In fact, I thought, it could be argued that other elements of the painting spoke of sadness, as well—each tiny, isolated figure painted on each of the Delft tiles that bordered the marble floor. The empty chair, the desolate landscapes, the opaque window—the way these things seemed to surround her like a wall. The rich colors, the white light seeping through the leaded window were almost unbearably poignant played against all this. But my appreciation of the painting was not heightened or lessened by the fact that I saw it differently that day.

"Buddha's Fourth Noble Truth," Ian had said. "Everything changes." The thought made me smile. He was right, as always. And as always, it was in my work that true things found a place at last, inside me. Loving art was safe, I'd thought. It never changed. Now, this morning, I understood that a painting was like a magic trick. Captured in its lines and forms and colors, in the brushstrokes, the arrangement of objects, the objects themselves, the light and shadow was everything the artist had known or felt as he had made it. Years of schooling, years of my narrow existence inside museum walls had taught me all the words, all the proper phrases with which to talk about art, had allowed me to believe that its value lay in its superiority to real life: Art is better than we are, better than we can ever be. Now I saw that, while the art historian, the conservator I was assessed and appreciated a painting, it was the person I was at that precise moment in time who actually experienced it. The deep, secret feelings each person brought to a painting were what made it come alive. Art is all we are, and ever can be— the sum total of every person who has ever been alive.

When Ian came by the lab later, I tried to explain all this to him, but he barely listened. "You know, Evie, you could do freelance work anywhere in Europe," he said, out of the blue. "Possibly, you could get on at the Courtauld, teaching. Would you like that at all? You'd be wonderful at it. Of course, you could come on board here. But that wouldn't be suitable, really, because you shouldn't be less than head of the department and that's impossible—"

I said, "Wait. I haven't said a word about changing jobs."

"But what you told me the other night at dinner, about you and Cliff. I've been thinking about it all weekend, fretting about it. Surely, some kind of change is bound to occur—"

"Probably," I said. "But I have no idea *what.*"

"That doesn't worry you?"

"Nope," I said, smiling.

He looked unconvinced. "You will, though," he said. "This blasé attitude isn't like you, Evie. And what about Jenny? You're not distressed about her leaving, either?"

"I'm sad," I said. "Very. That's what got me thinking about the painting this morning and how so much of what you see depends on who you are. Not to mention your state of mind on any given day. You know, what I was trying to tell you before you started in advising me on my career path. You were right about Jenny, by the way. I got myself all tangled up in her life. I think I'll probably stay that way, if she's willing. And, I don't know, something strange happened. I'm just not angry at my family any more."

Ian just stared at me. I could see there was no point in trying to explain to him that what I felt was a wonderful wobbly balance, the same dangerous exhilaration a child feels, standing in the exact center of a moving teeter-totter.

The feeling held. In the week following Jenny's departure, I finished cleaning the painting, and re-lined it. I had only to fill the damaged areas and give the painting a light coat of varnish before arriving at one of those rare moments I'd built my whole life around: the paintbrush in my hand, touching the priceless canvas, echoing the rhythm of the master's touch. With luck, I would experience that instant of connection—a yes-ness—reverberating down through time.

Each night I went home to Cliff's flat. Home. I was so comfortable there, Cliff and I were so happy there together that I had begun to think of it that way. He had moved his things back the day Jenny left. Neither of us had even mentioned my returning to Dolphin Square. We settled into a quiet existence. Without Jenny there to be entertained or educated, we stayed in and read, Mozart playing on the stereo. We made love, slept together easily, the natural fit of our bodies like colors that have come together on a canvas in a perfect blend. At least for the moment, I didn't feel the need to try to envision what the story of our lives would be after this idyllic time had passed.

The way I felt about Cliff during that week after Jenny left was mirrored in the way I came to feel, finally, about the Vermeer. After I understood that it changed constantly, the painting tricked me again and did not change at all. Now when I looked at it, the light held all the elements in perfect balance and created a stillness so complete and so satisfying that any desire I'd had for narrative was forgotten.

And I saw how this flawless equilibrium had been achieved: Vermeer had been capable of seeing one small thing at a time—the way two colors lay together on the plane of a woman's face, the triangular shape of a shadow. He had faith that the sum of a thousand fragments, clearly rendered, would make one beautiful, nameable thing: a woman, a necklace of pearls, a life. As I prepared to begin the last phase of the restoration, the last phase of my time with Cliff, this intuition seemed like a gift.

I hadn't mentioned anything to him about reading Metta's postcard, but as the date grew nearer, the return of his children was on my mind. August fifteenth passed, and the following morning Cliff phoned me at the lab to tell me that Metta had called his office. I still felt guilty about having read the postcard, but I was glad, too, because it had allowed me to prepare what I thought was the right thing to say.

"You'll want to have the children for the weekend, of course. That's no problem. I'll just stay at Dolphin Square."

I hadn't expected him to assume I'd stay at his flat while Robin and Monica were there. I certainly hadn't expected him to say, "Evie, please, will you drive over with me to get them?"

In the end, we compromised. I'd spend the night at Dolphin Square, but since it seemed so important to him, I agreed to spend Saturday with the three of them. That morning, he dropped me outside a pub in the busy village where they lived.

"Give me an hour," he said. "It's a ten minute drive from here to the house." He paused, abashed. "But Metta likes me to sit down and have a cup of tea. There are always things she needs to tell me."

"Fine," I said. So why did I feel abandoned, watching his Land Rover climb the hill and disappear? We had decided on this as the best plan. Metta knew that I was going on the outing with Cliff and the children, but although I was curious about Cliff's ex-wife, I did not want to meet her.

I did not want to go into the dark pub either, where I would sit alone imagining Cliff and Metta drinking tea in the house where they had lived together. I checked my watch and set out walking. The village was like any number of others I'd seen: pretty stone cottages with trellised roses, window-boxes bursting with bright flowers. Shop windows displayed pastries, antiques, crafts. It wasn't as if I were the only outsider there—big tour buses were parked all along the narrow streets. But I felt strange as I walked along, at the same time conspicuous and invisible. I thought, Cliff might have shopped at this hardware store I'm passing, Metta at this bakery. Her woven goods might be for sale in the shop advertising "Authentic Cotswolds Crafts." Her friends might be peering from the windows of these houses.

I followed High Street down the hill, turned into a cobbled lane, and walked along the low stone wall of the village churchyard. When I came to the open gate, I entered. The morning sun bounced off the windows of the church, pebbling some of the graves with light. The glare hurt my eyes, so I walked from the sunlight into the shadow of the church, and around to the side. Many of the tombstones there were tilted, chipped. They weren't white, like the tombstones near the church entrance. Lichens, mosses, molds had speckled them with gray and rust and gold and green. Tufts of grass grew up, lush, emerald, around them. Wild daisies floated above the green. I sat awhile on a stone bench, hoping to lose myself there among those finished lives, but I could not stop thinking about Cliff and Metta, talking.

I'd seen the living room of their house in photographs. Cut flowers on a table, light streaming in through mullioned windows. It wasn't the image of them, leaning toward each other—earnest, civilized—that I couldn't bear, that sent me from the shadowy haven of the cemetery, back to the glare of sunlight in the street. It was thinking, what are they saying?

When Cliff pulled up in front of the pub, Monica was in the front seat of the Rover. She stared straight ahead, as if she hadn't seen me; then Cliff turned and said something to her. She sat perfectly still for a long moment, while I stood on the curb. Finally, she opened the door, got out, and climbed into the back seat with her brother.

I said, "Thanks," and introduced myself to both of them as I slid into the car. Robin blushed and muttered hello. Monica just said, "Yes," and raised an eyebrow.

"Could you put this in, Dad?" she asked, handing a cassette tape over the seat. And Cliff did, filling the car with the worst music I had ever heard: discordant, screamy. Music I'd never have believed I'd be grateful to hear.

I watched them in the rear view mirror just as I'd watched Jenny a week before. Robin was a handsome, sturdy boy of eleven, with Cliff's blond hair and ruddy coloring. He did not appear to have been blessed with Cliff's personality, however, or his energy. He sat scrunched into his corner of the backseat, staring out the window, occasionally glancing at Monica, who completely ignored him. She moved in time to the music, her eyes blank. She'd probably been a sturdy child once, like her brother; but now, at fifteen, she was pudgy. Her complexion was spotty, her face peeling from overexposure to the sun.

"I'll wait here," she said, when we pulled in and came to a stop at the Cotswolds Farm Park. "This place is boring."

"Get out of the car, Monica," Cliff said, and opened her door.

She reached between the seats and took her tape from the tape deck. Then, with great deliberation, she inserted it into the Walkman she took from her purse. She put on her earphones. The music was turned up so loud, it seeped out of them in a whispery roar.

"Mummy said any time Monica's upset, she should just listen to her music and calm down," Robin said.

"That music?" Cliff asked. "That music calms her?"

"Mummy said—"

"Your mum's not here, is she?

Cliff was staring so hard at Monica that he did not see the misery that crossed the boy's face.

I said, "Leave her, Cliff. Maybe in a bit, she'll come after us."

"She'll come if she's hungry." Robin bent over and put his face next to his sister's. He puffed his cheeks out. "Fatty. Won't miss *lunch*, will you?"

Monica elbowed him in the chest so hard that, for a moment, I thought he might fall.

Cliff glanced back at his daughter one last time, then headed down the path, Robin and I trailing behind him. The farm park stood on a high plateau among the Cotswolds hills, and as we walked, I could see the tops of trees and houses nestled among them. A tiny village in the distance looked like a set of the pretty little ceramic houses I'd seen for sale in the shops.

"It's beautiful," I said.

"It is, isn't it?" Cliff stopped and looked out. "We used to come here all the time when the children were little. I mentioned that Bruce Watkins, the owner, is a friend of mine, didn't I? A colleague, actually. Amazing fellow. You remember Mr. Watkins, don't you, Robin?"

"Weird," Robin said. "Mucking about with all those chickens."

When I met the man a few moments later, my first thought was, Well, here's something Robin and I see eye-to-eye on.

He was tall and gaunt and balding, with skin so thin that the blue veins of his arms were visible. His face and scalp were pink from the sun. There were broken blood vessels, delicate as snipped threads, all along his cheekbones. We shook hands, and mine felt lost inside his huge one. His other hand was occupied keeping good hold of the goose he was carrying, tucked under his arm.

"Shetland goose," he said, as if introducing it. "Very rare indeed."

Cliff had explained to me that Watkins's farm park was dedicated to preserving breeds of animals that had once proliferated throughout England and were now threatened by extinction. Watkins bred them, and had built fenced walkways throughout the park so that tourists could view them in their natural surroundings.

"I want to show you something," Cliff said. "What Watkins and I have been working on together."

Robin sighed. "Can't I just go look round by myself?"

Cliff hesitated, then shrugged, releasing him.

When Robin was out of sight, Cliff took my hand and we followed Watkins, who led us to a barn. Inside it was dim and smelled of hay and manure. Light fell in slats onto the dusty floor. Watkins stopped before a pen, where a mother goat lay with her kid.

"She's smaller than normal, you'll notice," he said to me, still clutching the Shetland goose. "More compact."

"Yes," I said.

"It's what we believe goats looked like a thousand years ago."

"We call it the NIWRAD Project." Cliff grinned. "Darwin backwards. Watkins is breeding these goats and some sheep, as well, for a museum I want to open in a few years time. A Roman villa, exactly as it would have been. Even the animals."

Really, I was speechless. I listened to Watkins describe some ceramic tiles they'd excavated on the site of the nearby Chedworth Villa some years before, imprinted with the hooves of sheep and goats. "The animals probably wandered into an area where the tiles were drying. In any case, the imprints have been invaluable to me, breeding backwards. This little one—" He gestured toward the sleeping kid. "When he's full grown, we'll press its hoof into clay and see if it matches up with the original." He regarded me intensely. "I get closer and closer. I believe, in my lifetime, I'll accomplish it."

"Isn't that wonderful," I said.

When Watkins excused himself at last and went off to put the goose back in its pen, I asked Cliff, "Why did we come here?"

He looked surprised. "I wanted you to see the place," he said. "Meet Watkins. He's quite a character, don't you think?"

"You wanted *me* to see it."

"Yes."

"Look." I pointed to the big oak tree near the entrance of the park. Robin sat beneath it. Monica had emerged from the car and sat beside him, her yellow earphones still intact.

"They're being bloody difficult," Cliff said.

"But, Cliff, think. You brought *me* here. Don't you see? You want to show me this place, you want to visit with your friend, you want to have a pleasant outing with the children you haven't seen all summer.

You can't do all those things at once."

"I don't know why not," he said. "I don't know why I shouldn't try to salvage something of the day. And as for having a pleasant outing with the children, I assure you, they don't behave any better when I devote myself to pleasing them. They sit and stare stupidly no matter what we do. I pay for the house they live in, their school fees, their holidays—that's all I am to them, the person who pays the bills, the person who has to be appeased so that he'll keep on paying them. Metta preps them, you know. If Daddy does this, or Daddy does that—

"If Daddy upsets you, turn your horrid music as loud as it will go. Ah, bugger this," Cliff said, "Bugger it all," and stalked away toward the car park.

The children watched him pass, then looked toward me, waiting to see what I'd do. It occurred to me, suddenly, that I'd left the letter we'd gotten from Jenny this morning on the dash and, scattered with it, the happy photographs of the three of us together that she'd sent. Surely Monica must have noticed them there, sitting in the front seat on the way to collect me at the pub. Perhaps she'd insisted on staying in the car because she meant to look at them. The thought made me feel sorry for her. If she'd read the letter, she'd see there was a special connection between Jenny and her father. She'd feel like she was losing him all over again.

Cliff was right. Jenny would have loved today. That would be obvious to Monica from the pictures of her smiling at all the other odd places Cliff had taken her. She wouldn't have to think much further to figure out that Jenny was the kind of girl Cliff wished Monica herself had turned out to be.

Of course, she couldn't be expected to understand that affinity existed outside the realm of all rational human arrangements. I was the last person Monica would want to tell her that Cliff's affinity for Jenny did not negate or even subtract from his love for her. Still, if I'd been braver, I might have tried. I could have said, "Look at me and my Aunt Lily," and explained how I finally understood that she'd have been my favorite aunt, the most important person in my childhood, no matter what the circumstances of my life had been. I had more in common with her than with anyone else in my family. Peg was nothing like me at all. Even if she had been my real mother, we'd have had trouble getting along.

The irony of the predicament I found myself in now did not escape me. All those times I'd been snotty and stubborn, and now here I was face-to-face with the unhappy, recalcitrant children whose father I loved. What would Peg do, I thought, and saw myself, defiant, scowling. Mostly, she ignored my bad behavior. She carried on as if I were the most compliant child ever born.

On her worst days, she'd tried harder to please me than Cliff was trying to please Robin and Monica this morning. He'd disappeared completely. He might have doubled back to ask Watkins some pressing question about those ridiculous Roman goats, he might be lost in one of the ever-present books or magazines he kept at the ready wherever he went. Whatever. He'd honed a whole kit of avoidances; that, I knew.

I looked at Robin and Monica, sitting glumly under the oak tree and, as unpleasant as they had been to me earlier, I couldn't help but feel sorry for them. I couldn't bear to let the whole day be spoiled, without even trying to redeem it. I made myself smile. This might very well be the first of many appeasements that would fall to me should Cliff and I end up together, I thought, walking toward them.

Chapter Twenty-one

"*I* don't know, maybe they were stunned by my cheerful invitation to lunch," I said to Ian the next afternoon. "Or maybe I'll figure out eventually that this is some kind of ritual with them: aggravating Cliff to an explosion, then doing a Jekyll and Hyde on him and turning into virtual caricatures of meek English school children. In any case, they sat down and had their lunch and neither of them made a single nasty remark the rest of the time I was with them."

We were at the Tate. A busman's holiday, Ian called it. We made our way through the galleries at a snail's pace, not exactly looking at the pictures, but feeling the presence of them as we talked. The high drama of the magnificent Turners, the Pre-Raphaelites—Rossetti's Beatrix, Millais's lovely, dead Ophelia in her riverbed grave—fitted the mood I was in. Rather to my surprise, I found myself thoroughly enjoying relating the disastrous events of the day before, even though I'd been miserable living them and had spent a sleepless night re-living them, to boot.

"So you won them over then," Ian said.

"Round one, maybe. They were hardly forthcoming. I asked Monica if she'd enjoyed her holiday in France and she said, 'Oh, yes, it was lovely.' Period. I told Robin that my parents lived a stone's throw from the Indianapolis Motor Speedway—he's crazy about car racing, according to Cliff. 'Oh, really,' Robin said. Like, big deal. But they weren't horrible, as they'd been earlier.

"I mean, why *would* they like me? If there's one thing in the world I ought to know it's that children want their real parents together, and anyone who appears to keep that from happening is the enemy. How could it be any other way?"

"They are ghastly, though, aren't they?" Ian asked. "I told you."

"Oh, honestly, neither one of us know the first thing about children. You know that. So how would we know whether those two are any more ghastly than the norm? And I'll tell you something, Cliff doesn't know a whole lot more than we do. He's not very good with them, Ian. Impatient, and not very understanding. After the way he was with Jenny, it surprised me. But then I don't know all that's gone on because of the divorce, whether he's always been that way with them. Whether today was some kind of aberration. I guess I don't know very much about his real life at all—"

"Yet you're radiant," Ian said. "Look at you." He regarded me with an almost pensive expression.

"I'm just happy." I felt foolish saying it. My throat felt prickly, and my eyes burned, as if I might begin to cry. I remembered Jenny's convoluted explanation of the idea she'd learned in her world lit class: joy and sadness becoming one thing. Did it apply to yes and no, too? And to the dead weight of fear merging with this unstoppable rising, swelling, opening out? I wished that she were with me so that I could say, "I think I know now what you meant."

I got back to the flat first. It felt different inside now that the children had been there. I sat a long time in Cliff's bedroom, where the presence of my things made me feel less an intruder. I told myself that tomorrow the cleaning woman would come and make the children's rooms look unlived in again. But until then, Robin's bed was a tangle of sheets and blankets. In Monica's room, there was a dusting of powder on the dressing table, Kleenex with lipstick blottings in the wastebasket. She'd left a gold barrette on the bedside table.

I looked at the print of "Woman Standing at the Virginal" that was propped on the dresser, and thought of Vermeer, the man. I imagined him in his luminous corner, endlessly arranging and rearranging the little harpsichord, the blue chair, the paintings on the wall, the woman herself—her hands, her shawl, her hair ornament—until he hit upon the perfect balance of light and shadow, the perfect balance of horizontals, verticals and elegant curves. And all the while, there were children careening through the house, an art dealership to oversee, creditors waiting to be paid. When I considered what I knew of his day-to-day life, the wonderful, resonant stillness of the painting seemed inexplicable to me again. I tidied the kitchen, poured myself a glass of wine and carried the bottle and an extra glass with me into the darkening study. I thought, if I could only know whether that stillness had been born of the way Vermeer felt inside, or whether he had painted what he yearned to feel—what he desperately needed but knew could never be achieved in his real life—it might reveal something important about what was possible in my own life, with Cliff.

It was nearly ten when I heard his footsteps, then his key in the lock. I couldn't see him from where I sat, but I heard him take a deep breath as he closed the door behind him. I imagined him running his fingers through his hair, craning his neck from side to side, stretching. Then he took two steps forward into my vision. He had on a white T-shirt imprinted with the route of the Grand Prix at Monaco.

"Present from Robin?" I asked.

My voice startled him. "Yes." He moved toward me.

I said, "You look tired."

"Fagged. Had a bit of a scene with Metta, I'm afraid."

"Scene?" I poured him a glass of wine.

"Metta always wants to talk. She's a great one for *communicating,* as she says. I hate that bloody word. She's never figured out it's what you do—or don't do—that tells a person how you feel. In any case, despite the fact that we've seen the divorce through, she's decided she wants me to come back. She says if we'll just communicate, there's no reason we can't all get on. It's what the children want. Metta says I owe it to them to give it another try."

I looked at his face, and the pain I saw there told me what he could not say. "You're going then," I said.

"Evie—"

"Please. Don't even try to explain. It's my own fault, anyway."

"Evie," he repeated.

But I went on, an ugly bitterness bursting from somewhere inside me. "Such perfect timing," I said. "Another few weeks, and I'll be gone. You'll have had your fling and you can go back to Metta and the children and have the perfect family you always wanted and never, ever feel guilty again."

He touched my arm.

"Oh, I know. You'll think of me so fondly—"

"Evie, I love you," he said.

"Then God damn love," I said, and started to cry. I sat there, my face buried in my hands, and every hurt I'd ever known flooded into me. Every lost, loved face presented itself and faded away. "I hate this," I said, finally calming down a little. "I was stupid to let myself fall in love with you, when I knew—"

"Knew what?" said Cliff. "You don't know bloody Hell, Evie. Would you quit second-guessing me and let me tell you what I want?"

"To go on the way we are?" I said. "That's impossible, isn't it? To carry on an affair whenever it's convenient?"

"I *said*, would you let me tell you what I want?"

The urgency in his voice stopped me cold. I reached to pick up my glass, but saw that my hand was shaking, so I drew it away. "All right," I said. "What do you want?"

"You," he said. "My Romans. Some peace of mind. I'm not going back to Metta and the children, Evie. I can't."

"You're not?" I said. "Not ever?"

"No." He put his hand on mine, and I couldn't help it, I felt my fingers close around it. "Do you believe me?" he asked.

"Yes," I said. And I felt his words settle inside me, as if what we were together had finally claimed me, taken on a kind of weight. Strange, it didn't frighten me. I had no idea how it would all turn out, no idea what this moment would ultimately mean; but I felt a sense of calm descend upon me as Cliff talked to me about his life.

"Of course, it's ever so easy to see it now," he said. "Looking back, it seems I should have known right from the beginning that everything Metta believed in was worse than absurd. God knows, Ian saw it—as he likes to remind me. But I loved her then. And I wanted my own family desperately. I let her make that safe place for us and let her protect me and the children in it. It took me years to see Robin and Monica as they really were. And to see myself, too. To see that I was dying.

"Then, suddenly, I wanted everything. All the time. Rather like Jenny," he said, almost smiling. "Once I'd left Metta, there was no one who could equal my energy. I'd teach my classes and work in the library hours on end. Most days I'd pop over to some site and have a go at it with the diggers. I was out most every evening. There are any number of people who'll have you to a meal if they can count on your being charming, you know; and I was. Then I'd come back to the flat and be Giles Bardon most of the night.

"I was doing that when I met you, Evie. I'd been doing it for a long time and feeling quite exhausted, though I'd never have admitted it, even to myself. Then I met you and it felt like coming home.

"I run all this through my mind again and again. I can't go back to Metta and the children—I *won't* go back. But, at the same time, I know I can't go live your life in America, I can't ask you to stay here and live mine —"

"But I'm here now," I said. "We're here together."

He shook his head. "But how long? A month; two, if you drag things out. Then what?"

The sense of calm that had fallen upon me stayed with me now, amazed me when I looked at him and saw the doubt he felt, the fear he felt for us reflected in his face. It was his voice I heard inside my head, the voice I had begun to hear quite regularly now and knew that I would always hear. I couldn't help smiling at the comfort it gave me.

"Aren't you forgetting your own lesson?" I spoke his own words back to him. "Reality is this moment—any moment—underpinned by all that was. If you really believe that, isn't it enough to say that now will be the underpinning of what will come next? Whatever it is. So what's the problem?"

"This mess with Metta and the children," Cliff said miserably. "While they were gone, and it was only the two of us—and Jenny—I felt differently. As if there might actually be a 'next.' But now they're back, it seems I've got so much of myself tangled up in the bloody mess we've made of our lives that I don't know if I'll ever be fit to be with someone else. With you. It only seems fair—"

"Cliff," I said. "Please. I'm a middle-aged woman, remember? There's no father about to appear, asking your intentions. The person I am, the life I've led and mean to keep on leading—well, any kind of traditional relationship is out of the question anyway. Do you think I want children? A house in the country? You know I don't. Right now it's enough for me to know I want you in my life, to believe that it matters so much there's bound to be an answer—"

"Wait a minute," I said. "I want to show you something."

I went to the bedroom and brought back my print of the Vermeer. "That again," Cliff said, and smiled for the first time that evening. "That again. See that rectangle of light on the blue velvet chair?" He nodded.

"Look closely. There's no way to explain where it's coming from. Not from the famous Vermeer window, that's for sure. The angle's all wrong. But not knowing doesn't spoil the painting. If anything, it enhances the mysterious effect. And you certainly can't argue that just because you can't explain the light, it isn't there."

"True," he said. But he looked confused.

"Well, there's a wonderful story about the painter, Braque, looking at this picture with a friend," I told him. "The friend commented, with some aggravation, that the light on the chair had no logical source. Braque is said to have smiled and responded, "Ah, but it comes from another canvas. One you haven't seen yet."

"And you think another canvas will appear for us, do you? And explain everything?"

I went to him. "We'll paint it," I said.

He was quiet in the morning. Over breakfast, we talked about the week ahead, established the times our schedules would allow us to be together. I chattered about beginning the next phase of the repair. I'd mix a putty of the same composition as Vermeer's original ground, and use it to fill the gouged areas, building and shaving until they were perfectly level with the rest of the ground. Then, with a delicate tool, I'd etch the criss-cross pattern of the canvas onto the surface of the filled spaces.

"How long will it take?" he asked.

"The filling, maybe ten days. Then a coat of varnish. Then a few weeks for the inpainting."

"You'll be done with it all by the end of September, won't you?"

I nodded. The tears that stung my eyes caught me off guard, and I got up quickly to clear our breakfast things away.

Filling was tedious, and I could not concentrate for more than a few hours at a time. When my eyes hurt and my head ached, I'd leave the museum and walk the city, as I had during those first few weeks of my stay. The bright display of flags along Whitehall, the Royal Horse Guards in their red uniforms, the bronze Churchill caught in an eternal stride toward the Houses of Parliament—everything about London was familiar to me now, and almost unbearably dear. I'd pause on a street corner, the city whirling all around me, and I'd think, I am here. Not since my time in Florence, years ago, had I felt so present in my own life.

Evenings and stolen afternoons, I spent with Cliff. We went to the theater, to films. We had long dinners, took walks afterwards in the deep twilight. The day after I had completed the filling and given the damaged areas a thin coat of varnish to prepare them for the inpainting, we took a picnic to a spot Cliff knew along Pilgrims' Way. From where we sat, high on a hill, we could see the cottages and the church spire of the village, Shere. Green fields surrounded us, stretching all the way to the horizon, black flocks of birds wheeled and settled, wheeled and settled, and it occurred to me that the scene probably looked no different now from the way it had looked to the pilgrims who rested in this same spot hundreds of years ago. In the quiet I could imagine them, ghostly among the trees, looking long at the endlessness, the spires of Canterbury still no more than a dream.

I thought, surely any minute Cliff's going to tell me that Pilgrims' Way had sprung up over the remnants of Roman roads. Or say, "Listen! The mystery takes a turn and Giles Bardon finds himself with the American bride on a hillside near Shere!"

But he lay on the blanket we'd spread, his eyes closed. I longed for his electric smile. I wanted him to leap up and embrace the world again, to wrestle to understand it, dragging me kicking and screaming along. Instead, he drew me down to lie alongside him, held me so closely that I could feel his heart beating against my own.

Chapter Twenty-two

*I*knew how to grind the pigments exactly as Vermeer would have done three hundred years ago, how to add the correct proportion of nut oil and balsam and Venice turpentine to match the original colors for retouching. But oils darken and change throughout the whole life of a painting. If I used Vermeer's method, the old and new pigments would change at different rates, and in time the repaired areas would become obvious. What I needed was the illusion of a perfect match. So, for durability of tone, I chose tempera, a mixture of pigment and egg yolk that the medieval painters used. I would lay down the ground color, then seal it with a coat of shellac. When it dried, I'd set my palette with the blue of the woman's shawl, the wheat yellow of her satin skirt, the flesh tones of Cupid's foot, the gray-blue of the wall. I'd apply the color to the surface with the finest brush, isolating each layer with a coat of shellac so that the new paint could be easily identified by future conservators and, if necessary, easily removed. Last, I would work up the flat tempera in delicate oil glazes to give the colors a luminous quality.

I was ready to begin. The woman waited, tilted back slightly on the easel. But I could not bring myself to touch my brush to the palette. Had Vermeer ever known the grief that overwhelmed me? I closed my eyes and let the image of his sturdy milkmaid rise within me: the abundance of bread before her, her earthen pitcher spilling milk endlessly through time. I saw his pregnant woman in blue bent over her letter, washed in light. And his woman in gold and ermine, caught in an anxious glance—the fingers of her left hand still on the frets of her mandolin while accepting a sealed envelope with her right. He made them and had to let them go. How had he borne it?

I wanted to see those paintings again, to go back to that time when the daily sight of them had nourished me. I wanted to walk along the canals in Amsterdam and see myself moving, reflected in the water. To sit in Vondel Park under the trees, to while away a long rainy afternoon in a brown café.

"Go," Ian said when I told him. "Take Cliff with you."

"I don't know," I said. "Did the Romans get to Amsterdam?" I was only half joking.

Ian laughed, and answered in his most tutorial tone, "They certainly got to Domberg. There, in the harbor, archaeologists found the remains of votive statues that the Romans had thrown into the ocean as offerings to the gods when their ships landed safely. But full Romanization ended south of Leiden—"

"Are you making all that up?" I asked.

"Ha," he said. "You ask me that, knowing how long I've known Cliff? I know more about the bloody Romans by accident than most people learn on purpose in a lifetime. Really, take him with you, Evie. It'd do him good to get outside himself. To go someplace where he doesn't know everything and half a measure more."

At first, Cliff said no.

I said, "Come on. Just a few days. We'll fly, we won't waste any time that way. I really want to see those paintings before I start the inpainting. I want you to see them, too."

"I can't, Evie. I'm too busy." He started listing all the projects he was working on.

It was just an idea I'd had, going to Amsterdam to see the Vermeers. An impulse, not one I'd have necessarily acted upon if I hadn't mentioned it to Ian. And even then, I might not have assumed, when Ian suggested it, that Cliff would go along. But I was caught short by his peremptory refusal. "But you'd drop everything in a minute if what I wanted to do was go look at some Roman site," I said. "You would, wouldn't you?"

He didn't answer.

"Cliff," I said. "I've tromped all over England with you for months, looking at whatever you wanted me to see. Now I want *you* to go someplace. I want to show *you* something and you won't go. Explain that, will you? Because I don't think it's fair."

By now, I was shaking. "Well, *will* you explain?" I repeated, and when he didn't immediately, I got up and walked out of the pub where we were eating supper. Back at the flat, I started throwing clothes into my suitcase, muttering. I was going to Amsterdam, by God, and I was going to go to the airport now and get the first flight out. To hell with Cliff. No way I was going to be here when he came back from the pub. We'd just argue again. Or, worse, act like everything was fine.

Oh, why had I told Ian to discontinue the rent on the flat at Dolphin Square just two days before? It left me with nowhere to go but Amsterdam, even though it would be midnight before I could get there. And I had no hotel booked. And I really didn't want to be alone. I was feeling extremely sorry for myself, and more than a little foolish as well by the time I walked out the door.

When I saw Cliff sitting on the front steps, I felt myself go hollow inside. But I hesitated only a moment, then went on past him without a word. I didn't realize that he'd followed me until I got on the train at Sloane Square and he slid in the door just before it closed. He sat down beside me. "I'll go," he said when he caught his breath.

"You can't go," I said. "You didn't even bring anything with you."

"What do I need?" He shrugged. "I went in and grabbed my passport. I'll buy whatever I need when I get there. In any case, I'm going—"

"You are not," I said, too loud. I felt myself flush. The train was crowded and people were looking at us.

"I am."

I stared straight ahead. I wasn't about to be reduced to squabbling in public with him. We rode two stops to Gloucester Road, where we had to make the transfer for Heathrow. Cliff started to pick up my suitcase and carry it for me, but I glared at him. He pulled his hand back as if I'd slapped it. We walked through the tunnels to the platform in silence, boarded the train on the Piccadilly line.

"Evie, please. I'm sorry," Cliff said when we sat down. "I don't know why I didn't want to go with you. Sometimes I think I don't know anything at all."

His last words made me remember what he had said to Jenny at Avebury. They brought that day back to me—and Silchester and every other day we'd spent together in the past months. Now here we were on the train, hurtling toward Heathrow and Amsterdam. We knew as little as we ever had, but we were still together—as unlikely as the stone circle at Avebury, as real.

I felt the anger drain from me at last. But I felt weak without it, afraid to speak for fear that I would start to cry. I let Cliff put his hand on my hand, though. When we got to the airport, I let him take my suitcase. I followed him to the ticket counter where he bought two tickets on the next flight to Amsterdam, which would be leaving in less than an hour.

He knew not to talk to me. Not while we waited. Not on the flight over. Not even after he'd booked a room for that night at a hotel near the airport and we were alone there. By then, we were both exhausted. I turned down the covers on the big bed and lay down, still completely dressed. Cliff lay down beside me. There was the roar of the jets taking off and landing. The drone of traffic on the highway. An occasional rustling or bumping along the otherwise quiet corridor. The digital clock blinked: 12:06, 12:07, 12:08. Not far away, the still water in the canals shone in the moonlight and the tall, narrow houses stood silent, their stepped gables making dark patterns against the starry night. The Vermeers waited. Day or night, it was all the same to them.

"Evie," Cliff said finally, just my name.

I turned to him and wept.

Now I was the one drenched in sadness. The red crumble of brick beneath my feet, the flash of bicycle spokes in sunlight, the wavery reflection of trees in the water took me back to that earlier time. Every turning, every rise seemed to bring another memory, each one bursting full-blown, a perfect picture in my mind's eye. I stood before the house in the Jordaan, remembering the room I had lived in there. Spare, immaculately clean, with whitewashed walls and ancient Delft tile baseboards, my Vermeer prints propped on the scrubbed oak table I used for a desk. The room Joris had come to that one time.

I looked a long time at the mullioned window on the second story. Sometimes, in the very early mornings, I had stood perfectly still in the dove-gray light streaming through it and imagined I was one of Vermeer's women. The memory of this was so vivid that, if I'd been alone, I might have believed I was the young woman I had been sixteen years before, given myself up to the pure yearning of that more simple life.

As it was, Cliff held me in the present. Having decided to take the trip with me, he'd thrown himself into it completely, behaving as if we were on some kind of mission. He wanted to know all about the grant I'd won to intern at the Rijksmuseum, about the Vermeer that had been stolen from the museum in Brussels—sliced from its frame—and later found rolled up under a mattress in a dingy apartment above a gas station. He wanted to know about Amsterdam at that time—overrun with hippies, who'd set up camp in Vondel Park and wandered around the city all day, dazed and unkempt. The relief I felt seeing him exhibit his old enthusiasm, my joy at being with him did not diffuse my memories. Or shake my sadness. Rather, all these sensations mingled and made my heart race. My own voice seemed to echo inside my head, as if I'd been given the wrong dose of a potent drug.

"Lunch?" he said now. "Take me someplace you loved when you lived here. Your favorite place. What was it?"

I took him to a brown café on the Prinsengracht. Cool and dim and golden inside, it smelled of coffee and cinnamon, just as I remembered. Old Delft tiles of sailing ships decorated the walls, brass lanterns hung from the rough wood timbers. Cheerful waitresses served us plates of pancakes so thin that they curled at the edges—heaped high with sliced apples, covered with whipped cream. We sat near the window and, though the day was warm and the trees along the Prinsengracht were full and green, what came back to me was sitting in exactly the same spot with Joris on countless winter days—the bleak light seeping in through the yellowed half-curtains, illuminating the tangle of plants on the window sill, then a section of the thick red and blue patterned rug that covered the table, and then finally my own sweatered arm resting there. It was hard light with little warmth, but it suited me. I was filled up with the work we were doing together, I was burning. The cold winter light had calmed me.

Now, cannily, Cliff asked, "And when you used to come here, were you in love?"

I had not told him everything about my time here. When I'd spoken of Joris, it had been as my mentor, the person who had taught me how to work. But I saw now that Cliff had guessed how it really was between us.

"Yes," I said. "Not like we are, though. Joris and I did love each other, but he was happy in his family life, too. So all we felt for each other poured into our work. It was there in all he taught me. And it was enough; it was, in a way, better than what we might have had. At least, that's what I believed then.

"It's funny, though, how things look different to you as you grow older. Joris was in his late forties when I met him, just a little older than I am now. I've always thought of my year in Amsterdam from my point of view. I was still so young then. Barely thirty when I left. I knew how *I* felt. I accepted how Joris felt, but it's only now that I can really understand it—

"At this age, it's as if you have a box of time left, a certain size and shape of time, and you have to decide how you're going to use it. It's not the same as thinking about retirement: will you go to Florida or Arizona or the South of France? It's a pocket of time between the years of your life that make you who you *are* and the moment when you realize that everything that will ultimately define who you *were* has already happened to you. It's your last real chance for a completely different life."

"Mid-life crisis," Cliff said.

"I don't think it's that simple. Everyone has some kind of midlife crisis these days, but for most people it means little more than coming to accept the way things are. They slow down, buy an expensive sportscar or a new wardrobe to make up for waking up and realizing that they don't look so good anymore. They're growing old, someday they're going to die. This thing I'm talking about doesn't happen to everyone. It's like an opening, a secret doorway. It can come in the disguise of a person, or a city, or a job. Some kind of sickness, even. It can be anything that stops time for a little while and lets you see that you can still change everything, if you only have the courage—

"Joris didn't have the courage," I said. "That's what I see now. I don't mean what he decided wasn't right. It probably was right for him. Because you not only have to have the courage to do the thing, make the break with your own life, but you have to hold on and see it through. I don't think he could have done that. He loved his old life too well. But what I wonder is, once the window opens onto that other world,

can you ever forget it? I wonder sometimes whether Joris really did go
back to the way things were before we met."

"You don't know?"

"I never saw him again. We wrote for awhile, but his letters were,
I don't know, unsatisfying somehow. Cheerful, newsy. They didn't tell
me anything about the way his life with Anneke was going. But then I
didn't really know how it had been between them before. Their lives
seemed perfect to me when I knew them—serene and orderly."

"The doll, the book, the blanket again," Cliff said. "That still
center."

"Yes, I suppose so. I just know that, then, I'd have given anything
to live the rest of my life with him. And when any hope of that was
lost, I set him on the shelf in my mind with Rob and Aunt Lily, and
decided I would make my own still place."

"And you stayed there until I came crashing into it."

"True," I said. "Until you came crashing into it."

"It *is* the kind of moment you've described, though, isn't it? What's
happened to us these past months. The trick doorway suddenly opening. Could we go backwards? If we turn away from it now, could it be
as if we'd never met?"

"No," I said. "At least for me, that would be impossible."

"Then we're *doomed* to be together," Cliff said, but he was smiling.

More than an hour had passed since we'd sat down. We'd long
ago finished our pancakes, the last of our coffee had cooled. Now the
light shifted, and we were pooled in warm sunlight, almost too warm.

"So," I said. "What next?"

"The paintings. And go from there," he said.

We followed the Prinsengracht to Spiegelsgracht, which was lined
with antique shops and galleries. It had been my favorite route to work,
I told Cliff. I rode my old battered bicycle out of my way every morning to take it because I loved the moment when I turned onto
Spiegelgracht, and the Gothic towers of the Rijksmuseum rose up before me like a dream. Now bicycles and mopeds zoomed past us as we
walked toward the museum. We crossed the bridge over the
Singlegracht, where tourists gathered in droves, snapping pictures.

To the right of the main entrance and around the corner, hidden from view, was the long rickety green shack where museum employees kept their bicycles. There was the door I had entered every morning. I had walked a labyrinth of corridors, crossing through the museum proper at one point, to the elevator which carried me to the lab in the southeast tower. From there, the city had looked like one of those ancient maps that showed not only the ringed network of canals crossed by streets and alleyways, but green *pleins* and church spires and weather vanes and the red tile roofs of houses.

Once inside, Cliff and I walked straight down the long, skylit gallery, past the tourists standing ten-deep before Rembrandt's "Nightwatch," into the room where the Vermeers were hung, all four on one wall. It was crowded there, too. Waiting for our turn, I listened to the melody of voices speaking in a half-dozen different languages or more. *Lumiere, luz, licht.* In each one, clearly, repeatedly, the word for "light" emerged.

The paintings were just as I remembered them: jewel-like and at the same time utterly ordinary, more familiar to me than members of my own family.

"The Woman in Blue," pregnant, lost in her letter—oblivious to her abandoned pearls, the scarf, the wooden box with its lid tilted back, the wrinkled envelope that are arranged so beautifully before her on the table in the gentle light cast through an invisible window.

"The Milkmaid," her apron rendered in startling cobalt, the sleeves of her dress in velvety green. The plainness of her surroundings, her plain face, her muscular forearm tensed, the curve of her hand supporting the pitcher from which a thin bluish thread of milk pours forever into an earthen bowl cannot possibly add up to such aching loveliness, you think, looking and looking—amazed because they do.

"The Little Street," its geometry of gables, chimneys, rooftops, shuttered windows, and doors so pleasing, so completely evocative of the simple goodness of the people who live there, the richness of such lives, that it is jarring to look closely and realize that the people themselves are no more than quick gestures of color, mere suggestions of women working, children at play.

And "The Love Letter," the painting I had helped to repair. I had to clasp my hands behind my back to keep from reaching to touch the places I knew Joris's hand had touched so long ago, places my own hand had touched. I concentrated instead on the woman's lemon yellow dress trimmed in ermine; the maid behind her, one arm akimbo; the blue pillow, the laundry basket, the pair of slippers on the black and white patterned floor. I looked so long that there was nothing but color against color and I could see the way Vermeer had patiently constructed each figure, each object, each shadow, each point of light.

A sense of peace fell over me then. I was transported to the cozy stone library of my childhood. I was eleven again, sitting at one of the long tables—joyful, leafing through the big volumes of beautiful pictures I'd discovered. Mine. And I felt Aunt Lily near me, as lovely as the woman in blue. She *became* the woman, washed in light, the child she'd longed for now forever inside her.

Glancing at "The Milkmaid" again, I saw Peg.

I saw my young self, too, screaming at her. I hate you, I hate you! I couldn't remember why I'd said it, just the sound of my voice screaming. The way it felt in my throat. I saw Peg stop what she was doing in the kitchen and turn toward me, her hand still poised above the countertop. "Oh, Evie," was all she said.

I knew that I'd go back. Sooner or later I'd have to collect the things Aunt Lily had left me. I needed to see Angel, wanted to see Jenny. And it was time for me to set things right with Peg. I didn't know if I'd be able to say, honestly, that I loved her. I didn't know if I ever would. But I wanted to say that I finally understood that she had loved me. And that I understood, too, what it was like to fall in love unwisely, impossibly. To feel your life, your very destiny shift and fly away so that you had no choice but to follow it to a place so foreign, yet so immediate that your past would become like a story to you, not quite real.

"Look," Cliff said. "The bread. The way he's done those points of light along the crust—" He stepped away, then stepped up close again. "Odd, isn't it? From a distance it's perfectly ordinary bread. Up here, it's no more than dazzle. Just pure light."

"Light abolishes form," I said, clicking back into my analytical self. "See the way Vermeer made the point of focus fall on the back wall? The way the details there—right down to the cracks in the plaster and the nail holes—are all so perfectly defined? It's like a photograph: none of the objects in the foreground are in sharp focus. So where light strikes the bread, the face, the hands, it makes them quiver and dissolve—"

"It does abolish form," he interrupted. "You're right. But think of it, Evie: light. Couldn't you say love is a kind of light? Changing everything, changing its own *nature* in the process—which changes everything again. And again." He rushed on. "And if that's so, we go at it all wrong, don't we? Trying to box it up. Trying to give it some tried-and-true form when its very essence doesn't allow it."

He was thinking aloud, he didn't expect an answer. But all after-noon, I thought about what he had said. Everywhere, light seemed to break around me. It shattered the still water in the canals, shot win-dowpanes with silver. It haloed passers-by, so that the streets seemed to be filled with angels. Light gathered inside me, and I saw at last what Vermeer had known all along: If you are patient enough, brave enough to see what you love, it is possible to craft a world for it, a place where it lasts forever.

I did not try to understand this one small thing I knew. Not yet. Love was like a painting, I decided. There was a time when it was im-portant to look closely, to see how it was made, and there was a time when all that mattered was the lovely, quivering illusion that the light and line and color made. In London, Vermeer's woman waited. In New York, there was another life. But it was enough for now to walk through this city in the last light of the day, to turn and see Cliff shimmering beside me.

Acknowledgements

I would like to gratefully acknowledge the curators and conservators at the Indianapolis Museum of Art, the National Gallery of London, and the Rijksmuseum whose help was invaluable to me in creating a plan for the repair of Johannes Vermeer's "A Lady Standing at the Virginals." I am equally indebted to the work of countless art historians whose books and monographs provided information abut Vermeer's life and work, especially *Vermeer and his Milieu: a Web of Social History* by John Michael Nontias and *Vermeer and the Art of Painting* by Arthur K. Wheelock, Jr. Katherine Kressman Taylor's *Florence, Ordeal by Water* provided a wealth of inforamtion about the 1966 flood. A fellowship from the Indiana Arts Commission enabled me to do important on-site research in England and Holland.

I would like to thank my parents for the "war stories" they shared with me, many of which made their way into this novel; Patricia Cupp for her first memory, for stories of her early childhood during World War II, and for having been an excellent traveling companion during much of the research for this book; Charles Miles, whose knowledge of English history has been a great gift to me; Kim and Tim Lafferty, who have a knack for finding the most amazing picnic sites in the English countryside, Rebecca Ebert and her book club for critiquing an early draft of the novel; and Steve Shoup, who has always believed that I could do anything.